Beth Solheim

At Witt's End

Echelon Press

Publishing

AT WITT'S END
An Echelon Press Book

First Echelon Press paperback printing / March 2010

Cover Art © Nathalie Moore
Award winning Graphic Artist

Echelon Press
9055 G Thamesmeade Road
Laurel, MD 20723
www.echelonpress.com

ISBN: 978-1-59080-662-3
1-59080-662-X
eBook 1-59080-663-8

PRINTED IN THE UNITED STATES OF AMERICA

10 9 8 7 6 5 4 3 2 1

Dedicated to:
Jerry Solheim (the love of my life)

In memory of:
Gregg Pouliot (my father)

Acknowledgements

My tireless work buddies, who never complained
during numerous proofreading sessions,
offered advice, and urged me to persevere.

My sincere appreciation to my publisher,
Karen Syed, who made my dreams come true.

A heartfelt thank you to editor Kat Thompson
for her sage advice and guiding hand.

1

"Oh dear, not another one," Sadie said, parting the curtains in Cabin 14 and peering out the window. A man in a black suit stared back at her. Sadie's shoulders sagged as she signaled to her twin sister. "Jane, come here. Tell me if you can see him. In that fancy get-up, he's either one of them or he's an undertaker." Sixty-four-year-old Sadie cupped her hand over her forehead to prevent the sun's glare from obstructing her view.

The man looked back over his shoulder, clutching his leather briefcase to his chest. He took a few steps forward, hesitated, then cautiously edged off the walkway seeking cover behind a low-hanging pine. Bewildered eyes peeked through the boughs. He concentrated on a group of teens, toting inflatable rafts and skipping playfully toward the shore.

Jane edged closer to the window and nudged Belly LaGossa aside with her knee. The dog snorted at the intrusion. After sniffing the air, Belly waddled across the cabin floor, scratched on the screen door and waited for one of the sisters to let him out. His jowls fluttered a sigh of resignation when he realized they had no intention of honoring his request.

Jane followed the direction indicated by Sadie's finger. "Where? I don't see anybody."

Sadie hoped Jane would quiet her anxiety. If Jane could see him, he wasn't a crosser. If the man was invisible to Jane, it meant the fifth and final crosser was about to make an entrance.

Although most guests who failed to cross over were shocked to learn of their demise, they were generally harmless and agreeable. Not this week, though. Sadie already had Rodney, a crosser with an attitude, occupying one of the bunks in the inner room. She was sure Rodney had been destined for hellfire, but took a wrong turn on his way to meet the devil. The hateful twenty-one-year-old had stretched her patience to the limit, because he didn't give a rip. About anything. Or anybody. He took pleasure in making life miserable for the other crossers. Sadie turned back toward the window. If her hunch was right, another crosser was lurking outside her door.

"Right there." Sadie jabbed her finger in the direction of the walkway. She watched a courtesy-cart driver glide past the man in black.

The cart driver tapped his horn to alert four men laden with fishing gear that he was about to pass on their left. Chatting with excitement, the cart's passengers scanned the marina as the driver continued to transport them to their assigned cabins along the shores of Pinecone Lake.

The advertised check-in at Witt's End Resort was every Friday afternoon between 2:00 and 4:00 p.m. Because guests arrived promptly at 2:00 p.m. to take advantage of two extra hours of valued vacation, staff members scurried to accommodate the rush. Today was no exception. New arrivals crammed the walkways, the gift shop, and the marina.

Sadie tapped the window pane with her fingernail as Jane edged closer. "Just look over the top of my finger at that guy in the snazzy suit. Do you think he's a crosser?"

Sadie held her finger rigid to give her sister ample time to zero in.

"Well if he's a crosser, why do you bother to ask? You're the only one who can see the dead."

If Sadie could get her hands on the man who had deemed her a death coach, she'd staple his lips to his nose. It had to be a man bent on revenge. Who else would saddle her with the responsibility of guiding the dead on their final journey?

"Geez Louise. How come everything happens all at once? I've got a cabin full of crossers and now I have to deal with a new manager who can't make a decision. It makes me furious I let you talk me into hiring him to run the resort," Sadie said. "I gave in too easy. I should spank myself."

"Easy?" Jane's voice rose as she stared in disbelief. "That wasn't easy. It took me two years to convince you."

"Mother would kick the lid off her casket if she knew we hired a manager. Witt's End has been in our family for over eighty years."

"That's a bunch of hooey," Jane bit back. "Our manager does a good job. You make it sound like we sold the resort. We didn't. Besides, now we can go dancing. You were the one who complained we never went dancing on seniors' night."

"If that man in the black suit is another crosser, I won't be going to the Fertile Turtle any time soon," Sadie said.

"Well you better feel like it because Mr. Bakke's taking us dancing tomorrow night." Jane gestured toward Sadie. "And don't embarrass us by wearing any of your stupid outfits."

"This isn't stupid," Sadie argued. "It's new. It's all the rage." She smoothed the hem of the leopard print shirt over her mini skirt.

"You look like you're going on safari. Why can't you dress like me? Like a normal person."

Sadie wanted to comment on Jane's attire, but if Jane hadn't changed her appearance in thirty years, one more fashion tidbit wasn't going to help. Sadie had even gone as far as purchasing colorful outfits for her sister. They were still buried in the back of her closet behind the cadaveresque colorscape Jane referred to as beige, ecru, tan, and, on a real flamboyant buying binge, khaki. The bottoms were all worn with white blouses. Ironed, starched, lace-adorned blouses. With Jane's silver bob topping off the ensemble, Sadie often had the urge to poke her bland sister to make sure she was still among the living. Why look like a crosser if you could prevent it?

Before huffing away from the window, Jane added, "I still don't see a man in a suit. If he's got a suit on, he must be a crosser. Who else would wear a suit to a resort?"

"You've got a point," Sadie said. "But with four other crossers already in residence, I don't feel like dealing with a new one."

"Why? It's no different than any other time. You should be used to it after forty years." Jane walked over to the screen door and looked through the opening.

"I already told you those business types don't like being told they're dead," Sadie said. "In fact, they get downright belligerent. They waste time denying it when they should be making their death decisions."

"Do you think I'll end up being a crosser?"

8

"Not if you don't have unfinished business."

"Who made those stupid rules? And where does it say I need to have unfinished business? I don't understand why they didn't give you a manual so I could check to see if you're telling the truth." Jane waved her hand in dismissal before removing her glasses and rubbing her eyes.

Not only had Sadie not been given a manual, but the assignment lasted a lifetime. She would prefer to ignore the crossers, but she couldn't. If she didn't guide them through their death decisions in the allotted time, the crossers would never realize their death potential. They'd slip into oblivion.

"You've been in a foul mood ever since you got up this morning. Are you going to share your problem-of-the-day, or are you going to keep me in suspense?"

Jane lifted a *Victoria's Secret* catalog off the kitchen table and placed it under a stack of magazines.

"Put that back. I haven't decided what to order yet," Sadie said. Her gaze wandered to the window. The man in the black suit peered back at her. His demeanor had changed from confused to distressed.

"You're too old to be buying that kind of stuff." Attempting to straighten the rest of the items on the bookshelf Jane said, "Why don't you look at something intelligent?"

"Like one of your cooking magazines? I don't know why you bother to read them. You don't follow the recipes anyway." Sadie batted at Jane's hand as her sister tried to stop her from pulling the catalog back out of the stack. "You're driving me nuts. All you do is clean, clean, clean. It's to the point where I have to Duct Tape my undies to my butt. I'm afraid if I lost sight of them for one second, you'd

9

put them away and I'd never find them again."

When Jane's tidiness drove Sadie to distraction, Sadie countered by creating a mess. Even though Jane's exasperation resulted in a sermon clarifying the finer points of organization, Sadie took pleasure in flustering her sister. However, this sparring hadn't been intentional. Jane's worries had escalated to a feverish level because of a pending lawsuit, a lawsuit that could produce devastating results, and Sadie knew it would be wise to keep her retaliation to a minimum.

Sadie had dealt with crossers for forty years. That she could handle, but not the lawsuit.

2

Jane crossed to the door to let Belly out. "What a nuisance. He's been pacing for the past ten minutes. Everywhere he goes I have to wipe up a puddle of drool." She peeked through the screen. "Is the guy in the suit still out there?"

Sadie caught sight of movement near a Norway pine as she slid her feet into her rhinestone-adorned sandals and wriggled her toes. "He's still there. He's walking toward the parking lot, but he keeps looking back at our cabin."

"I hope he's not a crosser. I can't take much more stress. Besides, you've already got your hands full."

"I'm not the only one who's got my hands full," Sadie said. "Nan's got the Fossum family in storage at the mortuary. I don't know how she's going to manage. I still can't believe all three of them died in that accident."

"From what Nan said, Deputy Friborg stopped by twice to look at the bodies." Anguish tightened Jane's aged features. "He must really miss his friend to view his body twice."

"I don't think that's why Deputy Friborg wanted a second look." Sadie looked through the window at the mortuary next door. "From what Nan said, he's not totally convinced it was an accident."

"What?" Jane whispered. "Do you mean…?" Jane's mouth hung open in disbelief.

"Shut your mouth before a bird builds a nest and you choke on it. I'm not in the mood to do CPR."

"Not an accident?" Jane said. "When you told me Tim thought his dad was murdered, I didn't believe it. But if Deputy Friborg is concerned, maybe it's true."

Goose flesh rose over Sadie's arm as Jane's comment hit her. If the deputy's curiosity snowballed into a full-blown murder investigation, it would only add to her problems because Tim was one of her crossers.

Jane's gaze darted back and forth. "Who would want to hurt the Fossums?"

"Hopefully no one. I think Tim's imagination got the better of him." Tim Fossum's body lay in cold storage at the mortuary next to his parents. It wasn't unusual for crossers to deny their demise. The fact that Tim didn't cross over when his parents did made it harder for him to accept. If he fostered a notion of murder, it gave him something to concentrate on, other than his death decision.

"The poor lamb," Jane said. "What a terrible thing for Tim to go through."

"How do you think I feel? I'm the one who broke the news to Tim. To make it worse, he's forced to make a death decision that might prevent him from ever seeing his parents again." Sadie tipped her head upward and sighed. "It breaks my heart to see him so confused."

"That's the problem," Jane said, waving her arms in frustration. "I can't see your crossers but you can. Even that bothersome dog can see them. It's not fair."

"You missed your calling, Jane. You look like a traffic cop trying to get the Hell's Angels to turn in at the church."

"I do not. I'm upset because you're the death coach and I have no choice but to believe what you tell me." Jane looked out the window again, trying to spy the man in the black suit. "I'm too tired to deal with this. I couldn't sleep last night because I kept worrying about our lawsuit. Now I'll be worrying about a murder, too."

"Quit worrying. I told you our attorney will take care of it. And I'll bet it's not true about the Fossums anyway."

Sadie pushed back the despair that engulfed her every time she thought about losing the lawsuit. Putting forth a positive front was safer than thinking about the consequences.

"But what if we don't win? What if we actually lose the resort?" Jane slammed her hand down on the table. "How can you be so calm?"

Drawing on her reserve, Sadie said, "I'm trying my best not to think about it. There's nothing we can do until the hearing."

"That's what drives me crazy. I hate waiting." Jane fidgeted with her blouse collar, attempting to pull the points into alignment. "Our employees depend on us for a living. They'll be out of a job if we lose this resort."

Sadie sat in the chair next to her sister and folded her hands around Jane's fists. "You can't think like that. You've got to have faith it will be settled in our favor. We've owned this resort since Mother died. The judge will take that into consideration."

The women turned at the sound of Belly's bark. His stubby tail jerked anxiously as he sniffed the air.

"Judge Kimmer never liked us," Jane said. "He won't give a hoot how long the resort's been in our family. You know he's wanted to buy this property. The fact we turned him down won't help."

"The resort was never listed with a realtor. He had no

right getting angry when we turned him down." Impatience squeezed at Sadie like a vice. Witt's End was the most prime vacation property in Northern Minnesota. For over twenty years every developer in the upper Midwest had tried to buy their resort. Some of the locals, including Judge Kimmer, had also expressed an interest in the property, but Sadie held fast by declining their offers.

The resort featured three thousand feet of shoreline dotted with towering Norway pines and sheltered one of the most popular fishing bays on Pinecone Lake. A reservation list spanning two years, a lodge, a restaurant, a marina, a sand beach, and a gift shop guaranteed many return visits by satisfied vacationers.

"You were the one who suggested we get this over with as soon as possible. Because you were in such a hurry, they selected an earlier court date," Sadie said. "Now we're stuck with it. If we'd have waited, Judge Kimmer wouldn't have been assigned to our case."

Jane pushed back from the table. "I couldn't wait because I'm dying by inches every day. I can't think about anything but this lawsuit." As Jane paced, she fidgeted with a pleat in her tan slacks. "I know you're right. I know I have to put this out of my mind. You've got the crossers to keep you busy. I don't have anything to occupy my mind."

"It's not like I asked to be a death coach," Sadie muttered.

"Then why did you take the job?"

"Job? *Job*? Being a death coach isn't a job. It just happened."

"Well it sure seems like a job," Jane said. "You're busy every day dealing with them. And now you think there

14

might be another one out there. You need to find someone else to do it."

Through lips tight with exasperation Sadie said, "You know I was chosen to guide them. How else will they know how to cross over to the other side?"

"The fact they couldn't cross over shouldn't be your problem. Let them find their own way."

"I'd like to, but that's not possible. I've explained this a million times."

"I know you have. But it would sure make it easier if I could see them. It's embarrassing when I sit on them all the time."

"That's not going to change. I'm not going to be given an assistant, either. When the day comes someone else is designated to take over, I'll probably be long gone."

"How are you going to deal with the crossers if we lose the resort?"

"I don't know. I just don't know," Sadie said. "Why can't you be more like me and quit worrying."

"I don't want to be like you. I don't want people thinking I'm crazy because I talk to imaginary friends."

Glaring at her sister over the rim of her orange frames, Sadie said, "I think somebody messed up at the hospital when we were born."

"Oh not this again," Jane said. "I'm tall. You're short. Big deal. That doesn't mean we're not twins."

"At least I don't have your fat ass."

"At least I'm not a boobless half-pint. And don't tell me you're not jealous. I know better," Jane said.

Sadie stood and hurried to the door as Belly let out a high-pitched yelp. One end of the dog wagged frantically while the other end poked through the porch railing and whined at the man behind the Norway pine. A briefcase corner protruded from the edge of the tree.

To the right of the tree, several children in bathing suits jostled for position in front of an ice cream cart. Sadie winced with compassion when a child's chocolate ice cream tumbled from its cone and landed on the ground at the girl's feet. Heat waves rippled up from the pathway. The youngsters licked as fast as they could to catch the drops of melting ice cream before they trickled down their arms. The man peered around the tree at the children.

"I still don't understand why they picked you to take care of the crossers instead of me. I'd be just as good at it as you are." Jane nodded sharply.

Sadie stuck her little finger in her right ear and screwed it back and forth. "My hearing must be on the blink. I thought you said you'd be as good at it as I am."

"Maybe even better." Jane's voice caught in her throat. She frowned as three scantily clad teenagers hurried toward the beach. "Good grief," she said under her breath. Her gaze lingered on their thonged bottoms. "That's disgusting."

Filling a mug with coffee, Sadie placed it on one of Jane's lace doilies and motioned to her sister to return to her chair. "Drink this. Quit dwelling on our problems. Maybe you could call Mr. Bakke to see if he wants to go for a pontoon ride."

Sadie inched her fingers through her black hair. Black, verging on blue, happened to be the color-of-the-week at Big Leon's beauty shop. She picked at the gelled spikes she had created earlier in the day to make sure they were still standing erect. Glancing at her reflection in the window, she turned from side to side, eyeing the new leopard-print shirt the postman had left in her mail box. She made a mental note to order another push-up bra. Maybe one with a little more lift. She wanted to wow them at the Fertile Turtle. That's if she ever found the time to go dancing again.

Jane's hand suddenly splayed across her chest. "Have you told Nan about the lawsuit? If we lose, she could be evicted from the mortuary."

Sadie loved Nan Harren like a daughter. She cared for Aanders like the grandson she wished she had. The feelings were shared. Harren Funeral Home sat at the edge of the resort property next to Cabin 14. Nan and her eleven-year-old son occupied an apartment in the mortuary, originally designed to house mortuary science students. The land lease the Witt sisters held on the mortuary would be worthless if they lost the lawsuit.

Sadie's eyes sparked with anger. "Every time I think about Carl's lies in that lawsuit my head feels like it's going to explode. Carl Swanson is a demented rat. Apparently the money he inherited from his grandfather isn't enough."

Sadie pointed toward the bookshelf. "Did you see this morning's newspaper? That big liar's decided to run for sheriff. If you think Carl's a jerk now, wait till he's elected."

"I saw that. I can't believe he'd do something that stupid. Who would vote for him? Everyone knows he's a donkey's patootie."

Jane drained her coffee cup. "Well? Have you told Nan, or not?"

"Nan's got enough to worry about. She's got three bodies to prep and one of them is Tim. Nan loved Tim. He spent a lot of time with Aanders." Sadie tapped her ear lobe, setting the dangling beads in motion. "How do I tell a dear friend she might lose everything? I can't do it. What if I tell her and then the judge rules in our favor? The last thing she needs is more stress," Sadie said.

Justifying the reason she'd postponed the inevitable nagged her to distraction. Even though she knew her sister disagreed, Sadie was willing to wait for the pendulum to swing in favor of providence rather than misfortune.

"Nan's had to live with rejection all her life. Can you imagine what losing the mortuary would do to her?" Sadie turned her ear toward the door as she heard footsteps plink across the wooden porch.

Dread filled Sadie. She glanced through the screen door just in time to see the man in the black suit disappear into the woods.

3

Worry and dread caused the hairs on Aanders' neck to tingle as he stared at the basement door. A mix of curiosity and anticipation had him on the verge of ripping the door off the hinges and bounding down the stairs, but he knew he couldn't. He had made a promise to his mother and was trying desperately to keep it.

Think of something else, he thought clenching his fists. Anything else. Aanders' foot tapped rapidly against the stool's leg as he leaned on the kitchen counter. Maybe if he let the hateful words the new kid had shouted at him seep back into his mind, it would shove aside his present predicament. Aanders had looked forward to meeting the new guest at the resort, but when he finally did, all the kid did was tease him about living in a mortuary.

Aanders had learned to benefit from his unique surroundings. Not every kid lived in a mortuary. Not every kid was as brave as they pretended. Not every kid dared touch a dead body. For those brave enough to touch the lifeless flesh, Aanders charged a dollar. After all, hadn't his mother encouraged him to be enterprising?

A burst of sizzling grease signaled supper would soon be ready. Eleven-year-old Aanders watched his mother flip three pieces of chicken in the frying pan. He twiddled the salt shaker between his fingers until it tipped over. Sneaking a look at his mother he covered the salt with his hand, edged it off the counter and watched it sprinkle onto the floor. His blond bangs caught on his eyelashes, twitching when he blinked.

"I thought you'd feel better if I cooked your favorite meal," Nan said, reaching to brush the hair from her son's face.

Aanders appreciated that his mother wanted to lessen his sorrow, but food didn't appeal to him. If he admitted he wasn't hungry, he'd hurt her feelings. She'd worry. She already had enough on her mind without upsetting her more.

His stomach rolled a queasy warning as his gaze fell on the basement door. A whining dog wasn't making the situation any easier. Belly had parked his bulk in front of the basement door and insisted on being given access to the lower level.

"I don't know why you let that dog in here again," Nan said. "You know I've asked you not to do that."

"I didn't. He must have slipped in under the hearse door. I've seen him do it before."

Even though Belly's physique resembled a cement truck, he had a weasel's knack at sneaking into the mortuary apartment. The dog must have slipped in when he helped his mother transfer the heavy body bags from the hearse. Belly no longer startled Aanders when he appeared out of nowhere. At least not like his father startled him when he showed up uninvited. Belly's visits were welcomed. Not his father's.

Nan coaxed Belly away from the door with her foot. "After you finish eating, take him back to Sadie's cabin. He's going to ruin the paint on that door." Sidestepping the dog she added, "This is the second time I've found him clawing on the basement door. I don't know what's gotten into him. Usually he just sleeps in front of the fridge."

Belly's mission in life was to consume food. Lots of food. When not occupied with his vocation, Belly sought the luxury of a good snooze. Aanders often woke with Belly occupying more than half his bed and hogging the pillow. The defining property line between the resort and mortuary meant nothing to Belly.

Belly's heritage was a mystery. He had long legs, a stubby nose, a rotund body covered in brown spots, and a cropped-off tail with four elongated hairs growing out of a bald portion of its tip. When Belly wagged his tail, the black hairs flapped in the breeze adding to the dog's odd appearance. Aanders trimmed the black hairs, but they grew back with gusto. The dog also had only one testicle.

Aanders joined his mother as she stared out the kitchen window. They watched a young woman scoop a toddler into her arms after he wandered too close to the water's edge. The child giggled with glee. The lilt of children's voices echoed back and forth across the short span between the resort and the mortuary before it faded away. It was a sound that usually brought smiles to their faces, but not tonight.

Nan put her arm around Aanders' shoulder and pulled him closer. "We'll make it through this," she whispered, placing her lips against his temple.

Aanders blinked hard to divert the tears welling in his eyes.

Belly interrupted the silence with a muffled bark, prancing in front of the basement door. Aanders held his finger to his lips. "Be quiet. Mom's already mad at you." Belly continued to plead by alternating his soulful stare between Aanders and the boy's mother. Aanders slipped his fingers under Belly's collar. He led him to the pantry and opened a box of treats. Belly sniffed the offering. He gulped it down, snorted, then returned to the basement door.

Aspen leaves flitted outside the kitchen window as if mimicking the energy of the resort crowd. Wisps of wood smoke rose from a nearby campfire. Nan let out a deep sigh, focused her attention on the lawn, and peered at a small, riderless tricycle inching its way down the sidewalk. She leaned closer to the window. The vehicle's pedals turned in sync with the rotation of the tires as it crossed the grass and disappeared over a rise.

Nan stood on her tiptoes. She stretched her torso across the sink and peered sharply to the left. "That's odd."

Aanders plopped down onto a stool. He swiveled back and forth, staring at the window.

"I just saw a tricycle going toward the resort all by itself," Nan said.

"You mean that blue one?" Seeing his mother nod, he said, "I saw it going the other way when you put the pan on the stove."

"Who was riding it?"

"Nobody."

"Who was pushing it?" Nan turned to look at her son.

"Nobody." Aanders leaned against the back of the stool. "I thought it was the wind."

Nan frowned at the treetops. "It doesn't look that windy."

She placed a piece of chicken on Aanders' plate. "You've got to get some food in your stomach before you disappear altogether."

"You always tell me to eat more, but it doesn't help." Aanders leaned his chin on his fist, absentmindedly stabbing his fork into the meat again and again and again.

"You'll appreciate that when you're older." Nan stood two inches taller than her five-foot-four-inch son. Aanders had inherited her slim build and Scandinavian features. He bore no resemblance to his father's side of the family.

"Sadie called and asked how you were doing," Nan said. She brushed her thumb across Aanders' forehead to wipe the hair from his eyelashes. "She's concerned. She knows you lost your best friend."

"I know," Aanders said. "She and Jane brought cookies over while you were in the embalming room. I don't like it when Jane cries."

"She cries because she's sad for you. We're lucky to have the Witt sisters as friends." Nan smiled at her son. "Sadie is like the mother I never had. I think she likes to pretend you're her grandson."

"My friends think she really is my grandmother," Aanders said. "They say my Grandma is weird. It's embarrassing when they talk about Sadie and her imaginary friends."

"Sadie's not weird. She's eccentric. Sadie means well."

"But she dresses weird. Really weird. That only makes things worse. Why can't she dress like a normal old lady?"

"Sadie's unique. I admit she's a bit strange, but she enjoys life. We should all be more like Sadie." Nan poured milk into a glass and set it near Aanders. "She's concerned about us because I'm raising you on my own."

"Thank goodness," Aanders said.

"What did you say?"

"Nothing." Aanders directed his words toward his feet.

"That's not fair, young man. Don't criticize what you

23

don't understand. You know your father has issues."

"I'm glad he doesn't live here anymore."

"Me too. It's hard to believe it's been four years." Nan's voice trailed off. She lifted her hair from her neck, gathered it in her hand, and slipped a band around it. Her blond bob hung just above her shoulders. The damp air raised havoc with her thick, wavy mane making it impossible to manage.

Nan scooped a pad of soft butter from a dish and spread it over a slice of bread. "Put some chokecherry jelly on this. You've got to eat something." Her shoulders flexed in rhythm with the tapping of her fingers. "You doing okay?" She reached across the counter and patted her son's hand.

"Yeah." Aanders swiped the back of his hand across his cheek as a tear formed and fell to the counter. He fought the urge to run toward the basement door.

"I'm sorry, Aanders. I'm so sorry you lost your best friend. If it were in my power to change what happened, I would."

Sobs issued forth as Aanders pushed his stool back and walked toward the basement door. "Why did he have to die, Mom?"

"That's one of those questions I can't answer. Every time I work on someone who died unexpectedly, I ask myself that same question. You'd think a funeral director would be used to it by now, but I'm not."

"He's the only friend I ever had," Aanders cried, placing his palms on the door and leaning his forehead against the wood. "He liked me and didn't make fun of me like the rest of the kids do."

"You'll have other friends. I know you don't believe

that now, but you will make other friends."

"I don't want other friends. I want Tim back. I want my best friend back."

Running her hand across Aanders' hair and pulling him close, Nan said, "I know you do. I want him back, too. I want his whole family back."

Aanders leaned into his mother's embrace, once more fixing his gaze on the basement door.

4

After staring out the screen door with a coffee cup clutched in both hands, Sadie turned and whispered to her sister. "He's back. I don't know where he went yesterday, but he's back. I think he's ready to ask for help." A hinge creaked in protest when Sadie pushed on the screen door.

The man in the black suit shot a distressed glance at the door and then at the resort guests who scrambled past him on their way to the parking lot. His knuckles paled as his fist gripped the briefcase handle. He shouted at a nearby group of men. When they ignored him, even after a second attempt to get their attention, he stopped. Furrows of confusion crowded his narrow forehead.

"Is there something I can do for you?" Sadie repeated the question when he didn't respond.

The man shielded his eyes to focus on Sadie. He squinted and scanned Sadie from her spiked hair to her polished purple toenails. "I highly doubt it."

"You'll change your mind," Sadie said under her breath. She sat next to Belly on the top porch step. Keeping his gaze on the man, the dog's hind quarters wriggled in excitement. Sadie coaxed Belly into a sitting position, maneuvering him sideways until he panted in her face. "Oh pew, Belly. Your breath smells like Jane's rear end."

"I heard that," Mr. Bakke shouted through the screen door. "How do you know what Jane's rear end smells like?"

"Just a wild guess," Sadie answered. "From the size of it, I bet I'm right." She pushed Belly's head to the side so she could catch her breath.

Sadie inhaled deeply over her coffee, pulling in the rich aroma. Caffeine. Her vice. This was the one thing she refused to give up. Actually it was the second. She also refused to miss her weekly appointment at Big Leon's Beauty Shop. What he couldn't do with a curling iron and a bottle of dye.

She watched the man step back onto the paved path. He pulled a key ring from his suit coat pocket. Pressing a button on the remote attached to his key chain, he scanned the cars in the parking lot. He pressed the button again. Failing to hear the honk that signaled a programmed function, he stared back down at the keys.

"Are you sure I can't help you?"

Turning to respond, he said, "Madam, I already answered your question. It would be most unlikely that you could answer any inquiry I might have."

"Suit yourself." Sadie shook the last few drops of coffee from the mug and stood. "I'll be inside if you need me."

"Are we getting another one?" Mr. Bakke asked, as Sadie let the screen door slam behind her. She set the mug on the table.

"I think so, but he's one stubborn crosser."

Mr. Bakke dipped his hands into the dishwater and wrung out a cloth before wiping the length of the kitchen counter. He wore khaki shorts and a light blue polo shirt featuring a Witt's End Resort emblem. A ghostly-white, seven-inch section of exposed skin stood out boldly between his knee-high stockings and the hem of his shorts. His unusually large feet were clad in brown sandals. Sadie

27

blinked twice to make sure he wasn't wearing snowshoes.

Small-boned and height challenged, his head sported thin wisps of white hair that refused to lay flat against his scalp. Tufts of ear hair sprung from the sides of his head. *Were Belly and Mr. Bakke hatched from the same furry egg?* Sadie smiled at the prospect.

"I can't believe Jane's letting you do that," Sadie said, watching Mr. Bakke run the cloth over the counter. "She won't have a purpose if you clean. Why waste your time? You know she'll redo it when you're not looking."

"I'm trying to lighten her load. She's so worried about the law suit she's irrational. This morning she cleared the table and started the dishes before I finished eating."

"That's why I wolf my food down and bloat like a pig. You take in a lot of air when you're forced to shovel it in," Sadie said. "She's pressured me to eat fast ever since I can remember. Jane got that trait from our mother."

"I'll bet it drove your father to distraction," Mr. Bakke said.

"We never knew him. Mother refused to tell us who he was."

"She wouldn't tell me, either. I tried to trick her into telling me, but she never let it slip." Mr. Bakke joined Sadie at the kitchen table.

"Mr. Bakke," Sadie said, pointing across the table. "You might want to consider moving to another chair. You just sat on Lora."

Placing his palms flat on the table for leverage, Mr. Bakke planted his sandals on the floor and rose slowly. He turned to view the empty chair. "My apologies, Lora. I didn't know you were there. I thought Sadie and I were alone."

A hollow rap on the screen door interrupted their conversation. They turned to witness the man in the black suit squint with curiosity as he tried to make out the figures on the opposite side of the door.

Sadie pushed the door open.

"Excuse me, madam," the man said, his eyes lingering on Sadie's hairdo. "It seems I've had a lapse of memory. I can't figure out where I am." His shoulders jerked when a car door slammed behind him.

Sadie joined him on the porch. "You're at Witt's End."

The man tightened his grip on the briefcase. "I know that. I read the sign. I need to know where Witt's End is located."

"We're located on Pinecone Lake in Northern Minnesota."

Belly grunted, lifted his bulk from the rug, and rammed his head against the screen door. Sadie pushed it open to prevent the dog from ripping the mesh from the door's frame. Belly sniffed the man's shoes. He snorted against the back of his trousers as the man tried to push him away with his briefcase.

"That's not possible. I'm on my way to…" He paused. "Well it's none of your concern. I just need to get back to the correct highway."

Sadie watched him scan the parking lot again, desperate to connect with something familiar. She motioned at him. "Maybe you should step in for a few minutes to get your bearings. Then I'll help you select a route."

The man sat in the chair Sadie indicated and looked around the room. Noticing others present, he said, "I wouldn't have bothered you if I had known you had company. I apologize for the intrusion."

"It's not an intrusion. These folks are guests just like you," Sadie said, picking at a wad of dog hair that had stuck to her purple tube top. Sadie turned to point to Mr. Bakke on the davenport. "Well, everyone's a guest except Mr. Bakke." Smiling at the elderly gentleman she added, "He's family."

Mr. Bakke waved and continued to read without looking up from his newspaper.

The man studied the other guests. "A guest? I'm not a guest. I may be perplexed, but I guarantee I have no intention of becoming a guest."

"Nobody ever does," Sadie said gently.

Belly propped his chin on the man's leg and rolled his eyes coyly. Then he barked. The man's white knuckles jutted through his skin.

Leaning away from the dog, he said, "Please remove your mongrel from my pants leg. He's getting drool all over me." He grimaced as the slobber spot on his briefcase veined across the leather.

"He's not my dog," Sadie said.

"Then why do you tolerate him? He should be outside where creatures belong."

"He thinks he lives here." Sadie tugged on Belly's collar. "But he really belongs to the neighbors."

After situating Belly on the opposing side of the room, Sadie reached out to shake the man's hand. "I'm Sadie Witt," she said. She felt the clammy coolness of his skin when the man placed the tips of his fingers against her palm. "And who might you be?"

He looked up over the top of his glasses at Sadie's wrinkled cleavage and quickly averted his gaze. He shook his head. "It doesn't matter who I am. What matters is I'm obviously in the wrong place."

"For your information, you are exactly where you're supposed to be."

"I can't be. I haven't booked a vacation. And if I had, it certainly wouldn't be here. My arrival here was a miscalculation."

"I don't think so," Sadie said, edging closer to the man. "Let's try this again." Sadie reached her hand out. "I'm Sadie Witt. Who are you?"

Without extending his hand, the man straightened his shoulders, raised his chin, and said, "I'm Theopholis Jamison Peter."

"Well Mr. Peter, welcome to Witt's End. May we call you Theo?"

The screen door slammed and they turned toward the noise.

"Who called the undertaker?" Rodney Lassiter's footsteps fell heavily as he clomped over to Theo. "Black suit. Black tie. Did they let you drive the hearse, too?" A sneer portrayed his disdain as he ran his finger under the lapel on Theo's suit. "Nice threads, dude. I bet this cost you a wad. It ought to look real good where you're going."

"Sit down, Rodney, and be quiet," Sadie said. "Theo is one of our new guests."

Tugging on a chair with his boot, Rodney said, "Where do you find these losers, Sadie? The last one was a race car driver with his helmet melted to his head. Now you got one in a mortician's costume. How come you don't get no sexy broads coming to your cabin?"

Rodney's jeans hung low on his hips. As he moved, his hands grasped the waist band to keep from losing his pants. One of his t-shirt sleeves featured circles burned into it spelling the word 'kill' in uneven letters.

"Cork it, Rodney." Sadie put her fists on her hips as she turned to face him. "I don't want to have to tell you again."

With lightening speed, Rodney bounded back toward Theo and placed his oil-stained hands on Theo's leather briefcase. "What's in the briefcase?"

Recoiling, Theo said, "I beg your pardon."

Rodney wrapped his fingers around the padded leather handle. "Let's see what you got."

Gritting his teeth, Theo uttered, "Remove your hand from my briefcase."

Rodney tugged on the handle, trying to twist the case from Theo's grasp.

Theo clamped his hand on Rodney's fist and squeezed. Rodney yelped and pulled his hand away. Theo let out his own shriek. "Your hand. What's wrong with your hand?"

The twenty-one year old winced as he cradled his hand and tried to move his fingers. Rodney shouted, "You broke it. You broke my hand."

Frantically directing his question toward Sadie, Theo repeated, "What's wrong with his hand? It's clammy."

"You don't know you're dead yet, do you?" Rodney said. Stepping up to Theo, Rodney tapped the man's chest, pushing hard with each tap. "For your information Mr. Pansy-Ass-Big-Shot, you're dead. You're as dead as a mackerel. A stinking, slimy, rotting mackerel."

Theo squared his shoulders. "You don't know what you're talking about." Frustration smoldered as he continued, "Do I look like I'm dead? You, young man, wouldn't be talking to me if I were dead, now would you?"

Reaching toward the briefcase Rodney matched Theo's exaggerated tone. "I would and I am. You're just as dead as the rest of the losers in this cabin."

Rodney swatted at a greasy cluster of hair tickling the nape of his neck. A ragged shoulder seam on the left side of his t-shirt bragged of a recent confrontation, one of many the young man had started over the years.

Sadie's shrill voice interrupted the clash between the men. "Rodney. That's enough. Either go back outside or go to the inner room."

Glaring at Theo, Rodney said, "Loser. You're lucky I worked my ass off today. I'm too tired to deal with you." Retreating toward the inner room, he stabbed his finger in Theo's direction. "Later, dude. Count on it." He slammed the inner room door causing a framed picture to bounce and shatter against the floor.

Sadie patted Theo's chair to encourage him to sit down. "It's not wise to get into a pissing match with a skunk." She lifted a broom off a pantry hook and swept up the shards that had scattered across the floor. "Ignore him. He's got an attitude. He's cranky because his thirty days are slipping away." Sadie motioned toward the inner room door. In a low tone she added, "Whatever you do, don't let him know you're afraid of him.

"I'm sorry Rodney told you about your death. That information should have come from me." She grasped the back of his chair and again gestured for him to sit down.

"Most people are in shock when they learn their dead."

"Death? Are you out of your mind?" Theo rasped.

"Yes she is," filtered through the inner room door. "All you have to do is look at her. Any idiot could figure that out."

A gaunt young woman rose from her chair and touched Theo's fingers. As he jerked them from her grasp, Lora said, "Sadie's not crazy." Looking toward the inner room door, she leaned in and whispered, "Don't believe Rodney. Sadie's the only chance you've got to reach your destination."

Lora and her son Michael, the third and fourth crossers of the week, had arrived shortly after Rodney checked into Cabin 14. Lora was nothing like Rodney. Terrified and insecure, Lora needed constant encouragement. It didn't take long before Sadie realized the poor woman lacked the ability to make a death decision.

Lora's unwillingness to accept her new responsibility concerned Sadie. Sadie coached Lora at length to get her to understand the urgency of making a sound decision. The lectures failed. Lora leaned toward a decision that held risk.

Six-year-old Michael's objection to his mother's decision also added to Sadie's concern. Lora's decision led to doom. Her son's objections only added to the frail woman's dilemma.

Theo's toe caught on the rug as he hurried toward the screen door. His voice trembled. "What's going on here? Her fingers are as cold as Rodney's. They might be dead, but I'm not dead." His voice rose as he looked at Sadie. "I tell you I'm not dead."

"I know you're confused, but you've got to calm down. There's so much I need to explain." Sadie waited as Theo fumbled for the doorknob. "You have to make a decision and we're here to help you. The time you have left is limited. All my crossers are facing the same dilemma and will tell you about their concerns as the days go by. They expect you to do the same."

"Please listen to her," Lora said. "I didn't believe her at first, either. None of us did. But when you hear everything, you'll understand." Lora pulled her son to her side.

"When you died," Sadie said, "you didn't pass through the tunnel of light like you should have. You were held back. Some don't make it through the light because their issues are unresolved. It's up to you to figure out what that is. You've been given a time frame of thirty days to figure it out and make your decision."

"Decision." Theo rolled his eyes and looked away. "Your little fantasy game doesn't impress me in the least."

"Theo, you are dead. I don't know how you died, but believe me, you are dead. You have to decide whether you want to go back through the light or go to the parallel world." Sadie sat back in her chair, waiting for what she knew would come next.

"I've heard enough," Theo shouted. "Parallel world? What is this some kind of cult?" Theo flicked his hand toward the others. "If you've been taken in by this lunatic, then you're just as crazy as she is." He gestured frantically. "I suppose you're all waiting for an alien space ship to take you away?"

"No, we're not. There are no such things as aliens. But we know we need to make a decision so we can cross over." A blond, twelve-year-old boy rose and crossed the room toward Theo. "I'm Tim. I'm dead just like you." He pointed at Lora as he explained. "Lora and her son are dead. The guy in the inner room is dead. Sadie's our death coach and she's here to help us make our decisions."

A throaty laugh erupted from Theo as he threw his head back. "I just realized what this is. It's a bad dream. I've been having trouble sleeping and I'm on a new medication. I'm hallucinating." Theo tapped both cheeks rapidly. "I'll shake myself awake and end this nightmare."

"This isn't a bad dream. You died recently and made your way to my cabin." Sadie gazed up into his eyes to make sure he was listening. "I'm your death coach. You're a crosser and that's why you ended up in Cabin 14."

Sadie watched Theo's throat bob as he swallowed with difficulty. "I hope you look at your stay with us as an honor rather than a horror. You have the opportunity to make a major death decision. Most people don't have that luxury."

Sadie empathized with Theo as well as the other crossers. Believing the incredulous was difficult enough, but accepting the finality was next to impossible.

Theo's gaze moved around the room as Sadie pointed to Michael. "As you can see, crossers come in all sizes and ages." Michael tucked his head behind his mother's arm when Theo stared at him. Sadie put her arm around Tim's shoulder. "Tim and his parents were killed in a car accident. Tim's parents went through to the other side, but Tim remained behind. He wants to rejoin his parents."

Sadie nudged Belly away from Theo's leg as the dog pranced around Theo's feet. "And you've met Rodney. We don't know much about him," Sadie said, pointing toward the inner room. "He doesn't seem interested in sharing his intentions with the group."

Pulling Michael into her lap, Sadie said, "The five of you make up my guest roster for the time being. I'm only allowed five crossers at one time."

"But you have six," Theo said, pointing at Mr. Bakke.

"Mr. Bakke isn't dead."

"He's not?" Michael said, looking up at Sadie. "He looks dead."

Hearing his name, Mr. Bakke said, "What?"

"Our new guest thought you were one of the crossers, Mr. Bakke."

Mr. Bakke turned toward the kitchen table. "I'm not dead yet. I suppose that's not too far down the road, but as of today, I'm still kicking."

Sadie pointed at the door. "Theo's over by the door. You were talking to the chair Lora's sitting in."

"Is he the new one?" Mr. Bakke asked, directing his gaze toward the door.

"Yup," Michael chimed in. "He just got here."

Sadie patted Michael's leg. "Yes. He's our new one."

Theo nodded toward Mr. Bakke. "What's wrong with him? Can't he see me?"

"He can't see or hear you. He's a mortal."

"But you can," Theo argued looking at Sadie. "Your dog must see me because he keeps drooling all over my pants."

"All animals see crossers," Tim said. "Haven't you ever noticed how animals run and sniff the ground? It's because they smell a crosser and keep searching until they find it."

"That's preposterous." Glancing through the screen door, Theo spotted two men parking a golf cart next to the resort's shuttle van. He pushed through the door. "Excuse me. Can you give me directions to the nearest police station?" When they didn't answer, he shouted again. Rushing toward the golfers, Theo brushed past Jane.

When Jane opened the door, Sadie announced, "We have a new guest."

"That's nice," Jane said. "That must mean we have a full house."

"We sure do. Our latest guest is a bit skeptical. But he'll be back."

"Are any of them here now?" Jane asked.

"All of them except the newest one."

"Even Mr. Nasty?" Jane shifted the bag of groceries to her other hip.

Sadie sighed. "Yes, Rodney's here. He's in the inner room doing what he does best. Nothing."

Jane took the groceries from the bag and handed each item to Mr. Bakke. The elderly gentleman placed the canned goods on the shelf, taking care to turn each label face forward. He tapped the cans into alignment. As he stacked the smaller cans of dog food, he rotated them until the dog's heads aligned in a perfect column. Seven Spaniels stared back at him. He turned toward Jane and waited for the nod of approval before folding the paper bag and placing it on a shelf in the pantry.

"I think I'll go back to my cabin," he whispered to Jane. "I get nervous when Sadie has a full house. I keep sitting on them."

"That doesn't matter," Jane said. "Sadie told me the crossers are supposed to watch out for us. It's not our fault we can't see them. Besides, it's my cabin and I'll sit wherever I darn well please."

Jane directed her attention to Sadie. "What's the name of our new guest?"

"Theopholis Peter."

Splaying her hand against her chest Jane said, "How do you know that?"

"How do I know what?" Sadie turned to face her sister.

"About his peter?"

Placing her hands on her hips, Sadie said, "What are you talking about?"

"Well you said he had the awfulest peter. I want to know how you know that. Was he naked when he got here?"

"Good God, Jane. Sometimes I wonder if you're the crazy sister instead of me. I said his name is Theopholis Peter. Theopholis Jamison Peter. We call him Theo. Now do you understand?"

The men from the golf cart approached Theo. He repeated his request for directions a third time. "I'm sorry to bother you, but I seem to be lost. Can you help me?"

As Theo met the men, they continued without acknowledging him. Theo spun and reached out to grab one of the men. His hand clamped around the man's arm, but the man kept walking.

Gasping for air, Theo dropped to his knees. "It can't be. This can't be happening." He laid the briefcase in front of his knees, dialed the combination, released the latch. He inserted his fingers into the silk pocket lining the lid. He withdrew a small black bag. As he ran his fingers over the fabric, a tear dropped and beaded on one corner of the bag. He rocked back and forth clutching the bag. He sobbed, "Why? Why did this have to happen now?"

5

Deputy Carl Swanson sat hunched over an apprehension report, reading it through one final time. He scrawled his name across the signature line. Startled by a door latch clicking behind him, he turned to see his friend, Paul Brinks, enter and pause in front of a birch bark mirror.

A hot poker of envy stabbed at Carl. Paul had it all. All he had to do was smile and women surrounded him. Paul had been a babe-magnet in high school. He still was. Back then, Carl enjoyed sorting through Paul's castoffs. Not anymore.

Paul paged through a folder on Carl's desk while the deputy responded to an incoming phone call. He jerked his hand away when Carl slammed the folder shut.

"You don't need to look at anything on my desk," Carl said. "I don't snoop through your stuff, do I?"

"That's because you trust me. Trust is a good thing." Paul grinned slyly. "I hear the Witt sisters don't trust you. You're on their shit list. I still don't know why you think you're going to win that lawsuit."

"Don't worry about it." Carl slid the folder out of Paul's reach. "What makes you think I trust you? I'm not as dumb as Nan. I can't believe you dangled your money to get her to marry you."

"It's none of your business what I do. She'll come around if she wants the mortuary and the land it sits on." Paul propped his hip against the corner of Carl's desk. "Think about it. Before Nan's Dad died, he planned to buy the mortuary from the Witt sisters rather than continue the land lease. Now Nan wants to do the same thing. She wants to keep the family legacy alive, but can't afford it." Paul feigned a look of humility. "I'm a genius."

"Who'd want to continue the legacy of a mortuary, anyway? That's morbid."

"Her grandfather started the business a long time ago. Nan feels she owes it to him to continue their dream," Paul said.

Carl held his thumb and forefinger against his forehead to simulate the letter L.

"Nan's not a loser," Paul said.

"I didn't mean Nan. I meant you. Using something like that to get a woman to marry you is pathetic. But of course if the broad is dumb enough to fall for it, then she deserves you."

"I'm nowhere near as conniving as you are, my friend," Paul said. "I'm not the one going after two helpless, old ladies."

"Helpless my ass. The judge will determine who's helpless. You know how Judge Kimmer hates the Witt sisters."

Both men stopped as Angie, a twenty-three-year veteran with the sheriff's department, muted an incoming dispatch. Angie spun her desk chair around and signaled to Carl. Carl joined her behind the bullet-proof glass. Two 911 calls had been phoned in simultaneously. The callers indicated they had witnessed a vehicle cross the median, two miles north of town, and hit a pole.

They both looked back at Paul before Carl returned to his desk. "There was a car accident similar to the one the other night. Angie didn't want you to hear it. She didn't know how you'd react." Carl said.

"Who was it?" Paul pulled up a chair.

"Don't know yet. But it didn't sound serious. The victims didn't need an ambulance." Carl ran his hands over his face. "Thank God it wasn't as bad as the other night. I still can't believe the whole Fossum family was wiped out in that accident."

Carl tried to erase the image as he recalled the horrific scene of Richard Fossum impaled on a piece of splintered fencing. "It must be hard to lose your business partner."

"Yeah," Paul said, barely audible, as he stared at the folds of fabric in his lap.

"Want to talk about it? You know you should. He was your business partner. It's not good to keep it bottled up."

"Nope." Paul cleared his throat. "I still don't see why you think the judge will rule in your favor. If Sadie wouldn't sell him the resort, why would he want you to have it?"

"Because I put a bug in his ear," Carl said. "You know what a fishing fanatic he is. All the judge wants is a place to fish. He doesn't want the whole resort. I told him if I won, I'd make sure he had free use of one of the cabins." Carl smirked. "I also threw in a boat and all the bait he could use for the rest of his life."

"Judge Kimmer doesn't need any freebies. He's been rolling in money for the past several years."

"He dabbles in all kinds of things," Carl said. "I know he likes to putter with inventions. Or at least that's what he told me. Plus he's involved with a group of investors."

"Sounds like a conflict-of-interest to me," Paul said.

"Why? Because he tried to buy the resort? It was never

for sale. So it can't be a conflict. If Sadie uses that as a defense, no one will believe her. Who'd believe a crazy woman who babbles to invisible friends?"

"Her sister isn't crazy. Did the judge think about that?" Paul said.

"It doesn't matter. It won't come to that anyway."

Paul nodded his head toward an office near the dispatch desk. "What's Deputy Friborg doing in the sheriff's office?"

"He just finished a phone call. Apparently he wanted privacy." Carl flung the glass-paneled door open. It rebounded with a bang. "Hey, Lon. Did you see the front page of the newspaper?"

Startled, Lon Friborg pulled his feet off the sheriff's desk so quickly they hit the floor with a thud. "Holy balls. You scared me. I thought you were the sheriff."

"If I play my cards right, I will be." Carl leaned against the door frame. He crossed his arms and waited for Lon's reaction.

"You? The sheriff?" Lon put his feet back on the desk.

"If you'd pick up a newspaper once in a while, you'd see I threw my hat in the ring." Irritated at Lon's look of disbelief, Carl knocked the deputy's feet off the desk.

Carl was fed up with the shock everyone expressed over his entering the election. Lon was the third person this morning who acted surprised, and not one of them said it was a good idea. Stupidity. That's what it was. They weren't intelligent enough to understand the big picture. He absolutely refused to tolerate the laughter that gushed from his wife when he told her his plans. What did she know? She was so ignorant she couldn't remember to wear her underwear.

Lon bent to pick up the scattered papers. "Are you serious? You're running for sheriff?"

"Damn right I'm serious." Carl followed Lon back into the deputies' office. "I've planned a platform that'll guarantee victory. And in case you haven't noticed, I've started parking my squad car in my driveway instead of in my garage. It'll be good advertising. Kind of an 'in your face' approach."

"Your platform better include proving the Fossum crash wasn't an accident," Lon said.

Carl's jaw stiffened. "I thought I told you to drop it. The sheriff said it was an accident. Fossum hit a deer. That's all it was. An accident."

"And if you remember," Lon said, "I told you why I disagreed." Lon held up an index finger. "Skid marks for starters. I've known Richard for years. He was a good driver. The skid marks indicated a sharp wheel turn to the left. Richard knew better than that. He knew to tap on the brake and ride it out. Those skid marks didn't indicate braking."

Carl rolled his eyes. "That's lame. That's no reason to investigate. People swerve after hitting a deer all the time."

"What would it hurt to investigate a little further?" Lon said. "Did you see deer hair on the car? Or blood or skin? I didn't."

"You're blowing smoke out your ass," Carl shouted. "It was an accident. Get over it."

"Did you tell Paul about my concerns?"

"No he didn't," Paul said, looking at Carl for clarification.

"Paul's got enough grief right now. Losing his partner was bad enough." Carl glared at Lon as he returned to his desk. "And besides, it's bullshit."

"This needs to be investigated. If you're not going to do it, then I will."

Carl inched closer to Lon. "You do, and you'll jeopardize my chance of winning the election. People will think I'm not doing my job. I'm not about to go on a wild goose chase just because you've got a hunch."

"I'm telling you, Carl, Richard hadn't been himself before the crash. I'd never seen him so withdrawn," Lon said. "There's got to be something else going on."

"Richard was prone to mood swings," Paul said. "There was nothing else going on. I should know."

"Listen to yourself, Lon. You're just as loony as Nan's ex." Carl looked toward Angie as another dispatch call blared over the speaker. "When he made up stupid stories, everyone wrote it off to the booze. You're going to lose credibility just like he did."

Lon turned his back on the men and walked over to the coffee pot. He pulled three mugs off the rack and filled them with coffee.

"You need to hear my campaign strategy," Carl said. "It's based on what the people need." Drawing a sip of hot coffee, Carl spit it back into the mug. "Has this been brewing all morning? It tastes like mud. Make a fresh pot so we can have something decent to drink."

"Yes sir, Mr. Sheriff," Lon said. "Whatever you say."

Carl ignored Lon's remark. "I'm bored with being a deputy. I need a challenge. I happen to know what the bigwigs in this town want. That will be my platform. If I act

45

like I believe in what they want, I'm guaranteed a victory."

Grabbing the brim of his cap and raising it off his head, Carl scratched his scalp with his little finger. As he replaced his cap, he elbowed Paul. "Word has it the sheriff isn't going to run again. He's useless anyway. If I'm lucky, I'll run against some dumb stiff who thinks he can do a better job."

Lon slipped his Kevlar duty vest over his head. He reached around the corner and grabbed his shirt from a hanger.

Disgusted at Lon's lack of interest, Carl waited while he buttoned his shirt.

"Once I'm elected, I'm going to do what I want. I'm going to put them damn Indians back on the reservation where they belong." Carl sat forward in his chair. "Our current sheriff," he emphasized the word 'sheriff' by making quotation marks with his fingers, "isn't making them a priority. I know several council members who are upset with his attitude."

"You're not going to build a campaign on an issue like that. Pinecone Landing's got one of the biggest diversity groups in the state. Besides, the Indians have their own judicial system. It's federal law. You'd be a fool to think you can change it. And why would you? It works."

Paul piped in, "I think Carl's right. The sheriff is too lenient. We need someone in that office who's got big balls."

"That would be me," Carl said with raised eyebrows and a big grin. He watched Lon secure a wide leather belt around his waist and check the loops containing his cuffs and pepper spray. "I don't intend to change any laws."

He jabbed his thumb skyward. "You know how them Indians talk about Father Earth and all that other holy crap. It won't be God they fear, it'll be me. That's the key. It'll be a cold day before they break any more laws in my jurisdiction."

"You're going to get in a whole lot of trouble," Lon said. "You mess with the tribal council and you'll be pulled from office before you know what hit you."

"That's the trouble with you, Lon. You're such a pussy you've lost the ability to think on your feet." Carl leaned forward and grabbed his mug. "That's why I'm going to be sheriff and you're not."

"I don't want to be sheriff."

Surprised at the anger in Lon's voice, Carl said, "Nobody's going to miss a few renegades from time to time. I know enough to cooperate with the tribal council. I'll even help them locate their missing brethren."

"What makes you think they're the only ones who commit crimes around here?" Lon demanded. "Seems to me a few of your cousins were arrested last year."

"So?"

"If you look at the statistics, more crimes were committed by our locals than by the Indians."

"Then I'll just have to deal with the jack pine savages, too, won't I?"

"I guess," Lon said. "It seems to me you're seeking revenge on the whole tribe because of an indiscretion on your wife's part. You'd be better off cleaning up your own backyard first."

Carl was sick of Lon's blasé attitude. Nothing ruffled him. Yet he knew under that calm façade, Lon's brain churned nonstop. "Give me some credit. I intend to deal with all the crime. My plan will get press in the local paper. That'll make me look good. If everything goes the way I expect, there won't be a criminal left in Pinecone Landing." Carl nudged Paul. "I like the sound of that. Don't you?"

"Don't count on me to back your election," Lon said as he stood.

Carl grinned at Paul. "I think Lon's a little confused." Carl's grin soured as he directed his gaze toward Lon. "You and I both know you're going to be my strongest advocate. Not only are you going to support me, but you're going to head up my campaign."

Carl ignored the hateful look Lon shot in his direction. "I seem to remember an incident where you got carried away during an arrest." Faking curiosity, Carl said, "You do remember that, don't you? If I recall correctly, the Tribal Council had a difficult time believing your explanation."

Lon glared at Carl.

"Good. I see you haven't forgotten." Carl curled his fingers over his palm to examine his nails. He pulled a nail clipper from his desk drawer. "It goes without saying I expect results. If I get them, your past mistakes will remain safe with me."

"There's not one person in town who'd vote for you," Lon said.

"Two things will guarantee my victory. Your stumping efforts during my campaign and finalizing a piece of unfinished business right before the election. That'll be the clincher. Gaining ownership of that resort will be a major attention grabber and my name will be splashed all over the newspaper. Who do you think our fine citizens will vote for then?"

Carl dropped the nail clipper into the drawer. "They'll vote for the name they see most often. That's a proven fact. Why do you think politicians make themselves visible right before Election Day?"

"Because they can't win on their own merit?" Lon said. "I don't see why you're so determined to get control of that resort. I'm tired of your vendetta against the Witt sisters. You're obsessed."

As Carl groaned in disagreement, Lon added, "Those two old ladies wouldn't harm a bee if it stung them. Sadie may be a bit strange, but those sisters keep a whole lot of people employed year round. I think that's more important than your lawsuit."

"I don't care what you think. Sadie's mother got that property from my grandfather through illegal means. Granddad had a weak spot. He couldn't stand up to her mother's sexual advances." Slamming his hand against his desk, he said, "Mark my words. I'm going to make my grandfather proud. I'm going to get that property back."

As Lon walked through the door, he turned and looked at the dispatcher. "I'm on my way up north to pick up that perp." He nodded to the men at the desk. "Later, Carl. You, too, Slick."

"It irritates me when he calls me that," Paul said. He stared at Lon's back. "Lon hates me. He'd do anything to aggravate me."

"Hates you? What are you talking about?"

"He's got the hots for Nan. Ever since I started dating her, Lon's been giving me the cold shoulder."

"Quit whining. He's been interested in her for years. He

was the first one who approached her after she divorced his no-good cousin."

"I hate the way he looks at her. He's waiting for me to make a wrong move."

"You're crazy. He calls you Slick because you dress like you live in New York City." Carl's gaze ran the length of Paul's body. "You probably spent more on those pants then I earned last week. No wonder they call you Slick. I thought women were the ones who had closets jammed with clothes."

When Carl and Paul were in their early twenties, the two had been a formidable pair. Both men stood six feet tall. Between the two of them they possessed the attributes necessary to rank them high on the list of eligible bachelors. Paul had the money and the looks. Carl had the muscles and the swagger. Together they had been unstoppable and enjoyed a longstanding position at the top of the testosterone heap.

Paul fared well through time, but not Carl. His looks had curdled like cream. Over the years Carl had sprouted a protruding stomach, one that caused him continuous embarrassment. Women no longer found him desirable. Due to his wife's constant belittling and indiscretions, his confidence had eroded. He accepted his fate. Not because he wanted to, but because his wife would kill him if she found out he'd been with another woman.

Paul poured a mug of fresh coffee and looked out the window. Watching Lon slide into his squad car, Paul said, "Do you think he'll help with your campaign?"

Carl removed his cap and wiped his brow. "The way I see it, he doesn't have a choice. When he was accused of roughing up that perp last summer, I told the Tribal Council the perp had been in an altercation before he was arrested. They wanted to pursue it, but because Fading Sun's such a loser, they finally dropped it."

"I'm surprised the perp's wife didn't pursue it," Paul said. Staring at Carl with intense green eyes, Paul ran his hand over his hair before patting it into place. "You're not listening to me. I said I'm surprised his wife didn't pursue it. Mrs. Fading Sun usually doesn't put up with prejudice against her husband. She's one of those diversity crusaders."

"What gets me," Carl said, "is why a white woman with a good education would marry him in the first place."

Paul tipped his head toward his right shoulder, "At least the woman was smart enough to buy an insurance policy on her husband. Her payments are always on time. I can't ask for more than that."

"Yeah. I suppose," Carl grumbled. "That's all you think about is your insurance business."

"It's not just insurance. It's investments, too. And why wouldn't I think about it? I need to make a living, don't I?" Paul looked at Carl out of the corner of his eye. "Did Lon really rough up Fading Sun when the two of you arrested him?"

"That's none of your business," Carl said. "All that matters is that the investigation was dropped."

6

"I'm not hungry, Mom," Aanders said, pushing the plate with the uneaten chicken aside. Rotating the base of his milk glass against the counter top, he watched the white liquid swirl until it became motionless.

"Don't worry about it." Nan picked up her son's plate." I'll put it in the fridge. You might want it later." The ringing of the phone cut across her words.

Aanders crossed to the counter as the phone rang for the second time. "Harren Funeral Home."

The two-bedroom mortuary apartment made a shoebox look large, but Aanders had grown to love it. They had moved into the apartment after Nan's divorce. His mother installed a second phone line in the apartment to handle business calls after countless attempts at running from the apartment to the office had failed. Aanders knew his mother wanted to house hunt, but she told him the convenience of being on-site to run the business as well as the luxury of not having house payments was too good to pass up. Thoughts of relocation had been placed on hold.

While his mom and dad were still married, Nan had contracted with the University of Minnesota to provide internship opportunities to mortuary science students. She had added the apartment to the mortuary to house the students. Aanders' dad hated the apartment and called it an unnecessary extravagance. The apartment now made Nan's financial burdens easier to tolerate.

Aanders watched his mother jot directions on the

scratch pad she kept by the phone. Slowly, his gaze wandered to the basement door.

Nan folded the sheet and patted Aanders' arm. "I'm going to change and then I've got to retrieve a body at the nursing home. Will you be okay by yourself?"

"Yeah," he said, without meeting her eyes.

Nan lifted his chin with her fingers. "I want you to promise you won't go downstairs. I don't want you to see Tim till I've prepped his body." Kissing his forehead she added, "We'll have our own private viewing when I get back."

A tear rolled down Aanders' cheek. Nan brushed it away with her thumb. He leaned sideways to escape her hand. He didn't want to cry.

"I'm taking your silence as a promise." Nan lifted a black suit off a hanger and retreated toward the bathroom to change clothes. "I'll be back as soon as I can." As she reached to close the door behind her, Belly whined and made a feeble attempt to scratch behind his right ear. "Take that dog back to Sadie's while I'm gone. Why don't you ask Mr. Bakke to show you his new fishing rod? He bought it this morning. Maybe he'll let you try a few casts off the end of the dock."

Nan emerged from behind the door wearing a midi-length black skirt and a sleeveless white shell. Aanders watched her slip into a black jacket.

Aanders pressed the garage door opener while his mother climbed into the driver's seat. He waited as she propped a clipboard against the steering wheel and transferred the address from the note to the document on the clipboard.

"How long will you be gone?"

"I'm not sure. Maybe an hour. Two at the most."

As Aanders walked back into the kitchen, Belly let out a pleading whimper. Aanders brushed the dog aside with his foot. "You big fatty. You know he's down there, don't you?"

Belly circled in excitement, his toenails clicking against the floor. Raking his claws against the door's panel, the dog looked up at Aanders in anticipation.

"I can't let you go down there. Mom would kill me. Besides, I promised I wouldn't go down there." Clapping his hands together to get Belly's attention, Aanders insisted, "You heard what Mom said. I'm supposed to take you back to the cabin."

Belly lifted his chin and let out a piercing howl.

Aanders reached for the doorknob, but pulled back.

The four black hairs at the end of Belly's tail gyrated as his entire rear end swayed in excitement. When Aanders reached for the knob a second time, Belly began to pant.

A tiny sliver of darkness appeared and cool air wafted from the opening. Belly pulled at the panel with his paw. The door swung wide.

"Belly," Aanders shouted. "Come back here."

The sound of Belly's claws hitting the wooden stairs echoed from the opening before he landed with a grunt on the basement floor.

Shouting into the darkness, Aanders again said, "Belly. Get back up here right now. You'll get me in trouble."

Whimpers and barks of enthusiasm emanated from the shadows in counterpoint to the sound of his nails against the hard tile floor.

"You dumb dog. Come here right now." Aanders

placed a foot on the top step and strained to see past one of the nightlights twinkling in the darkness. "Right now. I mean it." Reducing his voice to a whisper, he repeated the dog's name and lowered his foot down another step. His finger twitched against the light switch.

The brightness momentarily blinded him and he waited for his eyes to adjust. He peered toward the embalming room. Unable to locate the dog, he whispered, "If you don't come here right now, I'm going to get mad. Belly? Did you hear what I said? Belly?"

A sharp yip caused Aanders to flip the switch off and hop toward the top step. He turned his ear toward the sound. "Are you okay down there?" He wiped his palms against his pants, waiting for the next sound.

Excited panting and more toe clicking enticed Aanders into turning the light back on. One by one, he descended the stairs. Whispering the dog's name, he continued to encourage Belly out of the embalming room. "I can't go in there. You have to come out. If Mom comes home now, she'll kill both of us. I mean it. We'll be really, really dead."

Growing fearful his mom would return and the receiving bay door would rise to expose him and the stubborn dog, Aanders grew more insistent. He approached the embalming room door. He snapped his fingers and crouched to Belly's level. "Come here boy. I've got a treat for you." The enticing offer usually did the trick, but Belly ignored the suggestion. His gyrating tail kept his rear in motion all the way back to the far corner of the room.

Belly put him in danger of betraying his mother's trust. The simple mission to find the dog and hurry upstairs before he saw the Fossums' bodies grew daunting. Two embalming machine lights blinked rhythmically casting an eerie green hue. The ceiling light from the hall adjacent to the embalming room added to his ability to recognize items as he gingerly moved forward.

A long, narrow embalming table stood in the middle of the room flanked on both sides by a bank of stainless steel cabinets. The back wall featured a massive, steel door. The door led to a walk-in, refrigerated storage bay containing two sliding body trays. Each tray pulled out and retracted for easy access. Because the cold-storage unit currently held two bodies, Nan had placed the third body on the embalming table in the center of the room.

Aanders spotted Belly in the corner of the room, pawing at the air. "There you are. Come here, you dumb dog." Aanders' hand brushed against the cold foot of the body lying on the steel table. He let out a gurgled cry. He backed away from the table and bumped against a cabinet causing steel tools to clank noisily against a metal pan. Another cry rose from Aanders' throat. He looked over his shoulder at the body on the table.

There he was. Tim Fossum. His best friend.

A white sheet covered Tim's body. Three of Tim's fingers protruded from beneath the edge of the sheet. The sheet clung to the boy's body, elevated by Tim's nose and his rigid toes. It looked like one big glow-in-the-dark lump, reflecting a green hue from the embalming machine.

A guttural wail rasped from Aanders. Sensing his legs about to give out, he grabbed the edge of the table and hung on. Nausea spasms rose in his throat. He had often helped his mother lift the heavier bodies when she was unable to manage them by herself, but no amount of exposure to mortuary procedures could have prepared him for the inconsolable loss he experienced. His friend was dead. His friend who he could tell anything to was lying next to him. Gone forever.

Sorrow flowed freely as Aanders' chest heaved with deep emotion.

Belly waddled over and poked Aanders' leg with his nose. Waiting patiently for his friend to sort through his emotions, the dog whined and lay down at the boy's feet.

Aanders knelt and pulled Belly close. "Why, Belly? Why did he have to die? It's so stupid. If he'd have just come home with me instead of going with his mom and dad, he'd be alive now."

Belly offered a slobbery lick in understanding before ambling back to the corner. His tail darted in a replay of excitement before he plopped down on his right haunch with his left leg splayed out in front. He stared into the corner. His head cocked back and forth.

Aanders touched Tim's finger tips, letting his gaze settle on the sheet over Tim's head. He grasped the sheet with two hands as he had seen his mother do when she uncovered the bodies for an initial viewing and folded the sheet back against Tim's chest. He gasped at Tim's pallor. Grabbing the table with both hands, he fought the lightheadedness that again caused him to tilt.

Waiting until he could stand unassisted, he said, "I hate you for leaving me. I hate you." He ran his hand under his nose and wiped it on his pants leg. "You were my best friend. You were my only friend." He shook as the angry words spewed forth. "We were going to be friends forever."

Belly again nudged Aanders' leg and snorted when the

boy bent to hug him.

Pulling Belly close, Aanders said, "We were going to invent a computer game and get rich. Tim said we'd buy matching trucks." As if reading from a list, Aanders continued, "We were going to have new friends. We were going to take our moms on a trip. We were going to do anything we wanted." He buried his face in Belly's neck and let the tears flow.

"Tim didn't care that I lived in a mortuary." Pounding the floor with his fist, Aanders shouted, "How could he have done this to me? I was his best friend." He threw his head back and gulped through the sobs. "What am I supposed to do now?"

"You'll always be my best friend, Aanders."

Aanders gasped, choking on air suddenly caught in his throat. His back grew rigid. He turned his head slightly to the right and peeked out of the corner of his eye.

Belly waddled eagerly toward the corner.

Aanders looked back at the body on the table. "Now I'm hearing things. I thought you said something."

Aanders snapped his fingers in command. "Come here you stupid dog. Right now. We've got to get out of here."

The voice from the corner said, "I did say something. I said you'll always be my best friend. No matter what."

Aanders screamed as he turned his head toward the corner. Trembling, he strained to see through the darkness and braced himself against a cabinet.

The voice from the corner also gasped in disbelief. "You can hear me? I can't believe it. If you can hear me, then you must be able to see me, too. Can you see me, Aanders?"

A fearful moan escaped as Aanders felt his way toward the door.

"Don't go," the voice begged. "Please don't go. It's me. It's me, Tim."

Shrieking louder as he looked from Tim's body on the table to the faint image in the corner, Aanders bumped against a cart containing embalming fluid. The cart toppled, sending plastic gallon jars rolling across the floor.

"You can see me, can't you?" Tim shouted. "You can see me!"

Aanders inched toward the door with his back hugging the counter. The figure shifted forward into the glow of the hall's light.

Aanders jerked his gaze from the figure to the body on the table. It was Tim. It was his friend standing there as well as his friend's body under the sheet on the table. "It ca-ca-can't be." He pointed in both directions. "You can't be in both places at the same time." He whispered, "Can you?"

"It's me. It really is. But guess what? If I'm dead and you can see me, then you're a death coach. Nobody else can see the crossers except death coaches." Tim grinned at his friend. "I can't believe it. Wait till I tell Sadie." He breathlessly added, "Maybe you already know you're a coach. Have you been keeping it from me all this time?"

Belly circled, stopping long enough during the rotations to offer a paw to Tim.

"Are you crazy?" Aanders shouted. "I don't know what you're talking about." He pointed to the body on the table and then again at Tim. "Are you dead or not?"

"I'm dead all right. But there's more. We were murdered and I've got to prove it."

7

Nan watched Mr. Bakke spray disinfectant over the embalming table and rub it vigorously with a white cloth.

A smile graced her lips as Paul Brink's words tiptoed into her mind. When Paul had generously offered to foot the bill for purchasing the mortuary and the five acres it sat on, Nan had refused. She wanted to do it on her own. Accepting his offer meant making a commitment. Her marriage to Clay had been a disaster and she wasn't ready to commit to someone else. Now she wished she hadn't refused. It was beginning to look like the dream of perpetuating her father's funeral enterprise would never be realized.

"I forgot to tell you Lon called," Mr. Bakke said.

"Did he say what he wanted?"

"Not really, but he asked if you'd finished with the Fossums yet."

"I had the strangest conversation with Lon yesterday," Nan said. "After he helped me load a body into the hearse, he told me he asked Carl Swanson to investigate the Fossums' deaths. Carl refused. He said Carl got really nervous when he brought it up."

"What did he tell you? Does he think foul play was involved?"

"I'm not sure. But I know he's investigating on the sly. He said if Carl finds out, he'll push to get him transferred. Or fired."

"I can't believe anyone would hurt the Fossums. Richard Fossum didn't have an enemy in the world," Mr.

Bakke said. "He's the kindest person I know."

"Lon said the same thing. That's one of the reasons he's puzzled. He asked if Paul ever discussed any problems he had with Richard."

"Did he?"

"None that he ever talked about. Paul's pretty quiet about his business. There's a lot of confidentiality issues in the insurance business, you know."

"I suppose that's true." Mr. Bakke tossed the cloth into a hamper.

"Lon said he wished he could get into Richard's office to look at his papers. He wants to see if he can figure out why Richard was depressed."

Sadie and Jane accompanied Nan, Mr. Bakke, and six men to the cemetery following the funeral of a woman who had passed and left no immediate family. She had been institutionalized and outlived the majority of her kin. Those relatives still living had long since forgotten her. Nan insisted that each client be treated with respect and dignity. This woman was no exception. Sadie, Jane, and Mr. Bakke willingly accompanied the woman on her final journey.

The tiny procession fell into place behind a patrol car with its flashers blinking rhythmically against the afternoon sky. Two cars followed the hearse.

After Nan parked the hearse at the cemetery, Mr. Bakke, still spry at seventy, walked toward the gravesite grasping Jane's arm with his right hand and clutching a psalm book in the other. Nan and Sadie followed close behind.

When Nan had offered Mr. Bakke a part-time job to

assist with funerals and body preparations, the elderly man jumped at the opportunity. He preferred productivity rather than wasting his time in a vacuum. He had proved to be a valuable assistant. Many times Nan had to insist he pace his workload.

Work wasn't the only thing occupying Mr. Bakke's time. Jane was his other project. The romance had brewed over two decades and turned into a satisfying convenience for them both.

Mr. Bakke lived in Cabin 12. Cabin 12 had been reserved for the resort's caretaker, but when Mr. Bakke could no longer keep up with the duties of the expanding resort, the Witt sisters let him live there permanently. The resort now had three younger men handling the caretaking responsibilities.

Two gravediggers stood off to one side at a respectable distance as the attendees gathered around the burial hole. Four gentlemen from an area church and two local businessmen who had offered to serve as pallbearers lifted the casket from the hearse and placed it on the supports straddling the hole.

Mr. Bakke recited a psalm as they lowered the woman into the ground. He leaned in and placed a rose on the casket. The group then recited the Lord's Prayer. A gravedigger winced and looked out of the corner of his eye at his fellow digger as Mr. Bakke solemnly offered an off-key rendition of Amazing Grace.

Heavy silence surrounded the site. Nan nodded to the gravediggers. The pallbearers quietly returned to their vehicle.

As Jane walked back to the car, she poked her sister

with her elbow. "Did you notice that car we met on the way to the cemetery?"

"What car?"

"That car with Carl Swanson and Judge Kimmer. Judge Kimmer was in the front seat with Carl. And Paul Brinks was in the back."

Sadie pressed closer to her sister. "Are you sure?"

"Positive. I know Paul and Carl are friends, but since when does Paul associate with Judge Kimmer?"

Sadie put her finger to her lips as Nan caught up with them.

"Thanks, Mr. Bakke. You did a wonderful job," Nan said. "I couldn't have done it without you." She nodded her appreciation to the sisters as she clasped their hands.

"Are you going to be home this evening?" Sadie asked.

"I have no choice. I've got a full slate with the Fossum family. In fact, Mr. Bakke, I'd like to take you up on your offer to help."

"I'll do it," he replied. "And I refuse to accept that raise you gave me. Just pay me what you paid me before. I do it because I enjoy it." He quickly added, "Not in a morbid sense, mind you. I enjoy it because I like being useful again."

Nan's eyes filled with gratitude.

"If you have a few minutes to spare," Sadie said, "we'll stop by after you finish with the Fossums. Jane and I have something to tell you."

"Great. I'll see you then." Nan slammed the hearse door and turned the key in the ignition.

Jane waved at Mr. Bakke as they drove off in the hearse.

8

Carl Swanson slowed his vehicle to a stop and turned off the overhead flashers. Reaching for his sunglasses, he shook them open and slipped the bows over his ears. "Where's my pen?" He ran his hand through a pile of debris strewn across the car seat.

Furious at being pulled over, Sadie hunched behind the wheel and waited for Carl to approach the passenger side of the Witt's End shuttle. She stared out the window as Carl rapped on the door.

"All right you old biddy, open the door." He stuffed his shirttail into his waistband and hoisted up his pants.

After Carl's second rap on the glass, Sadie grabbed the door's release lever and pushed it forward. "I see you took your sweet time getting out of your car. Your hemorrhoids acting up again?"

"Anything to prolong your agony, Sadie. You know my day's not complete until I make you miserable. Oh, and by the way, it's going to get worse."

Ignoring his face protruding through the opening, Sadie crossed her arms over her chest and stared through the windshield at a dead dragonfly that had taken one flight too many.

"I'll wait all day if I have to." Carl leaned his elbow on the door and scanned the seats in the van. He gave an exaggerated wave. "I suppose you've got a full load today."

"There's not a soul in here but me. I'm going to tell everyone you're waving at my imaginary friends."

"You be sure to do that. It adds fuel to my lawsuit. What judge would rule in favor of a crazy woman?"

After flicking a piece of lint from the dashboard, Sadie arranged the rearview mirror so she could check her image. She fluffed her spiked hair and turned her head from side to side before tapping on her ear lobe to set an earring containing zebra, leopards, and a menagerie of wildlife in motion. She cocked her head toward Carl. "You still here? I thought you'd be out chasing real criminals instead of preying on the elderly."

Carl placed a foot on the first step. "Get it out. Get it out right now." Beads of sweat formed along the brim of Carl's cap from the sun beating down on his dark uniform.

"Get what out?" Sadie said.

"It's so sad when old people become babbling idiots. Your Alzheimer's must be in full bloom." He put a hand on his raised leg. "You know what I want. Get it out." Carl leaned closer to the petite five-foot driver.

"Oh yippie. It's frisking time." Grinning, Sadie started to unbutton her shirt.

"What the hell are you doing?" Carl backed down one step.

"I know what you want." Sadie leaned toward him. Spreading her zebra stripe shirt, she said, "I'm ready."

Flinching as Sadie rose from the driver's seat, Carl shouted, "Sit down. Button your shirt."

Sadie pouted. "No frisking today?"

"I wouldn't frisk those saggy old breasts if you were the last woman on earth. I couldn't stoop that low."

Smiling, Sadie dropped back into the seat. "Maybe not. But it might bring back memories. Don't you remember the times you practiced becoming a deputy by frisking my daughter? Everyone comments on how she resembles me."

"That's disgusting," Carl said. "Your daughter is nothing like you. I remember every inch of her body."

"I'm sure you do." Pleased that Carl accepted the bait, Sadie added, "Don't you just love those old memories? And doesn't it just kill you that she dropped you flat on your face when she caught you two-timing with Bubbles Borque?"

The flush creeping over Carl's face matched the deep red embossing on his cap. He removed his hat and ran his arm across his forehead. "For your information, I was the one who planned on dumping her. Bubbles made it easier."

"Is that why I heard you crying outside her bedroom window night after night? You sure know how to beg."

Carl tugged his cap back into position. "Get your driver's license out."

"Not until you tell me why you pulled me over." Ever since Carl had filed the lawsuit, he made a point of pulling her over every time he spotted the shuttle van. "I haven't broken any law. What's the charge?"

"Same thing as last time. It amazes me someone as ancient as you still doesn't know the rules of the road." Without looking up, Carl wrote on the ticket. "Of course senility tends to do that, doesn't it? I think you need your driver's license revoked." Carl's gaze skimmed the bill of his cap and he looked up at Sadie. "I think I'll talk to Judge Kimmer about that, too."

"You're a good-for-nothing piece of sperm that didn't have the sense to quit swimming," Sadie shouted. Reaching under the driver's seat, she pulled out a ruler and waved it in Carl's face. "See this? I'm going to prove I didn't stop too far past the stop sign. I'm going to put an end to your harassment. I have no intention of paying the last two tickets and I don't intend to pay this one, either."

Descending the van steps, Sadie got down on her hands and knees and placed the ruler on the pavement. "There. Look at that." Waving at anyone who would listen, Sadie raised her voice. "Everybody look. Look at this ruler. This deputy is trying to give me a ticket for stopping too far ahead of the stop sign." Cupping both hands around her mouth she shouted, "Harassment. Blatant harassment. This deputy is preying on the vulnerable elderly."

"You idiot," Carl said, yanking Sadie up by her arm. Pushing her back toward the van's door, he put his mouth near her ear. "Get back in that van before I arrest you for causing a riot."

"Riot?" Sadie looked back over her shoulder as Carl squeezed her arm. "Seems to me everyone's avoiding you, not me. I'm a harmless old woman." She massaged the pain in her arm caused by Carl's grip. "I hope this turns black and blue so I can show my attorney what you did to me."

Carl's gaze zeroed in on the reddened area. "That's nothing compared to what you'll feel the day I escort you off my property after the judge rules in my favor."

"That will never happen." Sadie sat behind the steering wheel and glared at Carl. "You can make up all the lies you want about your grandfather, but you'll never get my land. Isn't it enough you got his money when your father died?"

"Not nearly enough," Carl spat. "Have you decided on a nursing home yet? You're going to have to go somewhere when I escort you off my property. Think of the fun you'll have playing Bingo while you piss in your pants. That should give you something to look forward to." Pushing further into the van he added, "Come to think of it, I'm going to have to evict old man Bakke, too. I hear you don't charge him rent. I'm not going to give him a free ride."

"I'm not worried. Judge Kimmer will rule in our favor."

Spittle flew as a hearty laugh burst from Carl's lips. "You really are stupid, aren't you? You're not one of Kimmer's favorite people."

"Then I'll ask for another judge."

"Won't help. The only other judge is retiring next week and the court calendar is full until Thanksgiving. Too bad."

Sadie pulled on the door lever and the panels closed against Carl's body.

Carl stopped the closure with his elbow and pried the door open. "My grandfather wanted me to have the resort. Your mother got him to sign over the deed by using sex. Everyone knows that. They also know that after granddad died, your mother ran the resort as a whore house."

"That's a lie, Carl Swanson. She did no such thing."

Carl interrupted. "For all I know, you're doing the same thing. But that will end soon." Releasing his grip, Carl added, "Be sure to take your imaginary friends with you when you go. I don't want people thinking I'm crazy, too."

Sadie tapped the face of her watch. "You just wasted twenty minutes of our tax payer's time. If you'd put that much effort into proving the Fossums were murdered, you might get someone to vote for you."

Carl stopped mid stride. "What did you say?"

"Lon thinks it wasn't an accident."

"Lon better keep his mouth shut. And so should you if you know what's good for you."

9

"Don't come any closer." The whispered warning was barely audible. Aanders hugged the counter and stared at the image. Through eyes glazed with fear, Aanders looked from the body lying on the embalming table to the pale image coming toward him. "I said stay there."

Tim moved closer to the embalming table, but hesitated when Aanders turned in withdrawal. "Please don't leave." He reached for his friend. "Please stay with me."

Unable to grasp the situation, Aanders blurted, "This can't be real. You can't be talking to me if you're dead." He squinted to bring the image into focus. "Are you dead or not?" The last word rose to a high pitch as Aanders saw Tim step closer.

"Yes," Tim cried dropping to his knees. The twelve-year-old rocked in place, sobs pulsing through his body. "I'm dead and I didn't go through the light with Mom and Dad."

"What?" Aanders bent down to look under the table toward Tim.

"I'm dead. I died in the car with Mom and Dad. We were murdered."

"Murdered? You weren't murdered. It was an accident." Aanders pointed toward the heavy steel door. "Your mom and dad are over there in cold storage. But what do you mean you didn't go through the light?"

"I was held back." Tim hugged his arms to his chest and looked up at his friend. "I need to find a way to go back through the light so I can be with Mom and Dad."

Aanders looked back at his friend's body on the embalming table and then at Tim crouched on the floor. "This can't be real. Wait till I tell Mom."

Sniffling, Tim scooted over to the wall. "You're not going to believe any of this, but boy do I have a lot to tell you. It's just like one of them scary movies."

Aanders backed away from Tim.

"Don't be afraid," Tim said. "Even though I'm dead, I'm still your best friend. Nothing bad will happen if you still like me."

Scowling, Aanders drew closer to Tim. He made sure he left a four-foot span between them.

Tim held his arm out. "Touch me."

"No way." Aanders leaned away from the outstretched hand. "I'm not going to touch a dead person who's talking to me."

"Why not? It's no different than those bodies your mom prepped last week. It'll feel just like that." Tim lunged forward and placed his hand on Aanders bare arm.

Aanders jerked his arm away. "Don't do that. Your hand's as cold as snow." Looking from Tim to the body on the embalming table, he said, "Quit scaring me." Aanders squared his shoulders. "I don't have to stay here and be your friend if I don't want to. I might take Belly upstairs and watch TV."

"Please don't go," Tim said. "I wanted you to touch me so you'd believe what I have to tell you."

Aanders appeared to look straight ahead into the darkness, but scrutinized his friend's every move out of the corner of his eye. He slowly unfolded his fists and inched his fingers across the span. He stopped when his finger butted up against Tim's hand. Mustering the courage to continue, he placed his hand on top of Tim's hand. "Wow. You feel just like that old man that got his leg caught under the mower and died in his yard. Remember that?" Aanders rubbed his index finger on the back of Tim's arm. "Mom says a dead person's skin is clammy. You're clammy, all right."

Tim felt Aanders' arm and then his own. "You're right. I am."

Aanders settled back against the wall, this time closer to his friend. "I guess that means you're dead."

"I already told you that." Tim watched Belly plop down between them and roll onto his side with a muffled grunt. He kneaded his fingers through Belly's coarse hair as he drifted off in thought.

Aanders hugged his knees to his chest and took advantage of the reprieve to contemplate this new revelation.

"The stuff I'm going to tell you will freak you out." Tim rose to his knees and faced his friend. "It's freaky that I'm dead and at the same time I'm talking to you. But what's freakier is you can see me. You don't realize what that means." Bouncing on his knees toward his friend, Tim added, "Man, are you in for a shock."

"You already said that. Nothing can shock more than a dead person talking to me. So what's the big deal?"

"Don't you think it's weird you're talking to a dead person?"

"Yaaahhh." Aanders rolled his eyes. Tim was his best friend, but he had a way of going on and on without ever getting to the point. "It's weird all right." His gaze shot toward his friend as he gasped, "Don't tell me I'm dead, too!"

"I never thought of that," Tim said. He took Aanders hand and ran his fingers over it. "Nope. You're not dead. Your hand is warm."

Belly snorted to remind the boys he was in attendance. He rolled onto his back. His left leg twitched as he wriggled back and forth, trying to find a comfortable spot on the tile floor.

Aanders pulled the dog near and rubbed his cheek over Belly's head. "You were trying to tell me he was down here, weren't you?" Tears brimmed in Aanders' eyes as he looked at his friend. "What am I supposed to do now?"

"Because I'm a crosser or because you're a death coach?"

"Because you're my friend and now you're dead. Who am I going to do things with? I don't want a new best friend. I want you to be my friend."

Tim and Aanders had become fast friends when they sat next to one another in kindergarten. Tim's Mom had been supportive of the friendship and encouraged Tim to include Aanders in their family outings after Aanders' father had abandoned his responsibilities. Other mothers had not been as supportive. They discouraged their sons from forming a relationship with the son of a mortician. Their whispered reasons included the mortuary being an improper place to entertain friends, or the fact that it was unnatural for a woman to ask her son to help with funeral preparations. Aanders childhood inched along a steep incline.

Tim leaned his head against the wall and looked at Aanders. "That probably won't matter once you hear what death coaches do."

"You keep saying that. What's a death coach?"

Aanders scowled as Tim finished explaining what he had learned during Sadie's round table sessions. "How do you know all this stuff?"

"I told you. I learned it from Sadie. She explains it after we come back."

"Come back from where?"

"The nursing home or the hospital. She takes us there in the morning and picks us up before supper. We're supposed to seek out the dying so we can cross back over with them. But first we have to make a death decision."

"You believed her?" Aanders said. "Everyone knows she's crazy. At least that's what they say." He paused. "Everyone except Mom. She thinks Sadie's a nice old lady."

"I knew you wouldn't believe me." Tim hugged his knees and rested his chin on one knee. "It's so freaky I didn't believe it at first, either. If you come to Cabin 14, you'll see all the crossers. There are five of us living there."

"Five dead people?" Aanders said with a gasp.

"Yes. There's a man in a suit who has a briefcase he won't let anyone touch. And there's a mom and a boy there too. The mom sits and cries all the time. She gets on everyone's nerves."

"What about the fifth dead person," Aanders said.

"That's Rodney. He's mean. I'm afraid of him, but I don't think the guy in the suit is. The guy in the suit talks funny."

"Like how?"

"I don't know how to explain it. He sounds kinda like the President when he's talking about important stuff on TV. You know. He uses big words."

"Does Rodney punch the other dead people?"

"Sadie won't let him," Tim answered.

Aanders struggled to grasp the information Tim had shared. "Can Mom see the crossers?"

"No. She's not a death coach. Sadie told us only death coaches can see crossers."

"That makes Sadie a babysitter for dead people." Aanders watched Belly paw at Tim to get his attention. "But Belly can see you. Is he a death coach?"

"There's so much to remember, I forgot to tell you about Belly." Tim picked at the four black hairs on Belly's tail. "Animals and death coaches can see the dead."

A sly grin formed as Tim said, "Man, is Sadie going to be surprised when she finds out you can see them, too. She told us there weren't any other death coaches in this part of Minnesota."

"I'm not going to her cabin. I don't want to be a death coach." Straightening his back, Aanders said, "I'm not going anywhere to be with a bunch of dead people."

"Well I'm dead and you're with me. And you've got dead people in your house all the time."

"That's different."

"No it's not. What's the big deal? You don't need to be afraid."

"I'm not afraid." Aanders' shout echoed through the embalming room.

"You are, too. If you won't go with me, then you're a big chicken."

Belly stirred at the outcry and thumped his tail vigorously against the floor.

"I'm not a chicken," Aanders said, cupping Belly's face in his hands. He pressed his nose against the dog's forehead.

"Then prove it."

As intriguing as the challenge was, Aanders felt his throat fill with acid. Over the years he had listened to rumors of Sadie's imaginary friends and had witnessed her waving her hands and talking into the wind as she stood on her porch. Now he understood why. He was cursed with the same powers. Sadie might be their babysitter, but he refused to take care of dead people.

Aanders pulled at his shoelace and flicked at Belly's ear with the stiff end of the lace. "Do you really have to make a death decision?" Gazing at Tim out of the corner of his eye he saw him nod.

"I either have to go back through the light or go to the parallel world. I don't want to leave you, but I have to find Mom and Dad. They'll miss me if I go to the other place."

"But they're in cold storage over there," Aanders said, pointing toward the walk-in cooler.

Tim sat with his legs straight and tapped his feet together. "That's just their bodies. Mom and Dad aren't in those bodies anymore. Their spirits went through the light when they died. I saw it happen." His body vibrated in rhythm with the tapping of his toes.

"You couldn't stay with me instead, could you?" A tinge of hope flickered across Aanders' face.

"No. Sadie said I don't have a choice. If I don't go through the light within thirty days, I'll fade away all together."

"Like a ghost?"

"I don't think so. Sadie said it meant I'd disappear into the air like campfire smoke. I'd never see my parents again."

Aanders swiped at a tear as it rolled down his cheek.

"I'm going to miss you, Aanders." Tim rested his hand on Belly's back and edged it toward Aanders until their hands touched. A sob escaped as Tim hid his face against his knees.

"Me, too. I still can't believe you're going to be gone for real."

"Me neither," Tim said, wiping his cheeks across the denim covering his knees. "We can still be together until I have to go."

"Really?"

"I bet you didn't know I slept in your room last night."

Aanders felt the hair rise on his neck as he stared at his friend. "In my bedroom?"

"Yes. And guess what. I saw your mom in her underwear when she came out of the bathroom."

"For real?" Aanders said.

"For real."

Both boys leaned their heads against the wall to contemplate the past few minutes. Grunts from the obese dog drew the lads from their thoughts as Belly struggled to get to his feet.

"Don't you wonder what the other world would be like? If you decided to go there, I could go there when I die, too."

Tim paused before he answered. "No. I think I better find Mom and Dad. I don't want them to get lonesome."

"Maybe they're already in the other world. Maybe you

76

should go there to find out."

"No, they're not. Sadie said only those who are held back from going through the light can go to the parallel world."

Aanders weighed Tim's answer. "You told me you had unfinished business. What kind of unfinished business would a kid have?"

"I wondered the same thing at first. I wasn't in business like my dad, but after I listened to the other crossers sort things out, I know why."

Both boys turned toward the sound of the hearse bay door rising.

"Mom's back," Aanders whispered.

"Be quiet and she won't know you're here," Tim said.

"She'll think we're crazy sitting on the floor in the dark."

Tim smiled. "She'll think you're crazy because she won't see me."

Footsteps shuffled past the door. Aanders held his breath. He listened to the sound of her shoes against the treads while she climbed and closed the door behind her.

Aanders exhaled, then he grasped the stainless steel counter. "I'd better get up there. She'll be looking for me." Before Aanders left the room, he turned back toward Tim. "What was your unfinished business?"

"I already told you. We were murdered. I saw something right before the car rolled over and I think I know who did it. But because I can't go to the sheriff, you've the only one who can help me prove it."

10

Mr. Bakke lifted the deceased man's shoulders while Nan slid an adjustment block under him to incline the body for better drainage. The elderly gentleman removed several tools from the drawer and placed them in a stainless steel tray.

"Looks good," Nan said. She checked the entrance incision for the embalming tube. She reached up and moved the overhead light into position before inserting the arterial tubing. Nodding toward Richard Fossum, she said, "His sister called this morning. She'll deliver the clothing for the family tomorrow afternoon."

Nan removed the cap from a jug of embalming fluid. "I can't imagine what Richard's sister is going through losing three loved ones at the same time."

"It's going to be one humdinger of a funeral." Mr. Bakke raised his eyes to meet Nan's.

"I've been so busy, I can't remember if I asked you to assist with the wake as well as the funeral. If I didn't, I apologize. I don't mean to take you for granted." Nan reached for a scissors and snipped the plastic tubing at an angle to accommodate the end of the pump's nozzle. "I'm glad Richard's sister agreed to one funeral rather than three separate ceremonies. I agree with her. It's easier for everyone to come together all at once. Some of their family's coming from quite a distance."

Mr. Bakke patted Nan's hand. "You did ask for my help and I'll be here. Jane sent my suit to the cleaners, so I should be good to go."

The embalming room door swung wide as Belly butted it with his head. He crossed the floor, with his nose skimming the tile. The dog snorted a wet spatter against Mr. Bakke's sandals before inspecting the far corners of the room.

"That dog seems to know how to get in when there's no possible way," Nan said. "Aanders must have left the door open again."

Belly made one final turn around the room before clacking his nails across the tile floor and grunting his way up the stairs.

"Apparently he didn't find what he was looking for," Nan said.

"Apparently," Mr. Bakke said, raising his gaze toward Nan and then back to the body on the table.

Nan closed the cooler door as she pushed the second cart into the center of the room. "Aanders asked me a question the other day I couldn't answer. He was wondering when Belly actually claimed ownership of the Witt sisters?"

Tipping his head in contemplation, Mr. Bakke said, "I would guess it was about seven years ago. My memory isn't that good, but I think it's been that long. Now he thinks he owns them."

Mr. Bakke handed Nan a catheter. "Once in a while I'd see him standing on the property line between Sadie's cabin and his other owners' house. He looked pathetic. He'd sniff toward his other owners, bark at them, and then go back to Sadie's. Sadie said he was giving them one last chance to beg him to come back."

Nan grinned as she pictured Belly's indecision. "Sadie

still insists Belly isn't her dog."

"That's true," Mr. Bakke said. "But don't kid yourself. Sadie loves that old dog. She uses it as an excuse when someone complains about Belly or when Carl threatens to fine her for not having a dog license."

Nan turned her attention back to Richard Fossum. She had retrieved his body from the hospital morgue several hours after retrieving Tim and his mother. Even though all three died at the scene, the coroner insisted on performing an autopsy on Richard to rule out substance abuse as a possible cause.

Mr. Bakke's hand brushed the autopsy sutures as he ran his gloved hand along the embalming tube. "I sure hope the results come back negative. I never knew Richard to be a drinker. His sister will have a hard time accepting it if alcohol was the reason. Or drugs."

"He was devoted to his family," Nan said. "I've always admired the way he treated Aanders like one of his own. He's been a Godsend since Aanders' father walked out on us. But I do have to say he seemed distracted when he picked Aanders up for the movie."

"Had he been drinking?"

"If I'd have thought that, I wouldn't have let Aanders go."

Mr. Bakke opened his mouth and then hesitated. Taking in a deep breath he said, "You know the Witt sisters think of me as family."

"I know that, Mr. Bakke," Nan said, smiling at the elderly gentleman.

"They tell me everything."

Nan looked up. "Meaning?"

"They told me about Lon Friborg investigating on his own. I'm guessing that isn't public knowledge, but they shared it with me because I'm family."

"You're right. I told them about Lon in confidence," Nan said. "I hope you're going to keep it to yourself."

"I will. You can trust me."

"Lon was in again this morning. He wanted to look at Richard's body," Nan said.

"Did you let him?"

"Of course. I didn't see any reason not to. If I'd have found anything suspicious during my initial prep, I'd have called the sheriff." Nan looked up at Mr. Bakke. "You know that's my policy, don't you?"

"I do," he said. "I wouldn't expect you'd find anything. Not much escapes our coroner. Did Lon find anything?"

Nan removed a length of tubing. "I don't think so. He did tell me Richard's sister was furious with him when he asked if he could have access to Richard's papers."

"Why?"

"Apparently she resented the implication that Richard might be involved in something," Nan said.

"I don't think that's why Lon wanted to see the papers. I'm guessing he's trying to prove Richard had an enemy."

"I agree. But I think Richard's sister was so overwhelmed she took it the wrong way."

"Speaking of accessing papers," Mr. Bakke said, "have you made any progress on finding that man who pulled a fast one on your dad?"

"Not yet. I'm still not sure what happened, but before Dad died, he spent a lot of time researching patents. I got the impression Dad actually designed something, but the guy filed the patent in his own name instead of Dad's. Dad never got credit."

"And you have no idea what it was?"

"Nope. When Dad caught me looking over his shoulder, he slammed the folder shut. He was either embarrassed he was duped, or he found out the guy made a fortune on the invention. Maybe it was someone local and he didn't want anyone to know until he had proof. I'm waiting to hear from the patent bureau."

Nan and Mr. Bakke's heads raised simultaneously as Belly's shadow crossed the basement window. Nan chuckled. "Do you think Belly ever sneaks back to his real home?"

"Would you if they didn't feed you?"

"No wonder he chose the sisters. By the looks of him, he hasn't missed a meal since he moved in." Nan began the repair work on Richard's face. She primed a handheld mechanism before securing his jaw into position with the spring-driven needle injector. She returned the tool to the metal tray and leaned closer to examine her work. "Didn't Belly's original owners ever complain that he opted to live with the sisters?"

"They bullied a few times with idle threats. But when Sadie told them she'd turn them in for cruelty, they didn't bother her anymore. In fact, when Belly sees them now, he turns and runs the other way. I think he's afraid they're going to make him come back."

The phone rang and Nan listened to footsteps above as Aanders crossed the floor to answer the phone.

"Mom?" Aanders shouted down the stairs. "Jane and Sadie want to know what time you'll be ready for them.

They want to talk to you."

"Tell them to give us another half hour."

"How's Aanders doing?" Mr. Bakke said.

"As well as can be expected." Compassion tugged at Nan as the agony of her son's sorrow engulfed her. Tim had been a constant presence in Aanders' life. Having a friend as popular and athletic as Tim had made it easier for Aanders to endure the taunting he'd suffered from his peers. At times, living in a mortuary had its benefits. But those times were rare. Aanders was courted yearly around Halloween when his friends wanted to prove they were brave enough to touch dead bodies or when they wanted to see who could endure a dead body when the lights were turned off. The rest of the year he was the mortician's son. An outcast.

"I was surprised to find Aanders in better spirits," Nan said. "Yesterday he was teary. This morning he was up early playing video games in his room."

Mr. Bakke held his gaze firmly on Richard Fossum's face.

"He hasn't asked to view Tim's body like he did yesterday. That worries me. It's like he's in denial," Nan said.

Nan ushered Mr. Bakke and the two sisters into her kitchen. Mr. Bakke pulled a chair out for Jane and lifted a pan of toffee bars from her arms.

Inhaling deeply, Nan said, "My favorite. My absolute favorite. You usually save these for special occasions. What are we celebrating today?"

Jane shot an accusing glance at Sadie as they sat at the table. Nan poured coffee and joined them as Jane cut into the warm bars.

"We thought you needed something special because of the Fossums," Sadie said.

"That's really sweet." Nan closed her eyes and savored the first bite. She realized this was the first good sensation she'd experienced since the accident had claimed the lives of the Fossum family. She let the pleasure surround her as she took another bite.

"It's nice to have Mr. Bakke help with the preparations, isn't it, dear?" Sadie said. She directed a scowl toward her sister who folded and refolded her paper napkin for the tenth time. "I know Mr. Bakke's certainly been a great help to us over the years."

Sadie reached across the table and patted Jane's hand. "Of course he's more than a handyman to you, isn't he, Sister?" Pulling her hand away, she yanked the napkin from Jane's grasp.

Jane's glare scalded Sadie. She picked up a table knife and sliced heavily through a toffee bar. She yanked a clean napkin from the napkin holder and placed the bar in the center. Leaning over, she laid the napkin on the floor. Jane patted Belly's back as he gulped the treat down in two swallows. The dog looked up anticipating more. Jane picked bits of shredded napkin from his jowls.

Mr. Bakke crossed his arms over his chest and quietly sank into his chair.

The group finished their coffee; tension grew between the elderly guests. "Nan, dear. We have something we need to talk to you about," Sadie said, ending Nan's toffee reverie.

"About the Fossum family?"

"Not specifically. But it does have something to do with your work," Sadie said.

The sound of baubles clinking against the table drew Nan's gaze to Sadie's wrist. Nan gently fingered one of the bright glass jewels. "You seem so serious. What's on your mind?"

As Sadie removed her bracelet and held it up for Nan to see, Jane blurted, "Oh for Pete sakes. Tell her. Get this over with before I faint."

Mr. Bakke leaned toward Jane. "I'm going back to my cabin while you ladies discuss business."

"What's going on, Sadie? Are you ill?" Concern crept across Nan's face.

"It's not that simple," Sadie said.

Jane's voice trembled. "We're going to lose the resort." Clutching her stomach she turned toward Sadie. "There. Now she knows." Flicking her wrist to dismiss her sister's inability to spread the word, Jane said, "You should have been the one to tell her. Not me."

"Why me? Why do I have to do everything?"

"Okay you two, quit bickering," Nan said. "This resort's been in your family for years. How could you possibly lose it?"

"Because of that horse's ass Carl Swanson. He insists the resort belongs to him." Sadie stood and walked to the window.

"What? Carl Swanson, the deputy?"

"That snake thinks our mother got the resort from his grandfather through illegal means." Jane wadded her second napkin into a tiny clump.

"The deed is in your name, isn't it?" As the question

escaped Nan's lips, another more pressing question surfaced. "What do you mean it has something to do with my work?"

Sadie inched her gaze from the floor to Nan's anxious face. "Carl told us if he wins the lawsuit, he won't honor our lease with you."

"What?" Nan reached for the back of the chair. "How could Carl possibly get ownership if it's in your name?"

"Because he filed a Constructive Trust Lawsuit."

"What on earth is that?"

"It's complicated," Sadie said, "but from what I understand, Carl's claiming his Grandfather told his aunt he planned to leave his estate and all his holdings to Carl's father. The aunt claims the grandfather never intended to give the resort to our mother. It's a lot of legal mumbo jumbo, but our attorney put it in simple terms so we could understand it."

Processing the information, a woozy heat engulfed Nan. The statement that Carl wouldn't honor the lease grew more menacing as she realized the consequences. "Did your attorney give any indication of how the lawsuit might turn out? Will there be a trial?"

"There won't be a trial. It's up to Judge Kimmer to make a ruling."

"Now I know why Carl's been avoiding me," Nan said. "The last few times I've stopped by Paul's office, Carl was there. He disappeared right after I got there. And, come to think of it, the other night he backed out of going to dinner with us. That's not like Carl to turn down a free meal."

"Carl's a weasel," Sadie said. "He knows there's a dirty deed afoot and he doesn't have the balls to talk to you face-to-face."

"Is this something you just found out?" Nan demanded.

"No," Jane said glaring at her sister. "She's known for quite some time and put off telling you. She thought you'd be upset."

"Upset? Of course I'm upset. If he won't honor the lease, I'll have to find a new location for the mortuary. I can't afford to do that." Nan pointed toward a cabinet drawer and said, "Thank goodness that funeral home in Minneapolis offered me a job. I got another letter from them last month. They're willing to provide housing for a year while we settle in. But if I have to move, I'll never realize my father's dream. He wanted this business to be passed on to Aanders."

Nan gestured in frustration. "I can't believe you held off telling me. Selling a business and relocating takes time." Fighting back the urge to cry, she added, "What am I going to do if Carl wins the case?"

Sadie watched fear cloud Nan's ability to think past the pending devastation.

"See. I told you. I told you to tell her earlier," Jane said. "Talk about not having balls."

"It's not a matter of balls," Sadie said. "It's a matter of setting off an alarm when it isn't necessary." Sadie stabbed her finger toward Jane. "If you thought she should know, then why didn't you tell her? You're just as much to blame as I am."

"Someone should have told me," Nan said. Placing her elbows on the table she buried her face in her hands. "Maybe Paul's marriage offer isn't such a bad idea."

"Don't you dare think that way," Sadie said. "He and

Carl came from the same thorny bush. You don't want to get tangled up with the likes of him."

The women turned toward Aanders' bedroom door as a peal of laughter echoed from the room.

"Was that Aanders?" Sadie exclaimed.

"Yes." Nan frowned. "I'm concerned about him. Yesterday he insisted on viewing Tim's body, but today he hasn't mentioned it once. I can hardly get him out of his room."

Another outburst rang from Aanders' room followed by a squeal of words.

"I don't think Paul's that bad," Jane said. "He impresses me as someone who's always neat and polite and dresses like a gentleman."

"Well then, that makes you a fool, doesn't it?" Sadie said. "If he's neat, he must be nice? He's not from here, you know. He's from some other part of the country. He's too sneaky to suit me."

"I don't understand what you're basing that on. You barely know Paul." Nan crossed to the pan of toffee bars and pulled a chunk out with her finger. "I've known him for over a year. He asked me to marry him several months ago and said he'd be patient while I sorted things out."

"That's a ploy. He wants you to think he's a good catch."

"You're wrong, Sadie," Nan said.

"If you're desperate, of course you think I'm wrong. Ask yourself why most of Paul's clients are over the age of seventy."

"Because he specializes in life insurance, investments, and endowment policies," Nan said.

"That's right. And why does he cater to them? Because they're old and vulnerable." Sadie joined Nan at the sink. "Paul came to the cabin last year and tried to sweet talk Jane and me into a policy. Jane was ready to write him a check right there on the spot, but I told her it would be over my dead body."

"What he had to offer seemed like a good deal," Jane said. "And besides, there's nothing wrong with life insurance."

"It's not a good idea if we can't afford the payments. Paul's sales pitch consisted mostly of sweet talk and compliments. You were ready to spread your legs for the man."

"I was not," Jane gasped. "You're jealous because he spent most of his time talking to me rather than you."

"My point exactly. You were literally drooling and he knew he had you wrapped around the axle."

"I was not drooling. I was interested in what he had to say."

"Stop it," Nan said. "Neither of you know the real Paul. At least we've got the option of staying in Pinecone Landing if I accept his proposal."

Nan's hand flew to her mouth. "Oh please forgive me. I was so worried about my own future I forgot about the two of you. Have you figured out what you'll do if you lose the lawsuit?"

11

Sadie eyed the clock as she pulled the final plate from the dish drainer. The previous evening's confrontation with Nan had drained her energy. The relentless humidity didn't help, either. She dabbed the towel across the floral design before placing the plate in the cabinet.

Mr. Bakke sat spread-eagled on the davenport attempting to benefit from a cross breeze filtering through the screen door. He had pushed his black socks down around his ankles so his white legs protruded like Popsicle sticks from below his Bermuda shorts. "I sure hope this storm brings relief. I don't have the gumption to get off the sofa." He fanned the newspaper in front of his face.

"I hear you," Sadie said. "I thought I'd feel cooler wearing a thong, but it doesn't seem to help."

"You mean a thong as in underwear?" Jane said.

"Do you see any thongs on my feet?"

Jane glanced at Sadie's feet before contorting her face in disgust. "Since when did you start wearing a thong?"

"Since I ordered one from the catalog. It came a few days ago."

"That's repulsive. A woman your age wearing a thong?" The furrows in Jane's forehead deepened. She lifted Sadie's purple miniskirt and took a peek. "Don't those sequins irritate your skin?"

"No. They match the pink in my shirt. It's called Pink Passion. Color coordination is all the rage. It also matches Belly's neckerchief." Sadie patted her heavily-gelled, pink-spiked hairdo and said, "Big Leon created this color to coordinate with my outfit."

"You look like a wad of bubblegum." Jane took three steps back toward the kitchen sink. "That's a waste of money. Who'd want to see your old butt in one of those things?"

"I'm sure they'd rather look at my butt than at your flabby ass in those panties you pull all the way up to your boobs. Humongous panties, by the way."

Mr. Bakke quietly raised the newspaper to shield his face.

Sadie reached for her keys. "I'm late picking up the crossers. When I get back, we'll look at my *Victoria Secret* catalog."

"No we won't," Jane said. "And let's hope you come back minus a crosser. Maybe one will have found someone on the brink."

"I hope so, too. Preferably Rodney. He frightens the others to the point where they can't concentrate on their declarations." Sadie bent and tugged at the rug, sliding Belly away from the door. He raised his head in acknowledgement as his stomach rose and fell with each pant. Patting Belly's head, Sadie said, "Rodney's as lazy as Belly. I wouldn't put it past him to crawl into one of the beds at the nursing home. He probably sleeps until it's time for me to pick him up."

Belly laid his head back on the rug, took a deep breath, and burped.

"I wish I could do that. I'd sure feel better." Sadie rubbed her stomach and looked at Mr. Bakke. "I think Jane's trying to kill us with her cooking." Sadie signaled she was heading out to pick up the crossers and let the screen door slam behind her

Mr. Bakke frowned at Jane over the top of the newspaper. "What exactly was it you served tonight for supper?"

"That recipe I showed you from the *Taste of Home* magazine."

"I don't remember the photo looking like that," he said. "What was all that blue stuff in it?"

"I added a few of my own ideas," Jane said.

"I'm glad to hear that. I'd hate to think there was a misprint."

"Nobody's forcing you to eat here, you know. If you don't like my cooking, you can eat at the lodge. Or better yet, if you're so darn fussy you can do you own cooking." Jane hung the kitchen towel inside the cabinet door before slamming it sharply.

Mr. Bakke patted the cushion. "Come and sit by me. You know I love your cooking."

Belly moved from the comfort of the rug and resituated himself in front of the screen door. His left rear paw scratched haphazardly at the pink neckerchief. As footsteps drew closer to the cabin, his tail thumped against the screen.

Aanders rapped his knuckles against the wood frame and looked through the screen door. "Sadie?" Seeing Jane approach, he asked, "Is Sadie here?"

She'll be back in about twenty minutes. Come in. I baked some cookies this afternoon." Before Mr. Bakke could comment, Jane held up a finger in warning. "I followed the recipe exactly the way it was written."

"How are you doing, son?" Mr. Bakke folded the

newspaper and looked up at Aanders.

Aanders stared at a peanut he pulled from the peanut butter cookie before breaking it in half with his front teeth. "I'm okay."

"You sure?"

"Yah." He drained the glass of milk Jane set in front of him and sought permission to take a second cookie.

The pair sat on the sofa and watched the last fifteen minutes of *Wheel of Fortune*. As each new letter was exposed, they shouted out their guesses. When the final commercial played across the screen, Mr. Bakke said, "If you need to talk, you know where to find me."

Nodding to acknowledge Mr. Bakke, Aanders crouched and let Belly lick the traces of cookie from his fingers. "I need to talk to Sadie."

"Here I am," Sadie sang out as she crossed the porch and opened the door. "I just got back from giving our guests a ride."

"I know," Aanders said with a smile.

"Want a cookie, Aanders?" Sadie handed the cookie platter to Aanders.

"No thanks. I already had a couple."

The van's occupants filed in behind Sadie and sat on the remaining vacant chairs. Belly placed his large head on Theo's leg and snorted a welcome.

"Keep your worthless canine on the other side of the room," Theo grumbled. "He's got drool hanging out of his mouth again. Can't you put that creature outside?"

"He's not my dog," Sadie said.

"Belly doesn't like to be outside when Sadie's in the cabin," Aanders said.

"I know that, dear," Jane said. "I didn't ask you to put him out."

"Theo wants me to put him out," Sadie explained. She turned and stared at Aanders.

Biting back at her sister, Jane said, "Well how am I supposed to know that? You didn't tell me they were back."

"What do you think I went to the nursing home for?" Sadie said. "To pick out a room for you?"

"To pick up the crossers," Aanders said.

Nodding sharply at Aanders' reply, Sadie's breath caught in her throat. She whispered, "What did you say?"

"I said you went to the nursing home to pick up the crossers."

Sadie's knees buckled before she moved toward Aanders. She grabbed at the back of a chair. "How do you know that?"

"Tim told me."

Theo looked at Sadie and pointed at Aanders. "Is he dead, too?"

"I'm not dead. I'm alive just like Sadie and Jane and Mr. Bakke," Aanders said, gesturing as he recited their names.

"Then why can he see us if he's not dead? I thought you said only death coaches can see the dead."

Sinking into the chair, Sadie grabbed Aanders' hand and pointed toward Tim. "Who's that?"

"My best friend, Tim." Aanders added, "I can see the other crossers in here, too."

"Oh my dear Lord," Sadie gasped.

"Would you please clarify this so I can better understand," Theo said. "You mean this child is a death coach? And he's challenged with the same responsibility you've been given?"

"Oh my Lord," Sadie said again. "This can't be. It simply can't be."

"What can't be, Sister?"

Moaning in dismay, Sadie said, "I refuse to accept it."

"Accept what?" Jane's voice rose with concern.

"This has got to be a mistake. Aanders can't possibly be the next death coach. Something's wrong."

"I tend to agree. I'm experiencing the same level of skepticism," Theo said. "A child assisting with decisions of such import? That's ludicrous."

"Aanders is a death coach? What are you talking about?" Jane said.

Music blared from the inner room, causing all heads to turn toward the door. Sadie shouted at Rodney to turn down the volume. When he failed to honor her request, she marched into the inner room, yanked the cord from the wall, and returned with the clock radio. She wrapped the cord around the red plastic before placing it in a drawer.

Rodney shouted from behind the door. "I'll get even with you, witch."

"Not if I get even with you first, you big toad." Sadie slammed the drawer and reopened it to stuff in the end of the cord.

Mr. Bakke said to Jane, "Let's go out on the porch. I'm confused." After folding his newspaper, he took Jane by the hand and led her through the door. He looked back over his shoulder before whispering, "Did I hear Sadie say Aanders is a death coach?"

Looking toward the inner room where Rodney's

rantings continued to build, Sadie warned Aanders, "You stay away from Rodney. He's one mean crosser and I don't want you anywhere near him. Do you understand?"

"I won't. Not after what Tim told me," Aanders said. He looked around the room. "I don't want to be anywhere near these people." His gaze lingered on Theo and the briefcase. "I didn't ask to be a death coach. I'm just a kid."

"You're a loser, too," emanated from the inner room. "I've seen you moping around like a girl since your buddy died. Get a life, kid. Your friend's dead. Too bad."

Tim rose and walked to the inner room door. "Leave Aanders alone. Leave us all alone. I hate you." Tim leaned against the wall, sobbing.

Laughter came from behind the door. "You big baby. Now why did you go and hurt my feelings? You ruined my day."

Aanders joined Tim near the door and put his arm around him. "It's ok. I'll stay away from him."

Theo sat erect and pulled his briefcase close to his chest. "Just what we need. Additional conflict. It's hard enough recalling Sadie's instructions without worrying about Rodney."

Sadie joined the boys. "You're not exactly my choice for a death coach, Aanders. I would have preferred someone more mature."

"I'm not going to do it." Looking at the crossers sitting around the table, Aanders said, "I'm going to pretend I never saw you. Nobody asked if I wanted to be a death coach so I'm not going to do it." Setting his jaw, he declared, "You're going to have to find someone else."

Sadie shook her head slowly. "You don't have a choice.

You've been selected. That's all there is to it."

"You can do it, Aanders. You can learn from Sadie. She knows everything," Tim said. "She's been doing it a long time and will be a good teacher."

Lora leaned forward. "Tim's right. I trust Sadie. She taught me how to make a death decision. I know what I want, but I have to wait to find someone on the brink before I can complete my journey."

Michael looked up at his mother and then at Sadie before scuffing his shoe against the wooden floor. He hid behind his mother and peeked out at Sadie with concern.

"I've got more years of experience than I care to remember," Sadie said. "You've got a big job ahead of you, Aanders, but I'll be here to guide you as you learn."

Sadie winked at Michael. It was time to get Michael to admit his true feelings. Every time Lora talked about rejoining her husband, Michael appeared agitated. If she could get him to draw on his inner strength and admit his true feelings, it would give the child a chance to have a say in his death decision. Sadie knew it would be the opposite of his mother's. She also knew she needed to force the subject at the next round table session.

12

Paul Brink's secretary ushered Carl into Paul's office. She placed two folders on the hand-carved mahogany desk before asking Carl if he wanted a fresh cup of coffee.

"How'd you manage to train her to do that? Most secretaries won't offer coffee anymore. That equal rights thing is way overrated," Carl said.

"No training involved. I hinted at what I liked during the interview and she listened."

"What else did you hint at?" Carl didn't need to ask because he often saw Paul's secretary leave the building after hours. Paul's previous secretary suddenly left his employ after an irate husband stopped by the office and found a locked door.

Paul's penchant for finding voluptuous secretaries chewed at Carl as envy crept back into his thoughts. When they were younger, every time Carl zeroed in on a new conquest, he was bombarded with questions about Paul. Without even trying, Paul fascinated women with his dark, brooding looks and penetrating green eyes, and Carl had to struggle to keep his jealousy at bay. Waiting for the opportunity to provide comfort to Paul's rejects seemed the best way to score.

"None of your damn business, Carl. What happens in this office stays in this office."

"Just like Vegas," Carl said. He sat on the leather sofa and put one foot up on the coffee table.

Carl knew Paul had dropped a bundle of moola on the

furniture in his office. The room contained leather items purchased from a showroom in New York. The furniture was grouped around an ornate area rug, imported from Italy, sitting under a heavy iron and glass coffee table. A mahogany desk finished out the room's grand design.

"Get your foot off the table. You'll scratch the glass." Paul batted at Carl's boot.

Carl stretched his leg further over the table, placing his foot on a magazine. He pulled it over with the weight of his heel. "Satisfied?"

"I said put your foot on the floor."

"You're not threatening the future sheriff, are you?"

"Believe me Carl, your manners won't improve when you win the election. If it takes a threat to keep your feet on the floor, then that's what I'll do."

Carl slapped his thigh. "Now that's what I like to hear. You said when I'm elected, not if I'm elected."

"I don't know why you want the headache of being elected. It's a lot more responsibility."

"It's double the salary, too. I'm not like you," Carl said. "I didn't come into a lot of money over the past five years."

Paul tapped his temple. "I used my brain. I picked the right deal." He cast an accusing glance toward Carl. "Kind of like the way you're taking advantage of Judge Kimmer's passion. I had coffee with Kimmer this morning. He droned on and on and on about fishing. The worst part was I couldn't talk that cheapskate into a new investment." Paul lifted a letter opener and ran his index finger over the sharp tip. "A whole half-hour listening to that crap. He talked about this piece of tackle and that piece of tackle. Like I care. Every time I tried to change the subject, he'd butt in and start all over again."

"I knew it. I knew it." Carl cast a line over the coffee table and feigned battling a big catch. "He fell for it. I knew he would."

Shaking his head in amazement, Paul said, "I like your idea of timing it right and having your name splashed all over the front page. Getting that resort away from the Witt sisters will be a major coup. A reporter will be all over it."

"You know me. I always get what I want. Why are you so surprised?"

"I'm not surprised, I'm skeptical." Running his hands over his hair and patting down the back, Paul said, "Just what exactly does the lawsuit say?"

Carl plopped his foot on the table again and put his hands behind his head. "It's called a Constructive Trust. In other words, a judge has to determine if a constructive trust can be imposed. He can impose one if he believes it morally wrong for the current owner to retain ownership of the property."

"Morally? Like if the current owner is committing a crime?"

Carl had the same misgivings when his attorney explained it so he understood Paul's skepticism. "It's a lot of legal stuff, but it made sense when he put it in terms I could understand." He leaned back trying to remember how the attorney cut through the legal terminology.

Lifting his cap and scratching his scalp with his little finger, Carl said, "When a person tells a family member he wants his property disposed of in a particular manner and that family member doesn't act upon those wishes, that family member is guilty of unjust enrichment."

"But the judge who handled your grandfather's estate acted on his final wishes."

"That's true. But my attorney said because my aunt has a different version and because she wasn't present during the hearing, it caused the Witt sisters to benefit from an unjust enrichment."

"What kind of money did you promise your aunt to make that claim?" Paul said.

Leaning forward Carl said, "Wipe that smirk off your face. Do I question your business ethics? Besides, anything can happen. My attorney said I had about a seventy-percent chance of winning. I figured I upped that percent by reminding Judge Kimmer about the fun he'll have if I win the lawsuit."

"You wouldn't stand a chance if a different judge heard the case."

"I lucked out when the Witt sisters moved the date up," Carl said. "The court assigned Kimmer to the hearing when the other judge decided to retire."

"You are one lucky dog."

"My attorney admitted this isn't exactly how the constructive trust law is interpreted, but with a little manipulation he could get the judge to see his point of view. All the judge has to do is re-evaluate my grandfather's intentions and determine whether or not the Witt sisters got what they didn't deserve."

Paul paged through his phone messages as he listened to Carl.

"I don't think the Witt sisters can afford an appeal. I guess this will be the end of it. If nothing else, maybe I'll get a cash settlement out of the deal." Grinning, Carl added,

"Don't forget, the key to the whole case is the fact the Witt sisters deprived Judge Kimmer of the property he wanted."

"I still say that's a conflict of interest."

"I already told you they never listed the property and Kimmer never officially talked to a realtor. Nothing was ever put in writing."

"Their word against his?"

Carl nodded. "Something like that."

The vision of changing the resort's name back to its original name brought a smile to Carl. Swanson's Resort had a nice flair. His smile was short-lived when he pictured the Witt sisters' mother wrapping his grandfather around her little finger with sexual favors. His poor, pitiful grandfather. No one would ever know what guiles the whore had used to seduce him. Carl spent a lot of time imagining what his grandfather had endured.

Carl scanned Paul's profile as his friend stared vacantly out the window and drummed his thumb against the desk. Carl had learned to tolerate Paul's mood swings and knew when to keep his mouth shut. Paul's business partner had been buried earlier in the day. Paul had served as one of the pallbearers.

The funeral for all three members of the Fossum family was the largest funeral in Pinecone Landing in over a decade and was held in the high school gymnasium to accommodate the massive crowd. The school's parking lot filled to capacity. Carl and several deputies had directed traffic to an outer lot behind the school's property to handle the overflow.

Paul's secretary rapped lightly on the door and reminded him she was leaving early for an appointment.

"You sure you're going to be okay?" she inquired, poking her head through the opening.

"I'm fine. Thanks for covering for me this morning." As she lingered in the doorway, Paul shooed her away with a flick of his fingers.

"I put a couple messages in your mail slot. One's from an out-of-state client who hadn't heard about Richard's death." Her voice trailing off down the hall, she added, "See you in the morning." A click of the latch signaled she had left the building.

Staring into his lap, Paul sighed. "That was really gruesome."

"The funeral?"

An annoyed glare darkened Paul's expression. "What else would I be talking about?"

"The accident?"

Spreading his hands as if to explain what should have been apparent, Paul said, "I wasn't there. How could I talk about the accident?"

"Well I was there. And believe me, it was gruesome. I'll never forget it. I've seen some pretty bad wrecks, but this was by far the worst." Carl removed his cap and rested his head against the back of the sofa. "Dispatch got the call from a guy who came upon the accident. Angie couldn't locate anyone to take the call, so I took it."

Paul swiveled his chair and stared out the window.

"The first thing I saw was Richard impaled on that fence post. It had gone clean through his gut. Then I saw his wife. Her head went through the windshield and I'm guessing she died on impact."

Carl could see Paul's head over the back of the leather

chair rotating back and forth. He waited for Paul to comment. Getting no reaction, Carl said, "When I opened the back door, I found their kid leaning against the seat with his eyes open. It looked like he was looking at his dad. There wasn't a scratch on him. I took his earphones out of his ears and tried to get him to talk before I realized he was dead."

Paul swiveled back toward Carl. "What did you find at the scene?"

"I'm guessing he swerved to avoid a deer. You know how many deer wander in and out of that area." Carl breathed deeply trying to erase the memories. "The sheriff agreed. He didn't see any reason to investigate further."

Carl raised his eyes to meet Paul's gaze. "Has Lon talked to you?"

"About what?"

"About the fact that it might not be an accident."

"No. But I thought you told him to drop that idea." Agitation tinged Paul's voice.

"I did. I just wondered if you heard any more about it. Lon's as crazy as Nan's ex-husband. You can sure tell they're related."

"Lon has no right to spread rumors," Paul scowled. "Who else has he told?"

"No one, as far as I know."

"I'm counting on you to put a stop to it, Carl. Losing my partner is more than I can handle."

Paul drummed his fingers on the desk. "What about the car? What about Richard's belongings? He'd been in the office earlier that day and I wonder if he had any business papers with him."

"It was the usual stuff. I saw a purse and a shopping bag on the floor next to Richard's wife. The kid must have been at a movie, because there was popcorn all over the back seat." Carl shifted in place before adding, "I think one of the deputies pulled a briefcase from under the front seat."

"Where is it?"

"Richard's sister has it. I sent all that stuff with her."

"Is Richard's sister staying at the Fossums' house?" Paul said. "I need to go through his briefcase to see if there's anything I need to take care of."

"She'll be out of town for at least a week. Then she'll be back to finalize their affairs. She left right after the funeral."

The phone rang and Carl watched Paul put the receiver to his ear.

Paul swiveled the desk chair placing a barrier between the two men. He stared out the window. "It was devastating, wasn't it? It took a lot out of me, too." Listening before he answered, Paul said, "I'm okay. You don't need to worry." He shifted the receiver as his thumb drummed against the armrest. "I understand. You get a good night's sleep and I'll see you tomorrow."

"Nan?"

"Yeah," Paul said quietly. "She's too tired to see me. The funeral took a lot out of her and she wants to be with Aanders tonight."

"She shouldn't work so hard. She needs to quit taking care of everything by herself." Carl sneered as he added, "That old runt she hired can't be much help. Speaking of Nan," Carl said sitting forward, "you still interested in buying the mortuary land when I win the lawsuit?"

"Of course. We'll need to form another partnership as soon as that happens."

"I don't think so." Noticing a slight lilt in Paul's voice, Carl realized the man appreciated the change of topic. "We never did anything with the old partnership, and if all goes well, I might not need your money."

"Or you might. I've got a few marketing ideas. That place could be a goldmine if you promoted it."

"I offered you the land outright. We don't need a partnership for that," Carl said.

"I don't plan to form a partnership for that. We already have a deal in writing for the land the mortuary sits on. I intend to see you keep your end of the bargain. Just as soon as the judge declares you the new owner, that property is mine."

Carl pushed against his knees for leverage and stood up. "There's got to be other land out there. Why waste good lake-front property on a mortuary?"

Carl put his hand on the doorknob. "What I don't understand is why you're using that land to get Nan to marry you. You've got all those other women hot on your trail. Why give everything up to get married?"

"It's part of the game. I'm like you, Carl. I always get what I want." Paul rose and joined Carl. "What makes you think I intend to give anything up? After you evict the Witt sisters and Nan finds out I bought the mortuary land, she'll fall into my sweet little trap."

"Nan's not an idiot. She'll catch on eventually."

"That'll take a few years. And then I might be the one needing fresh air. At that point, I'll make sure she wants out as much as me." Paul's smile carried an edge of deceit.

13

When crossers arrived at Cabin 14, they possessed a state of strength to help them through their thirty-day journey. It was to their benefit to make their declaration early, because their strength dwindled with each passing day. A crosser became a crosser lost if they were unable to cross back over through someone else's light. Crossers lost faded into oblivion. Rodney's lack of interest in his thirty-day time span concerned Sadie. He obviously had no intention of making a declaration.

As the crossers gathered around the kitchen table for their nightly round table session, Sadie noticed Rodney plop down on the recliner and grab the remote control. He aimed and clicked, paging from channel to channel with rapid progression.

"Wait. I wanted to hear what he had to say." Mr. Bakke looked from the television screen to Sadie. "I've been waiting all day to see how it turned out."

Marching over to Rodney, Sadie grabbed the remote and handed it to Mr. Bakke. "Mr. Nasty did it. Not me."

"You stupid bitch," Rodney shouted. "I wanted to watch Monster Garage."

"You're supposed to participate in the round table discussion. Not watch TV." Sadie pointed at the table. "How many times do I have to tell you to quit calling me a bitch?"

Mr. Bakke summoned Jane. "Let's go for a walk. It sounds like Sadie's got her hands full."

Jane closed her magazine and placed it on top of the others in the stack. She ran her knuckles down the edge of the spines to align the magazines before taking Mr. Bakke's outstretched hand and following him out onto the porch.

The evening breeze lifted Mr. Bakke's hair into wisps that remained afloat as the elderly couple paused at the bottom of the stairs. He placed a gentle kiss on Jane's cheek. His new orthopedic shoes stood out prominently, with the thick black soles appearing to anchor him firmly to the ground. Two knobby knees peeked out below his plaid shorts. He tucked the back of his striped shirt into his elastic waistband.

With Jane sporting a crisp white blouse, khaki slacks, and brown sandals, the pair represented a walking contradiction.

Sadie swung the screen door open and shouted to her sister. "Take Belly with you. He just lifted his leg on Theo's briefcase." She tugged at Belly's collar and pulled him over the threshold.

"Now maybe we can get going with our session." Sadie looked at Rodney. "Get over here and join the group." She pulled out the last empty chair and pointed at it.

"I can hear you from here. Besides you aren't going to say anything new anyway." Rodney slumped lower in the recliner and bobbed his dangling leg up and down.

Sadie grabbed the remote he'd retrieved when she let the dog out and switched off the television. She tucked the remote in her waistband.

"What's wrong with your dog's balls?" Rodney said.

"Nothing. What's wrong with yours?" Sadie cocked her head and watched his puzzled expression.

"There ain't nothing wrong with my balls. At least I've got two. What did you do to that mutt?"

"The same thing I'm going to do to you if you don't follow the rules."

Rodney taxed the limits of his imagination as he stared out the screen door and watched Belly's lone testicle sway as he followed Jane down the path.

"I wish I could get out of this dump," Rodney muttered, dropping into the kitchen chair.

"What a benevolent fellow you are, Rodney. And so eloquent. I'll bet you went to Harvard," Theo said.

"Where?"

"I'm sure everyone in this room would like to see you leave this dump. I hope you don't mind my quoting your ingenious use of the English language. If there truly is a Higher Power, and I'm beginning to doubt there is, maybe he'll accommodate us by granting your wish." Theo tipped his head, staring at Rodney.

Rodney opened his mouth and then closed it. A confused expression pinched his features. "You better speak English so I can understand you."

"That was perfectly clear to me," Sadie said.

Lora buried her lips in her son's hair, the corners of her mouth moving upward.

Rodney turned his chair so his back was against the table. He looked at Sadie. "Well? What are you waiting for? Aren't you going to bore us again?"

Theo tugged on Rodney's chair attempting to turn it around. Gritting his jaw as he grasped the wood, he said, "You are such a twit."

Rodney grabbed the edge of the table to thwart Theo's

effort. He grasped Theo's hand and squeezed it. "Twit?" When Theo let go of his chair, Rodney repeated, "Twit? I'm insulted. Couldn't you come up with a better word?"

Rodney butted his chair against Theo's chair. Dropping back into the chair, he pushed hard against Theo's black-suited shoulder. "Now I suppose you're going to call your mommy so she can come and beat me up."

Without flinching at the intrusion of Rodney's nose three inches from his face, Theo said, "I wouldn't think of exposing my mother to the dregs of society."

"I don't blame you," Rodney said. "She might ruin my reputation."

Theo looked at Rodney over the top of his glasses. "I'm sure she'd be quite distraught to hear that even though it made no sense whatsoever."

"Twits and dregs. I suppose you think that's a good description of my family."

"I have no doubt of its accuracy."

Sadie tried to interrupt the verbal volley by stepping toward Rodney.

"My parents are great people," Rodney shouted, startling the others at the table. "My old man was the boss of our family and we listened to what he said."

"Surprise, surprise," Theo said. "And I bet your mother's a quiet little church mouse who caters to his every need."

"Absolutely not. She's a large woman with great big tits and can open beer bottles with her teeth."

Theo spread his palms and scanned the others at the table. "Need I say more?"

"Are you criticizing my parents?"

"No. I don't need to. The image of your family portrait is repulsive enough."

"You worthless pig." Rodney grabbed the briefcase handle and snatched the case from Theo's lap.

Theo's large hand clasped down on Rodney's fist before Rodney had a chance to flee. Holding the thief's gaze, Theo whispered, "Do you remember what happened the last time you took my briefcase?"

Rodney stared back and slowly let go of the handle. "You're a bunch of losers. Every one of you." Punching his fist into the back of the chair, he stormed into the inner room and slammed the door. "I'll get even with you if it's the last thing I do."

Theo returned to his chair and placed the briefcase between his leg and the chair. He straightened his suit coat and smoothed his hand over his pants.

"I'd appreciate it if you wouldn't rile Rodney anymore." Sadie nervously picked at her hair.

"Madam. You are mistaken. It wasn't me who started that altercation."

"You're right," Sadie said. "Now that we've got some quiet, let's begin."

Michael came out from behind his mother and looked at her for reassurance. Lora took him in her arms and hugged him. "It's okay now. Rodney's in the inner room."

Theo, Lora, and Michael eagerly edged closer to the table. When Tim first joined the evening session, he had occupied the chair farthest from the table. He remained in the same chair, showing little enthusiasm.

When the crossers began to discuss their day's experiences, Sadie noticed a change in Tim. It was unusual for a crosser to experience a high level of fatigue before the second half of their thirty days. Why hadn't she noticed the change sooner?

"Tim? Did you make any progress finding someone on the brink?"

Tim looked at his lap. "No."

"I can't hear you, Tim. Can you speak louder so the group can hear you?"

Michael pushed a spoon along the table's surface with his index finger. "He played with Aanders all day at the nursing home." Michael hid his face against his mother's shoulder and peeked out at Sadie.

"Is that true, Tim?" Sadie's glare sparked disapproval.

Tim looked up at Lora and Michael and then down at his feet.

"Michael knows better than to tattle on his friends, but because this is important, I think it's okay." Lora looked at Tim and then back at Sadie. "The boys haven't been working on Tim's declaration."

"Tim. You've got to concentrate on your decision," Sadie said.

"I already made it. I'm going back through the light to see Mom and Dad."

"Then you need to find someone on the brink. If you don't, you'll never find them again. But first, you need to determine why you were held back."

"I already know why," Tim whispered.

"I doubt that," Sadie said. "We haven't even discussed it yet."

"Aanders spent the day pushing him around in the wheelchair," Michael said. "They thought it was funny because everyone asked why he was pushing an empty chair."

"I'm disappointed, Tim." Sadie raised his chin with her finger. "You know better than that. So does Aanders. We let him sit in on our round table sessions so he can learn the rules. If he's going to be a credible death coach, he needs to either help you find someone on the brink or let you finish your business."

Sadie realized her original concerns were coming true. She resented the fact she had been sent an immature death coach. Aanders was no more ready to take on the responsibility of recommending death alternatives than she was ready to relinquish the deed to the resort to that no-good Carl Swanson.

Aanders had no interest in learning. He was more interested in cramming a lifetime into the short span he had left with his friend. Reality would soon set in. The death-coach-in-training was too young to comprehend the gravity of this new responsibility. Tim's loss would set him back even further.

With tears welling, Tim said, "Aanders doesn't want me to leave."

Hearing Tim's outburst, Michael buried his face against his mother's arm.

"I know he doesn't. But he doesn't have a choice. Neither do you." Sadie tugged at Tim's chair, pulling it closer to the table. "I'm concerned about how weak you're getting. You need to concentrate, and Aanders is going to have to understand."

"But I don't want to go. He's my best friend and he'll be alone when I leave." Tears dripped onto Tim's lap.

Michael laid his cheek against the table as he listened. "No he won't. He'll make new friends. Every time we moved, I made new friends. Dad made us move lots of times." Michael continued with excitement, "When we moved, I walked up to a kid and asked him if he wanted to be my friend. Then we played."

Lora pulled Michael back onto her lap and smoothed his hair. "You're a wiggle worm. You've got to sit still." Turning toward Tim, Lora said, "Michael and I made our declaration. We've chosen to go back through the light to find Michael's father."

Michael pulled away from his mother's grasp. "No, Mom. I don't want to." A look of terror overtook him as he tugged on her blouse. "I want to go to that other place. Please Mom? Can't we go there instead?"

"I can't believe you said that. We don't have a choice, Michael. We have to find Dad."

Thrusting his head back Michael cried, "Nooooo! Please can't we go to the other place?"

"He'll be mad if we don't find him." Lora held her sobbing son. "He'll be glad to see us. I promise."

Sadie watched apprehension settle over Lora.

The inner room door banged open against a side table and rebounded toward Rodney as he bolted into the room. "That's all you do is whine, you stupid woman. I'm sick of it. Make a decision so you and that brat can get out of here."

Lora grabbed at Rodney's arm as the enraged man rushed toward her.

Rodney caught her arm in motion. "You try that again and I'll make sure you don't go anywhere."

As Theo opened his mouth, Sadie held up a finger.

"Don't say a word. We don't need any more conflict."

Attempting to curtail her frustration, Sadie turned to Lora. "You really need to take Michael's opinion into consideration. This is his decision, too. Michael's got reasons for not wanting to find his father."

"Let the loser go," Rodney said. "If she's that stupid, then that's what she deserves. Good riddance."

"Noooooo," Michael moaned, clutching at his mother.

"He'll change. I know he can change." Lora pleaded with Michael to stop crying. "It'll be different. I promise."

Sadie crouched by Lora's side "Don't make promises you can't keep. Michael deserves better than that."

"But he'll be mad if we don't join him."

"It's not his decision, Lora. It's yours and Michael's." Sadie put her arms around the desperate woman and hugged her. "Why would you subject Michael to that when you have another option?"

"Because she's stupid. And so are you if you haven't figured that out yet," Rodney said.

"I've had enough." Sadie emphasized each word. "If you don't stop…."

"Go ahead and tell me what you're going to do," Rodney said. "You can't hurt me. I'm already dead. If you think I'm going to leave peacefully before I go to the parallel world, you'd better think again."

"Just how big is the parallel world?" Theo asked.

"Will Rodney be there?" Michael's voice cracked as his lower lip curled upward.

"You don't need to worry about it, Michael," Lora said. "We're not going to the parallel world."

"Oh yes you are," Rodney said. "I'm taking you with

me."

"That's enough," Sadie said. "Go back in the inner room and quit wasting your energy. Instead of arguing, you should concentrate on finding someone on the brink."

"I have," Rodney challenged. "I found you."

"You can't go through my light. I'm not dead."

Rodney held Sadie's gaze. "Not yet."

14

Nan watched the bank information disappear from the computer screen and tapped her finger on the log-off bar. She moved to the next item on her list. Because her to-do list was always in flux, a day of leisure was rare. Nan jotted an appointment on her calendar for Mrs. Fading Sun, who wanted to make a final payment on her husband's funeral bill.

Smiling at Paul as he walked through the office door, Nan closed her laptop. "I received a few more payments today. If I have another good month like last month, I can make a down payment on the mortuary land."

"I already told you I'd loan you the money," Paul said. "If you'd quit being so stubborn and marry me, you wouldn't have to worry about money."

"We already talked about that. I need to do this myself. Marrying you and getting a loan are two entirely different things."

Nan stood. Paul pulled her close and kissed her forehead. "Does that mean you're still considering my offer?"

"Maybe," she answered, tapping his nose with her index finger and wriggling free. "Sadie and Jane had some devastating news. But I guess you already know about it."

Laughter filtered into the mortuary office followed by mumbled words and the sounds of engines racing. Paul turned toward the sound.

"That's Aanders," Nan said. "He's in his room playing

one of his video games."

"Who's with him?"

"Nobody. He must be talking to the characters. You know how he gets into that stuff."

Paul lifted one of the mini blind vanes before turning the wand to let the sunshine in. The highlights in Nan's blond hair shimmered in the rays of light settling on her shoulders. His gaze turned to concern. "How's Aanders doing since he lost his friend?"

"Actually, he's doing amazingly well." Nan paused, concern pushing confidence into a dark corner. "I expected more tears. I think his way of dealing with it is to play video games. That was their favorite pastime." Nan placed two documentation sheets inside a folder, wrote a name on the tab, and filed it in the drawer. "It's going to be pretty harsh when reality sinks in."

Turning her chair to face Paul, Nan put her hands on her desk and clasped them in a fist. "How come you didn't ask about Sadie's bad news?"

"I got distracted by Aanders."

Nan nodded briefly toward the apartment and lowered her voice. "Did you know Carl is trying to get the resort away from the Witt sisters?"

"He mentioned it last week."

"Last week? You mean you knew about this for a week and didn't tell me?"

"It's never going to happen. Carl's obsessed with making the Witt sisters miserable, it's just a phase."

"Miserable?" Nan gazed again at the apartment. Leaning closer to Paul she said, "I would call losing a livelihood more than miserable. They've lived at that resort their entire lives. What do you think they'll do if they lose it?"

Paul gently folded Nan's pointed finger back into her hand. "You're angry at the wrong man. I'm not the bad guy." Placing his hands on her shoulders, he guided her around the desk and eased her into one of the visitor's chairs. "Just because Carl is my friend, doesn't mean I agree with what he's doing."

"If he wins the case, the Witt sisters will lose their resort. Sadie said he's not going to honor my land lease and I'll have to find another location for the mortuary." Nan sank lower into the chair. "I can't afford to do that. I'll have to take that job in Minneapolis."

Paul took Nan's hand and gently kissed her fingertips. "Let's wait and see what happens. I still don't think you've got anything to worry about."

"But it's my dream, Paul. You know how much I want to keep my family's business alive."

"I know," Paul said. He ran his finger down her cheek and over her lips.

The warmth of Paul's hand felt reassuring. He nodded in understanding. "I need to leave something of worth for my son. Something he can be proud of. That's another reason I need to keep this alive." Nan moved to the edge of her seat. "Aanders wants to become a funeral director. I know he's young to plan his future, but he's the one who brought it up. If he follows in my footsteps, then he can continue Dad's dream."

"Does Aanders know I've asked you to marry me?"

"I told him a couple weeks ago."

Laughter once again echoed from the apartment

followed by screeching tires and a cheering crowd.

"And?"

"He didn't seem to have a problem with it. He wanted to know if he could have his own bedroom if we moved into your house. He also wants a dog. He has his priorities, you know."

Paul laughed and leaned forward to kiss her. "Now I've got an ally. I bet Aanders and I can talk you into marrying me in one week."

"Don't you dare make any promises. Aanders' father made promises all the time, but he never kept them. Let's see what happens with the lawsuit before we make any decisions." The phone's ring interrupted their conversation. Nan leaned across her desk to answer the call.

Paul watched her jot directions on a piece of paper.

Nan tore the sheet from the pad. Grabbing her purse from the desk drawer, she said, "That was Lon. I've got a retrieval. The coroner's not available so I need to sign off on the body and take care of the paperwork."

Paul accompanied Nan to the hearse bay and held the door while she climbed into the Suburban.

"Did you know Lon's investigating the Fossums' car accident? Apparently Carl refused." Nan dug for her keys and placed them in the ignition. "Lon's trying to prove Richard had enemies."

"That's ridiculous," Paul said. "Richard didn't have a mean bone in his body. Besides, Carl told me he put an end to Lon's investigation."

"Well he didn't do a good job, because Lon's still investigating. I would think you'd want to know if Richard was involved in something. After all, he was your partner. It could reflect badly on you if he was doing something illegal."

Paul stood outside the hearse bay and waited until Nan backed the Suburban out of the garage. "I'll see you later. Like I told you before, I don't think you have to worry about the Witt sisters."

Before Nan's vehicle rounded the corner, Paul dialed Carl's cell phone.

When Nan finished at the scene, she removed her latex gloves and dropped them into a bin at the rear of the Suburban. In rural areas and small towns, funeral directors were often called upon to act as deputy coroners when the county coroner was unavailable. Nan filled out the required paperwork and closed her briefcase.

Lon assisted Nan with the gurney by pressing a hinged mechanism allowing the legs to fold. Together they slid the body bag into the compartment.

"Any progress in your investigation?"

Lon stepped away from the other deputy who had also assisted at the construction accident scene. "I have a few ideas, but can't talk about them yet. I'm sure you understand."

Nan nodded. "If it wasn't an accident, I hope you get the person who did it. Let me know if I can help." She waited until Lon unhooked a section of the yellow tape surrounding the scene before she backed up and edged her vehicle out onto the highway.

Nan had a history with Lon and there were times it was uncomfortable being near him. The past twenty minutes had been one of those times. She had loved Lon before leaving for college and making the mistake of her life by marrying Clay Harren. That didn't stop Lon from keeping the passion alive. He promised he'd always be there. It was obvious he still cared.

Nan backed the hearse into the hearse bay. She knew the family of the man who died and didn't envy Lon telling them about the accident.

She recognized Aanders' voice as she ascended the stairs and strode into the lobby. Mrs. Fading Sun sat across the desk from Aanders and listened in earnest as Aanders told her about the accident that had taken his friend's life.

"I'm sorry I'm late, Mrs. Fading Sun. I had business to attend to."

"Don't worry about it. Your son was telling me about his friend. What a sad situation." Mrs. Fading Sun shook her head in disbelief. "The whole family gone in an instant. Makes me wonder what the good Lord was thinking."

"It's tragic," Nan said. "We can't believe it, either."

"And to think that poor man was impaled on a fence post. What an awful way to go. At least my husband's death wasn't quite that violent. God rest his soul," she said, as she unfolded a tissue and dabbed at a tear.

Nan frowned in Aanders' direction. He averted his gaze and left the office. Nan took a seat across from the woman.

"I'm so sorry I had to pay in installments. I would have preferred to pay in full right after the funeral." Mrs. Fading Sun's lower lip trembled. "It's embarrassing to be in a financial bind. I value the fact you didn't tell anyone."

"I'm always willing to make arrangements. Some people can't afford to pay all at once," Nan said. "Please don't be embarrassed."

Mrs. Fading Sun signed the check and tore it from her checkbook. She slid it across the desk and waited for Nan to mark the invoice 'paid-in-full'. "This is a relief. I hate owing money. We always paid our bills on time."

The widow watched Nan pull her husband's funeral folder from the drawer and make a notation in the corner. "I took care of our finances. If I'd have let my husband have the checkbook, he'd have spent every penny we owned. But you already knew that. I think everyone in the county knew that. Gambling should be outlawed."

"People have nothing but high regards for you, Mrs. Fading Sun. You've done wonders promoting diversity. There aren't many white women who have the fortitude to crusade as hard as you have," Nan said. "You've even won awards for what you've done. Bringing those inner-city kids from Minneapolis to experience the Native American culture was an excellent idea."

The woman smiled. "My husband was proud of me. He had his problems, but I always knew he loved me. We had a good life together." She dabbed at a tear with her finger. "I miss him so much."

"We can consider this file closed." Nan smiled at Mrs. Fading Sun. She paged through the alphabet and inserted the folder in the file cabinet.

"I still can't believe his life insurance policy was for $10,000 instead of $100,000."

Nan watched the woman's shoulders sag. "You were expecting $100,000 and received a death benefit of $10,000? Did you check your policy to see if there were any typos? Maybe the numbers said ten thousand, but the words spelled out one hundred thousand." Nan reached across her desk and patted the woman's hand. "Insurance policies are confusing. Too many fancy words. I've processed some after funerals where I can barely understand them."

"It's the oddest thing. I was sure we had received a copy of the original policy. But after my husband died, I couldn't put my hands on it. When I called the insurance company, the man said he'd send a copy when he sent the check."

"Did you ask if the amount on the policy was ten thousand?" Nan gazed with concern, waiting for an answer.

"That's what he said," Mrs. Fading Sun answered. "I suppose I shouldn't have taken out that policy without meeting face to face with an agent. I did it on line. But I guess it worked out because I got the ten thousand."

"I seem to remember another client having the same problem," Nan said. "He thought his wife's policy was for more than he actually received. He was sure he'd paid premiums for a larger death benefit." Uneasiness gnawed at Nan as she recalled her conversation with the man. "He couldn't find any copies of the papers he'd signed, either."

"I thought my payments were awfully high for the small death benefit I got," Mrs. Fading Sun admitted. "Rather than make a fuss, I let it drop. I didn't want people thinking I was greedy. And I certainly didn't want them knowing I was cash poor."

Mrs. Fading Sun folded the paid invoice and tucked it in her purse. "Let me give you a hug," she said. "I couldn't have made it through this without your guidance."

Nan ushered her to the door. "What was the name of the life insurance company?"

Pausing, Mrs. Fading Sun said, "If I remember right, it

was called Gessal Life Insurance. I sent the premium checks to an address in Minneapolis."

As Nan closed the lobby door and secured the lock, Aanders came up behind her.

"I'm going over to Sadie's for a while."

"Okay. But I'm disappointed you told Mrs. Fading Sun about the accident. You know that's private information and isn't supposed to be released to the public. You could get me in trouble. You know you're not supposed to read my files."

"I didn't, Mom," Aanders said.

"The fact that Lon thinks it might have been murder isn't common knowledge. You must have taken a peek at that folder."

"No. I didn't. I know I'm not supposed to do that." Seeing his mother's skepticism, he repeated, "I swear I didn't look at it, Mom. I must have heard it somewhere."

Angry, yet bewildered at the look on Aanders' face, Nan decided to let it go. The finality of easing her son through his friend's death was more important.

15

Sadie removed a new lipstick tube from its wrapper and twisted the stick into view. "What about this one? Do you like this color?" She dabbed the tip on the back of her hand and held it out for Jane to see.

"That's nice," Jane said.

"What do you mean, that's nice? You didn't even take your eyes off the ironing board long enough to see it. I could have had poop on my hand and you'd say 'that's nice'."

"It's too hot to look at lipstick." Jane turned the cotton dish towel over and ironed the back side. She matched the corners before folding the fabric and running the iron across the top of the last fold.

"I would think looking at lipstick is a lot cooler than ironing." Sadie balled her fists and placed them on her hips. "Any nitwit would know that."

"How would you know? You never iron." Jane cocked her head and glared at her sister.

The intense humidity and the intestinal cramping from Jane's latest culinary experiment taxed Sadie's patience. "Your clothes are too big. If they were smaller, I might help."

"My clothes are bigger because I am bigger. Any nitwit would know that." Jane's smirk signaled satisfaction.

Sadie stood in front of the mirror and applied her new purchase to her lips. Smacking them together and wiping away the excess with her fingernail, she turned to Jane.

"Don't you think this makes me look younger?"

"No," Jane answered. "You know who you remind me of in that lipstick? You remind me of Hollywood Johnson. Remember her?"

"What a terrible thing to say," Sadie said. "She looked like a walking skeleton with that pasty makeup and those huge purple lips."

"E-x-a-c-t-l-y," Jane said. "Now you know what I think about your lipstick." She collapsed the ironing board frame and leaned it against the sink.

Sadie used a tissue to remove the color from her lips. She pulled a second tube from her purse and applied it to her pursed lips. "What about this one? This deep violet goes better with my outfit."

"That's even worse. Now you look like Hollywood's mother."

"Mr. Bakke, take Jane down to the lake and throw her in. Maybe that will change her mood." Sadie grabbed her neckline and fanned the fabric, forcing air to flow under her shirt.

"Do you actually know someone called Hollywood Johnson?" Theo said as he pulled out a chair and sat at the kitchen table. "Observing you is like watching a sleazy 'B' movie." He looked at Sadie's hair and then considered the length of her purple and lime mini dress. "Since you've got the staring role in this comedy, I recommend you take that new push-up bra back to the store. Something must be wrong with it. Nobody has breasts that lopsided."

Sadie turned to hurl an insult back at Theo.

Mr. Bakke said, "It's the weather. The sultry air makes Jane testy."

"If Jane wore shorts like the rest of us, she might be more comfortable."

"I wouldn't be caught dead in shorts at my age. And neither should you," Jane said. "Look at yourself. When you bend over I can see your butt. It looks like you don't have any underwear on."

"I don't," Sadie said. "Too hot."

"Oh, good Lord," Theo said with a rasp.

A knock at the screen door interrupted the bickering.

"Are you ready to leave yet?" Aanders said. He crossed the span from the door to the cookie jar in three long strides, allowing the screen door to slam behind him.

Sadie knocked on the door to the inner room and shouted to the crossers. "It's time to go. Get in the van." She pointed a finger at Aanders. "I'm counting on you to help Tim. He's getting weak. It's your responsibility to see he finds someone on the brink. If he doesn't, he might not find his parents."

"I know," Aanders answered. "We'll try. When we get back, we need to talk to you. Tim knows why he was held back. He wants me to help him prove it, but I can't do it unless you help, too."

"I'll keep an eye on them," Lora said as she climbed into the shuttle. "Maybe if they think I'll tattle, they'll try harder."

Rodney jumped in the van, slumped down, and kicked his legs across the aisle, propping his feet on Lora's seat. "Are you going to snitch on me, too?"

"I don't think she's concerned with what you do, Rodney," Sadie said.

"Yes she is. She has the hots for me."

Michael tapped Sadie on the back. "Do you have to take Belly to the dog doctor?"

Puzzled, Sadie turned around to look at the boy. "What for?"

"You told Mr. Bakke that Belly got his nose bent out of joint. It got bent when you made him go outside because he rolled in rotten fish on the beach. Remember?" Michael put his chin on the back of the seat. "I looked at his nose, but I couldn't tell if it was bent. Maybe you should have the doctor look at it. I want Belly to get better."

"I think you're right," Sadie said. "I'll take care of that while you're at the nursing home. When you get back, he'll be fine."

"Dumb kid," Rodney said and leaned his head back on the van's window.

At 5:00 p.m., Sadie returned to the nursing home to gather the crossers. She pulled in under the portico, descended the van's steps, grabbed the no-parking sign, and tugged it down the driveway away from the van.

Theo climbed the van steps and sat in the first seat next to the door. His head swiveled back and forth while Sadie carried on a conversation with the residents under the portico. "What a pitiful situation," he said when Sadie returned to the driver's seat. "A bunch of old people sitting around waiting to die."

"Would you prefer they waited out on the street?" Sadie shot Theo a 'you're as dense as a doorknob' look.

Theo sat with his knees tight together and the briefcase resting on his lap. "I see you failed Humor 101."

"Coming from the master of comedy, that's a pretty strong statement." Sadie looked toward the portico and tried to see beyond the residents clustered near the doorway.

Sadie patted her hair. "Notice anything new?"

"Other than that skunk on your head?"

Sadie turned her head back and forth and gazed in the rearview mirror. "I can't help it if most of the highlights ended up in a row on top." She picked at the blond spikes and tried to move some of them sideways. "Big Leon said it'll look better after he cuts off some of the streak."

"I'd schedule that appointment if I were you." Theo sighed impatiently then tipped his wrist to look at his watch. "What's taking them so long? I don't have all day."

"You have thirty days," Sadie said. "And you've used up about 10 of them. How come you're always the first one back on the van? Are you sure you're putting your energy into finding someone on the brink?"

"Spare the sermon. I've had all I can tolerate for one day. Lora is sobbing in one of hallways because Rodney's harassing her again. That wretched creature has enough to worry about. And the boys are hatching a plan to find a murderer."

"A murderer?"

"Tim's convinced his father was murdered."

Staring at Theo, Sadie said, "Did he tell you that?"

"No. But I overheard them talking about it. Something about a rifle."

"A rifle? That doesn't make sense. Richard wasn't shot. But Tim's not the first to question his father's death. Nan's friend, Lon, is concerned, too."

"It's amazing how little minds fabricate huge scenarios, isn't it?" Theo said.

Sadie bit at the corner of her mouth. Theo riled her. His

contempt for those beneath him increased by the day causing him to lose sight of his declaration.

Sadie pushed the release lever and the van's door swung shut. She grabbed the keys off the dash, started the van, and pulled away from the no-parking zone.

"What are you doing?" Theo cried. "What about the others?"

"They'll have to wait. I've waited for them, so they can wait for me." Sadie drove two miles before bringing the van to a standstill at Nordeen Point, a public park situated on the north side of Pinecone Lake.

Sadie got out of the driver's seat and sat directly across from Theo. "I want to know how it went today, Theo. Were you able to zero in on anyone near death?"

"Aren't they all?"

"You're quick to criticize, but they're not all waiting to die. What makes you think their lives weren't as good as yours."

"Because they're not me," Theo said under his breath.

Sadie sat on the edge of the seat with her legs dangling in the aisle. "Did you ever enjoy yourself? Or did you spend your entire life with that steel rod up your butt?"

"There. That's exactly what I mean, Sadie," Theo said. "You're as crass as they come. Your language is repulsive and you have no respect for anyone's feelings. Put yourself in my place and see how it feels to find out you're dead."

"You put yourself in my place and think about taking responsibility for one crosser after another," Sadie said. "That's not a bed of geraniums, either."

Theo cringed. "Roses. It's roses. If you have to use a tired cliché, at least get it right".

"We're not going back to the cabin until you tell me something about your past."

"What do you need to know?"

"Tell me about your life. Did you marry? Do you have children? If you do, that must have been a miracle because I can't picture you having sex with that rod up your butt."

"Are you sure you're not Rodney's mother?"

Sadie grabbed her breasts and shook them. "Positive. Rodney said his old lady had big tits. Remember?" With palms up, Sadie wriggled her fingers to indicate she wanted him to talk. "I'm prepared to stay here all night if that's what it takes."

Staring out the window at the children playing on the swings, Theo said, "I'll allow two questions. Then I want to go back to the cabin."

"Were you married and do you have children?"

"That's two questions. But because they're related, I'll allow it as one."

"Are you a judge?" Sadie asked. "You've made a few comments that make me think you're a judge or a lawyer."

"Is that one of your questions?"

"No. But I need to know because I have some questions unrelated to being a crosser."

"If you want legal advice regarding that lawsuit, I'm not going to make any comments."

"Do you think we have a chance?"

"Not if the judge knows you." Theo smiled.

"We're going to talk more about this later."

"I don't think so," Theo responded with a slow shake of his head.

Theo and Sadie turned to watch a procession of cyclists

ride past the van. Sadie grinned broadly and waved as one of the cyclists recognized her and shouted a greeting.

"I need sound legal advice. Maybe you're not intelligent enough to help me."

"I beg to differ. And quit using reverse psychology. It won't work."

Setting her lime crystal earrings in motion as she sat forward, Sadie said, "Tell me about your family. The more I know, the easier it will be to help you."

"I don't need your help. I've already made my declaration. I'm going to the parallel world." Theo held his hand up. "Before you ask, it's none of your business why I've chosen to go there."

"What if I ask that as one of my questions?"

"I don't think you will. There are too many other things you'd rather know, so think before you ask."

He placed the briefcase on the seat and turned to face Sadie. "I didn't marry until later in life. My wife had two children from a previous marriage. They became the scourge of my existence. So did my wife. From the day they entered my home, my life became a living hell." Theo turned to watch a child spin the merry-go-round. "This past year I actually considered divorce. They had nearly drained me financially, but then something happened that made it impossible for me to divorce her."

Sadie drew in a quick breath.

Theo held up his hand in warning. "You have one question left. If you ask the correct question, it will answer the others."

"I'd like to know what happened so you couldn't divorce her. I'd also like to know how you died. That's more a curiosity question, so I guess that's not important."

"Like I said, if you ask the correct question, you'll have the answers."

Tilting her head upward, Sadie closed her eyes and tried to paint a mental roadmap of what Theo had told her over the past ten days. Her first impressions clouded the image. "You haven't given me any clues so I have to go with my gut. What little I know about you leads me to believe I know the correct question."

"Get on with it," Theo said. "I'd prefer not to stay here all night."

Sadie tapped her teeth against the tip of her violet fingernail and took a deep breath. "What's in the briefcase?"

16

Theo clapped his hands together in a genteel manner. "Sadie you amaze me. I didn't think you'd ask the right question. I should repent for my erroneous first impression, but I'm not going to."

"I don't understand why everyone thinks I'm such an odd duck," Sadie said.

Theo shook his head. "Do you really not understand? Do you think everyone is wrong?"

"They're wrong if they form an opinion and refuse to change it." Frustrated with Theo's high view of himself, Sadie blurted, "My first impression of you was dreadful. Your attitude stinks."

"My attitude? What about Rodney's attitude? That man's dangerous and you're questioning my attitude?"

"Rodney doesn't hide his feelings like you do. We may fear him, but we know exactly what he thinks."

Theo's scowl indicated disagreement as he placed the briefcase back on his lap. He thrust his chin in the air and turned to stare at the barefoot children running along the beach.

"I think people form first impressions with their eyes instead of their brains," Sadie said. "When I don't understand something, I don't trust it. But at least I talk about it. You're hiding something. That means turmoil."

Theo's indifference irritated Sadie and she kicked at the edge of his seat until the tip of her sandal connected. "It's fear, you know. It's fear that makes you put on that macho mask. You're afraid of what lies ahead, but you won't admit it. I can wait. I've got enough patience for both of us."

Sadie scooted back across the van seat and leaned her head against the window. "It's too bad patience hasn't put an end to my concerns about Aanders seeing a rainbow at midnight."

With mouth agape, Theo let out a sharp breath. "My dear woman, what on earth are you talking about?" When Sadie didn't answer, he said, "I shouldn't have to clarify myself. I don't have the faintest idea what rainbows have to do with Aanders or patience."

"Aanders is a death-coach-in-training. They aren't allowed to counsel their own crossers until they've seen a rainbow at midnight." She watched Theo's head shake in disbelief, his chin swiveling against his fist. "Trainees have to work under the guidance of another death coach. They train until they're deemed worthy. A rainbow at midnight is a sign the trainee has earned the right to counsel their own crossers."

"Absurd," Theo said.

"Skeptic," Sadie said, wagging her finger back and forth in front of her face. "I learned this when I was in training. I haven't made anything up. It's the way it is."

"Maybe you should rewrite the book."

"There is no book."

"Then how do you know you're doing it right?"

"Quit asking questions." Sadie stood and moved back into the driver's seat. Turning to look at Theo she said, "Tell me what's in the briefcase."

Theo ran his hand across the leather. He placed his finger on the gold numbers and rotated three dials in sequence to complete the combination. The clasps snapped open.

Sadie rose and stood on her tiptoes. She peered over his shoulder. Theo unfastened another clasp and slid his hand into a silk pocket lining the lid.

He removed his hand and held up a small, four-inch-square black bag. He grasped it gingerly between his thumb and forefinger before cupping it in his other hand.

"You've been protecting your briefcase because of a little black bag? What's in it?"

"Diamonds," Theo closed the lid. "Diamonds worth a fortune."

Sadie dropped into the seat across from him. "My Lord," she gasped. "Are you sure?"

"Would I protect this briefcase if I weren't sure? Of course I'm sure."

Sadie reached for the bag. "What will you do with it?"

"I'm not giving it to you, if that's what you think. This bag is going with me." He placed the velvet bag back in the case. His tone oozed bitterness as his resentful glare settled on Sadie.

No wonder the man wore black. It matched his disposition. "You can't do that. Give it to your family. We'll make up a story and I'll make sure they get it."

"That's out of the question. I refuse to let them benefit from my hard work."

"Do they know about the diamonds?"

"They do. But they'll never get their hands on them. That's the good thing about my death. I was upset when my wife found out a client left me an inheritance. That was supposed to be my secret. My private bankroll. After I claimed the inheritance and had the diamonds valued, I hung on to them for several days trying to decide what to do." Theo spun the combination and checked the clasps to see if they had locked.

"If you remember, I told you I couldn't divorce my wife. Because I received the inheritance while we were married, she's protected under the fifty-fifty divorce statutes. My wife gets half. There's no way to fight it. She and those self-seeking ingrates of hers would drain me financially all over again."

Theo set the case on the floor. "Then I had a change of plan. I decided to cash in the diamonds and file for divorce. They could have their half and I'd enjoy what was left after taxes. I'd be rid of those egotistical leeches and have funds left to live out the rest of my life. That decision was like a last-minute reprieve from the death penalty."

"Give it to charity. Give it to a church," Sadie said. "At least you'd know your life was worth something."

"Like I said before, that's out of the question. I clawed my way to the top by sheer determination and I'll be damned if I'm going to share it with anyone."

"But Theo…"

"I don't want to hear it. People have taken advantage of me all my life. I'm sick of it. My wife and her children lived beyond our means and expected me to cover their debts. I was forced to do it so I wouldn't become the joke of the judicial system." Stabbing the air with his finger Theo said, "I lived nine years of pure hell because of those bastards."

"Can't you draw up another will and back date it? I'll take it to your attorney. He won't know the difference. As long as your signature's on it, it's valid."

"Sadie. Shame on you." Theo grinned. "I could do that, but I won't."

"You can't cash them in the parallel world."

"Do you know that for a fact?" Theo asked. "Nevertheless, my satisfaction lies in the knowledge my wife won't get her hands on the money. My will stipulates I bequeath the balance of my holdings to my wife. When she finds out there are no holdings left, my revenge will be complete. All that spending will come back and bite her in her greedy Gucci pocketbook."

A crooked smile formed on Theo's lips before he broke into a broad grin. "I think I'll compose a letter telling her I've hidden the money in one of my law books. I'm gambling she got rid of them. She hated that library. We had many a squabble over the hours I spent in there."

"That's downright mean," Sadie said.

"It is, isn't it? Let them pine over the missing money." Patting his briefcase he said, "These gems are going with me."

17

Carl and Paul leaned against the hood of the patrol car. Waves of heat emanated from the vehicle, adding to the discomfort of the humid summer afternoon. Carl pointed at the marker indicating the resort's boundary line and fanned his arm the entire length of the beachfront. "Then starting right there, the next hundred feet of shoreline belongs to the mortuary. When Judge Kimmer rules in my favor, I'll own that, too." Carl rubbed his hands together. "It can't happen soon enough for me."

A green Buick slowed to a stop. The driver leaned out and asked for directions to the lodge. "Make a right at the next driveway. You can't miss it. Enjoy your stay, it's a great place," Carl said.

Paul elbowed Carl. "Now that's good marketing. A thumbs-up from a man in uniform should bring them back next summer."

"You know that book you told me about? I bought it last week. I can sum it up in two words."

"Two?" Paul asked. "That's all you got out of it was two words?"

"Kiss butt. Customer service means kissing your customers' butts and doing it with a smile."

"I suppose you could look at it that way. Your customer is your meal ticket. Don't ever forget that. The resort business is a service industry and your customers expect to be waited on."

"Bull," Carl spat. "My staff is going to do the butt-kissing. I'm going to sit behind that big oak desk and give orders."

A truck towing a boat trailer edged its way to the far side of the parking lot before backing down the access ramp. The passenger got out and gestured directions to the driver. As Carl approached the truck, the driver shouted, "Are they bitin'?"

The passenger tugged on the boat to loosen it from the trailer. He guided the boat toward the dock.

Carl reached out and flagged his hand, indicating he wanted the man to throw him the rope. He pulled the boat to the dock and secured the rope.

"I saw some big fillets coming out of the cleaning shack," Carl said. "Some of the biggest I've seen this summer."

"Hot damn. We drove all the way up from Minneapolis. Them babies better be hoppin' in the boat."

Carl pointed to one of the two large, red tackle boxes sitting on the boat's floor. "With that gear, you won't have any problem."

"We're not coming in till we catch our limit," the man shouted over the roar of the motor. He fastened his life jacket, pushed the lever forward and glided past a row of yellow boundary floats.

"Good luck," Paul shouted, joining Carl at the end of the dock.

Paul pointed at the sign over the marina. "The first thing you need to do is get rid of that sign."

"Why? I like it."

"'EAT, GET GAS AND WORMS' isn't exactly a great endorsement. I'm surprised anyone dares stop."

"It's a landmark. It's been there since I can remember," Carl said.

"Who do you want to cater to, the pro fisherman or the rednecks?"

"It doesn't matter as long as they've got money. Speaking of money, I need a business manager like your partner. Too bad he kicked the bucket."

"I still can't believe he's gone," Paul said. "Have you heard any more on the investigation?"

"Nah. I'm guessing Lon dropped it. He must have realized he'd be a bigger ass than he already is if anyone got wind of his suspicions."

"Let me know if you hear any more," Paul said.

"Quit worrying. Lon's a dufus. Besides, I've got more important things on my mind. I need to plan the eviction. I want to evict the Witt sisters the day I win the lawsuit."

Paul grabbed Carl's arm, his eyes brimming with annoyance. "Haven't you listened to anything I've said? If you evict them right before the election, you won't stand a chance. People respect the Witt sisters. You need to wait until after you've been declared the winner."

"Paul," Carl whined, "you're ruining my day."

"If you don't start using common sense, you'll lose everything." Paul threw his hands up in the air. "You're hopeless."

The two men turned to walk back to shore. Carl tripped over a red tackle box and fell to his knees. Tackle rattled as the case tipped sideways and skittered to the edge of the dock. Paul scrambled to keep the box from falling into the lake.

"What the hell?" Carl looked out into the bay. "Isn't

that one of the tackle boxes they had in their boat?" Carl scanned the horizon for the boat.

"That's what I wondered," Paul said. "How'd it get here? Maybe I should get one of the dock boys to take it out to them?"

"Nah," Carl said. "If they're that dumb, that's their problem. Besides, as soon as they realize it's missing, they'll come looking for it. We'll leave it on the dock."

A deer bounded out of the woods and skidded on the tarred access ramp. Startled by the figures on the dock, the doe tried to regain her footing while simultaneously spinning back toward the trees. Pushing off with her hind legs, she hurtled twice and disappeared back into the underbrush. The thick growth parted and swayed as the deer vanished.

"Holy balls. Where did that come from?"

"I think the deer flies are driving them crazy," Paul said. "They dart everywhere trying to get away from the flies. I'm guessing one bolted out in front of the Fossums' car."

Carl scanned the underbrush. "Did you ever get Richard's briefcase from his sister?"

"Not yet. She left town to take care of her father. When she gets back, she'll let me in so I can load up the stuff he had in his home office."

A rustle of leaves drew their attention back to the woods. A deer hesitated before bounding through an opening and running across the parking lot into the woods on the north side of the resort.

"That reminds me," Carl said, faking a shot at the fleeing animal. "I need to borrow your rifle again. I'm competing in a tournament next week. I have better luck with your rifle than I do with mine. With your scope and my dead aim, it's a given I'll walk away with first place."

"I lost it," Paul said.

"Lost it? How could you lose something like that?" Carl removed his cap and scratched the top of his scalp with his little finger. Paul had probably spent more on that scope than he had earned last month. Heat welled up around Carl's neck. It was an angry heat triggered by Paul's blasé attitude toward his possessions.

"I took it out to the woods to adjust the scope. It must have shook loose and fell off my four-wheeler when I drove home."

"Did you look for it?"

"No, Carl," Paul said. "That scope set me back three-thousand bucks. Why would I look for it? I thought I'd just leave it there until the next time I needed it."

"How am I going to win the tournament without your rifle? That was one fine piece of hardware." Carl kicked at a dock board in disappointment. "I'd use my own, but the rifles the sheriff gives us are crap. You had your scope aligned so perfectly, I could shoot blindfolded."

Two colorful rafts, toting coolers, floated past the dock. Paul waved at the occupants as they slid off and carried the coolers up the access ramp.

"If you were smart, Carl, you'd capitalize on that access ramp to make extra money."

"What do you mean?" Carl set the red tackle box on the end of the dock.

"Most people think that's a public access. But it's not. That access is on the Witt sisters' property. They've been letting people use it for years. If I were you, I'd charge per boat to access the lake. In the winter, I'd charge five bucks per vehicle during ice fishing season."

"Why didn't I think of that?" Carl said. "Got any more ideas?"

"Maybe. But they come with a price."

Carl watched Aanders head toward Sadie's cabin, playing a video game as he walked. When Aanders noticed them, he quickly averted his gaze back to his video game.

"Isn't that Nan's kid?" Carl asked. "Who's he talking to?"

"You got me. Must be the game," Paul said. "Did you notice how scared he looked? It's almost like he wanted to take off running."

"Give him a break. He just lost his friend. Tell me more about your ideas."

"The reason you didn't think about the access fee is because you haven't challenged your brain. You might have potential, but you don't know how to use it." Paul tapped his temple. "It's all about manipulation."

"You mean like how you're going to buy the mortuary and trick Nan into marrying you?"

"Something like that."

Paul pointed toward a cluster of children standing around an ice cream cart. The two men sauntered over to the cart. Paul stooped to look into the case. He gestured toward the chocolate tub and pulled a ten from his wallet. Carl waited for his cone before catching up to Paul. "Well?"

"Like I said, it'll cost you. Genius isn't cheap."

"Bull," Carl uttered. He wiped at the cone with his tongue.

"I could find another location for the mortuary. It isn't set in stone that I have to buy the existing building."

"You backing out on me?" Carl's nostrils flared as his voice rose. Red splotches edged up his neck and onto his cheeks.

Paul grimaced and looked around. "If I were you, I'd keep my voice down. You'll never keep employees if you react like that. You'll scare them away."

Carl slid his mouth around the cone to catch the drips. "Well golly gee, mister businessman, I disagree. I have no intention of changing my ways."

Paul and Carl watched a young woman in a bikini cross in front of them and walk toward the beach. Carl pursed his lips. "Oh baby. Come to papa. To think they'll be parading in front of me all summer is better than a wet dream. I'll be so busy entertaining I'll have to sleep all day to recuperate."

"You talk big, but your wife would chop you into bait and feed you to the fish."

"She'll never know." Carl pulled a tablet from his back pocket. "I need to add bikini babes to my list of things for the judge. He's coming for dinner tomorrow night. I try to sweeten the pot every time I talk to him."

Carl jabbed Paul with his elbow. "Look who's coming."

Mr. Bakke met the two men on the walkway and nodded as he continued. He shifted a bag of groceries from one arm to the other.

Carl shot his fist in the air. "Yes. How perfect is that?" He turned to watch Mr. Bakke step up onto Sadie's porch. "I hoped one of them would see me. He'll run in and tell them

I'm here. That made the drive out here worth it. I'd do anything to aggravate Sadie."

Paul stopped at the edge of the resort property and gazed at the mortuary. "It's a shame to waste shoreline on a mortuary. That hundred feet of beach front could generate a lot of income if you didn't sell it."

Carl scanned the shoreline. "So you're saying if you don't buy the land and building I should do something with it?"

Paul tapped his temple. "Think, man. That building could be used for lodging or it could be rented out to corporations for meetings." Paul tapped his temple again. "If you don't start thinking like an entrepreneur, you'll never succeed."

"I'll think about it," Carl said as he walked toward the patrol car. "My problem is cash. I was counting on cash from the sale of the mortuary land to pay my bills. If I don't sell it, I'll have to come up with the money. You know I don't have money." He grinned across the top of the car. "Not that my wife knows about."

The two men opened their doors. Suddenly, Carl let out a yell. "What the...?"

The contents of a red tackle box were strewn over the car's interior. Most of the barbed hooks were deeply embedded in the car's upholstery and fishing line had been entwined throughout the interior forming an impenetrable web. Carl's clipboard dangled from the rearview mirror. Each numbered citation had 'PIG' written across it in bold, black letters. Mermaid lures hung from the ceiling with dried-up minnows on the tips of the barbs.

"That witch," Carl shouted.

"Who?"

"Sadie. She did this," Carl yelled.

The Witt's End van pulled into the parking lot, stopping next to the patrol car. One of the resort's guests climbed out of the van. "Thanks for taking us into town, Sadie. We got some great pictures to show the folks back home. I'll bring them over as soon as I get them developed."

Sadie followed the woman out of the van. Theo, Lora, and Michael trailed close behind.

Carl grabbed Sadie's arm. "Were you in town all afternoon?"

She slapped at his hand and pulled free. "Yes, I was. What business is it of yours?"

"Do you have any witnesses?"

"For what?"

"To vouch you were in town all afternoon."

Sadie looked up at Theo, who stood next to her with a big smile on his face. "What are you grinning for?"

"Grinning? I'm not grinning. Do I look like I'm having fun?" Carl's voice rose with each word as he glared at Sadie.

Theo gestured toward Carl's patrol car. "You better take a peek in there."

Sadie raised up on her toes and looked in the window. She let out a hoot. "Did you leave your car unlocked?"

"No, Sadie. I always drive a car that looks like a tackle box."

"That's really stupid." Sadie reached in and pulled on a tightly wound portion of fishing line. The line twanged like a guitar string setting several lures into motion. "Those minnows stink."

Sadie shouted toward her cabin. "Jane. Call the

newspaper and ask them to come out and take a picture of Carl's patrol car. Maybe we can get the idiots who plan to vote for him to change their minds."

Carl spun to face Jane. "If you call them so help me I'll get ten more patrol cars out here and make a big scene. I'll tell everyone there's a murderer on the loose. Your guests will cancel their reservations and leave."

"At least they'll leave laughing." Sadie dabbed at a tear.

Carl opened his pocket knife and began cutting the tightly wound strings away from the steering wheel. "Look at this mess. It'll take me a week to find everything. I'm going to catch whoever did this. You can count on it."

"I doubt it," Sadie said, catching a glimmer of Rodney dangling a fishing lure as he leaned against a tree.

Carl cursed under his breath. "First I find out I can't use your rifle and now this." Carl stopped cutting and glared at Paul over the top of his patrol car. "How the hell can you lose a rifle?"

"I already told you. It must have jarred loose from my four-wheeler. I backtracked, but I couldn't find it. There's so much hazel brush along that trail, it's impossible to find anything."

Rodney swung a dangling fish hook in a wide circle waiting for Sadie and the other crosssers to close the door on Cabin 14. He checked the area to his left and then his right before reaching behind the tree. He jerked his hand back to his side. Aanders hurried past the patrol car, hopped up onto Sadie's porch, and yanked the door open. Rodney scanned his surroundings one more time. Reaching behind the tree, he pulled out the rifle he had taken from Carl's patrol car and disappeared into the woods.

18

The massive glass doors swooshed closed behind Lora as she began one more unbearable trek down the tiled corridor. Michael dragged his feet in resistance. Impending disaster circled his young shoulders like the time his dad suffocated his cat. Nursing home employees hustled past the pair, intent on keeping to their daily schedules as the ever-intrusive call lights blinked impatiently.

A nurse aide emerged from one of the resident's rooms pushing a wheelchair. She situated the resident, a man in his late eighties, next to the wall in the hallway. Another aide selected a clean set of sheets from a linen cart before entering the man's room. The man's chin rested on his chest. He sighed deeply without waking.

Michael paused in front of the man and looked up at his mother.

"I think he's sleeping. I don't think he's the one we're looking for," Lora said. She put her ear close to the man's face for a moment before continuing down the hall.

Lora walked in and out of each resident's room, Michael leaned on the door jamb. He'd let her walk three to four doors down the hall before running to catch up. He stayed close, but out of her way. On previous visits he had squatted on the floor creating a make-believe gravel pit with make-believe front-end loaders like the one his dad drove. When that bored him, he spread out on a bed and counted ceiling tiles with his fingers. This time he created a new make-believe Dad. One that wouldn't hurt them anymore.

Lora poked her head around the door frame. "Don't go too far. I don't like it when I can't see you." She continued down the hall to investigate the condition of each resident.

Lora walked deeper into the skilled-care unit. She scanned the length of the hall hoping to see staff scurrying to a resident's room. Sadie had told the crossers that a sudden gathering of medical staff could be an indication of someone on the cusp.

Michael hooked his fingers on each side of a door frame and swung like a hinge into one of the resident's rooms. He lost his grip and tumbled to the floor. With lightning speed, he sprung upright, retreated back into the corridor and pressed his back flat against the wall.

He heard sobs and sniffles coming from the people standing around the bed. He looked for his mom. He didn't see her. Michael slinked back into the room and inched his way closer to the bed. He skirted two pairs of legs so he could see why the people were crying.

The daughter of the dying woman held her mother's hand to her cheek and sobbed. "We're here Mother. We love you." The words came in gasps. The others in the room brushed at tears and held fast to one another.

Michael listened to them tell the woman she had suffered long enough. They told her to let go. He tiptoed closer and peeked around one of the men.

A nurse entered the room and took the woman's vital signs. She jotted the information on the chart. She motioned for the woman's son to join her at the rear of the room and whispered something to the man. The man moved back toward his sister and embraced her as he burst into tears.

Michael moved to the bed and looked at the woman.

She looked just like Sadie did when she was sleeping. He leaned against the bed and propped his chin against his fist.

The woman's daughter reached down and smoothed her mother's hair before placing a kiss on her cheek. She straightened her gown and gently pulled the covers up to her chin. Each family member took turns planting a kiss on the woman's forehead saying their final good-byes.

Michael's index finger tapped its way along the bed sheet until it was within inches of the deceased woman's hair. He casually looked up at the daughter, who stood next to him as he wound his finger around a strand of white hair. Chin bobbing against his fist, he said, "Are you dead?"

The nurse asked the family if they had a funeral director they wanted her to contact. One of the woman's daughters pulled a cell phone from her purse. With fingers shaking, she dialed the first of many.

The deceased woman opened her eyes and smiled at Michael. He smiled back and nudged the toe of his tennis shoe against the tile floor. "Are you dead yet?"

The woman sat up effortlessly and moved to the edge of the bed. "You were waiting for me, weren't you? I saw you go by several times the past few days." She placed her hand on Michael's head and ran her thumb through his bangs. "I'm glad you waited. Now I don't have to go alone."

She slid from the bed. When her feet touched the floor, she reached for Michael's hand. "Are you ready?" The light around the woman began to intensify as she effortlessly walked away from the bed.

Michael looked toward the door. "We need to get Mom."

Michael felt a cool breeze spread through the room and

he noticed the woman's gown moving with the air currents. A thunder rumbled in the distance. Michael ran to the door. "Mom. It's time to go. There's a dead lady in here who wants us to go with her."

The woman's family gathered around her bed one more time, their tears flowing without reservation. A few family members milled outside the door to escape the sorrow. The finality was more than they could bear.

The nurse gently guided one of the woman's daughters to a chair. "You don't have to leave yet. Take all the time you want. The funeral director won't be here for another half hour." She gave the daughter a brochure from the mortuary they had selected. She circled the phone number. "The funeral director will contact you to make arrangements if she doesn't hear from you by tomorrow morning."

The deceased woman's body wavered and rose off the floor, spears of light penetrating her translucent image. The intensity of the rumbling drew closer.

Michael looked back at the lady who held both arms out to him. She shouted, "Hurry, Michael. I can't wait much longer. We've got to go."

"Mom. Hurry," Michael screamed, his gaze darting frantically down the corridor. Hearing his name called by the dead woman, he looked back toward the intensifying glow. "Wait. Wait for us. Mom's coming."

"Now, Michael. If you're coming, you've got to come now." The strength the breeze spiraling through the tunnel pulled her further into the light. "I can't wait any longer," she shouted over the rumble filling the room.

Michael ran toward the light shielding his eyes.

"Wait. Wait for me." He reached toward the woman.

153

"Step forward, Michael. Step into the light." She continued to shout encouragement to the boy as she slipped further into the vortex. Her hair lashed like a pennant in the wind. She stretched to reach for Michael's hand.

As he grasped the woman's hand and was lifted upward by the current, Lora rounded the doorframe. She screamed in horror. "Noooo. Michael, noooo. Don't go."

Michael reached for his mom, fighting against the vortex pulling him backward toward the woman. "We have to go, Mom. Hurry and come with me."

Lora tried to grab her son, struggling against the wind that now drew her toward the light. Her clothes whipping in frenzy against her body, Lora shouted, "Don't go. We have to find your father."

Tears streamed down Michael's face as he fought the momentum. "No Mom. I don't want to. Please come with me to the other place."

Lora dropped to her knees and cried out against the roar. "I can't. I can't go against his wishes." She reached toward Michael. "Grab my hand." Seeing Michael fight to reach her, she said, "Come on, baby. Just a few more steps."

His fingertips brushed briefly against the back of his mother's outstretched hand, then Michael's arm dropped to his side. The momentum of the wind pulled him back toward the dead woman. His chest heaving with sobs, he turned away from his mother and reached for the woman's hand. "I'm ready."

Michael looked back toward his mother as they faded into the distance. "I love you, Mom," he shouted. "Don't let Dad be mean anymore." The pair faded into the tunnel, beginning their walk down the corridor of light.

19

Mr. Bakke and Jane swayed rhythmically on a suspended wooden swing, a rusted chain squeaking in protest with each forward movement. The unbearable humidity had even drained energy from the resort's guests. Vacationers had switched from high-speed to slow-motion to surrender. Jane fanned Mr. Bakke's newspaper back and forth attempting to stir the air. A group of guests meandered by the cabin and Jane waved the newspaper in greeting.

With one leg tucked under her and the other tapping against the wooden planking, Sadie sat next to them in an Adirondack chair. Billowing thunderheads clustered on the horizon.

"I sure hope that thunderstorm gets rid of the heat," Jane said. "I've never sweat so much in my life."

"If you'd wear shorts, you'd feel better," Sadie said without looking up from her magazine.

Belly waddled up to Sadie, licked her red toenails, and plopped down by her side. He looked from sister to sister, panting with discomfort.

Even though warm weather was good for business, the hot spell had been around too long. Sadie looked forward to a break. Earlier in the day she had assisted the resort manager with an unusually high volume of calls from city dwellers. Seeking relief from the heat seemed a priority. More than likely the weather was as hot at the resort as it was in the city, but the fact guests could spend time on the water made a trip up north worthwhile.

"You know I refuse to wear shorts. I don't want to become the brunt of jokes like you are."

"I beg your pardon." Sadie closed her magazine and dropped it on the porch floor. "I'll have you know, this is a first class outfit. I paid good money for it."

"If that's what you think, then you need new eyes. You're wearing white pants." Jane pointed as if that explained everything.

"I already know that," Sadie said.

"Every time you walk in front of me, I can see your red thong through the fabric. You look ridiculous." Jane nodded with conviction.

Sadie stood and walked over to Jane. "First of all these are Capri's, not pants." She turned around and bent over slightly. "Second of all, my red thong matches my red shirt and sandals. The waist part of the thong is supposed to show above my hip huggers. It's all the rage. If you'd read my fashion magazines once in a while, you'd know that."

Mr. Bakke rested his head against the back of the porch swing while his foot kept the swing in motion. As Sadie presented her fashion commentary, Mr. Bakke slid his glasses off the top of his head and positioned them over his eyes.

"Well don't go anywhere looking like that. And don't tell anyone you're related to me. I'd die of embarrassment if they found out," Jane said.

"I think they already know that," Mr. Bakke said.

Jane clucked her tongue in disgust. She glared at Mr. Bakke. "Put those glasses back on top your head and mind your own business."

Wrinkling her nose and fanning the air, Sadie said,

"My goodness, Belly is rank tonight. Did you pawn your cooking off on him again?"

"A little bit," Jane said. "I let him lick your plate since you didn't eat it. You shouldn't let good food go to waste."

Jane bent to pick the magazine off the porch floor and flicked at the dirt particles clinging to the cover. "Weren't you too hard on Aanders this afternoon? You had him in tears. I still think you should apologize."

"I'm not going to apologize." Irritated Jane brought it up for the second time, Sadie said, "Tim's got Aanders believing his father was murdered. That's all he talked about on the way to the nursing home this morning. "

"But that's what Lon Friborg thinks, too."

"I understand that," Sadie said. "That isn't what Tim and Aanders need to worry about. Tim's got to concentrate on his death decision. Time is growing short."

"From what you told me, Tim's imagination got the best of him," Mr. Bakke said. "If he thinks he saw a rifle before the car rolled, I'll bet it was that movie that put those thoughts in Tim's head."

"I told Tim and Aanders that same thing. They refused to listen. How is Aanders going to learn to become a death coach if I'm not firm with him? He clearly doesn't grasp the importance."

Mr. Bakke pushed his glasses back on his nose. "I got the impression he doesn't want to serve as a death coach. He told me he was going to ask you to find someone else."

Jane took the newspaper off Mr. Bakke's lap and fanned the paper between them, causing his hair to stand erect with each swirl of air. "Why don't you do that, Sadie?"

"Do what?" Sadie waved at another group of guests

passing by. The guest's dog bounded toward the porch and Belly uttered a half-hearted growl before laying his head back on his paws.

"Find another coach, so Aanders doesn't have to do it."

"In case you didn't notice," Sadie said, "there isn't a Death Coaches-R-Us store in Pinecone Landing. I can't pull one off the shelf."

Aanders kept his gaze on his feet as he walked up to the porch and took both steps in a single stride. When Tim didn't follow, Aanders shot a quick glance at Sadie before hopping back down to assist Tim up the stairs. "He's weaker today."

"You've got to remember what we talked about," Sadie said. "It's crucial the two of you concentrate on Tim's task." Sadie watched Aanders put his arm around Tim's shoulder and guide him into the cabin.

A young couple walked past the porch and waved at the trio. "How you doing?" Sadie shouted.

The young man paused, dabbed at his face with the bottom of his T-shirt and said, "I'm really hot."

Nodding as she tapped her lip with her finger, Sadie said, "That's a bit vain. But if it works for you I'm okay with it."

Curtains of confusion fell over the faces of the young couple before the man began to laugh. As they walked away, the young man put his arm around his girlfriend. "That's the lady I've been telling you about."

The crossers gathered for their round table session. Rodney propped his feet on an adjacent chair and leaned against the table. Tim and Aanders sat opposite Rodney.

"Lora," Sadie called out, "we can't get started until you

join us."

Rodney pointed the remote control at the television and selected a rock video channel. He thumbed the volume button until the others cringed from the noise. Heavy bass rattled the windows.

Sadie grabbed at the remote, but Rodney raised it above his head. As Sadie jumped to reach the remote, Theo snatched it from Rodney's grasp. He pointed it at him and clicked furiously.

Rodney stomped toward the inner room and kicked his foot against the wooden door. "Let the cry baby stay in her room. She's been bawling all day. She cried at the nursing home and then we had to listen to her all the way home. I'm sick of it." Rodney slammed his fist against the door. "You should be glad you're rid of that little prick."

A gasping sob came from behind the inner room door. Sadie opened it and reached for Lora. "You need to join us so we can make sense of what happened." Sadie eased Lora from the room and guided her to a chair. "You've still got a decision to make."

"She already decided to go with her old man," Rodney said. "She told me that when we got back. Let her go. Maybe he can set her straight."

Sadie ran her hand up and down Lora's back. She asked her to explain the exact circumstances that led to her son passing through to the other side. Lora relived the afternoon's events through heavy weeping.

"Why didn't you go through the tunnel at the same time?" Aanders said.

"Because I knew he wanted to go to the parallel world. I tried to get him to come back. At first he tried, but then it looked like he gave up," Lora said.

"I don't think he gave up. He wanted to go to the parallel world. He was afraid you'd make him change his mind." Sadie waited while Lora tried to regain her composure. She also waited for the denial.

Tipping her head back Lora burst into tears again. "My husband is going to be so angry. He always said I was a terrible mother." She placed her fists on the table. "He'll never forgive me."

Curiosity flickered in Aanders' eyes as he looked at Sadie. "Why didn't she go to her husband the same time Michael went to the parallel world?"

"I'm glad you're asking questions. It's the best way to learn."

Sadie pulled her chair closer to the table. "Crosssers can't step into the tunnel unless they've made their declaration. It's the same as if they never found someone on the brink. It results in death without purpose. But if someone who has already made their declaration steps in ahead of them, that person determines the final path." Sadie reached for Lora's hand. "I think Lora remembered that whoever steps into the tunnel first makes the decision. She knew Michael wanted to go to the parallel world."

"I begged him to come back. He tried, but the power of the tunnel was too strong." Lora buried her face in the crook of her elbow.

"Lora you know that's not what happened. Michael made a conscious decision. It was a sound decision. He didn't want to live in fear any more and knew what had to be done. You should be proud of him."

Theo looked at Aanders. "If you're going to help your

crossers, you'd better listen to everything Sadie tells you."

Raising her brows in astonishment, Sadie bit her tongue to keep from commenting on Theo's observation. Theo wanted Aanders to pay attention, yet Theo refused to listen. The bitterness and penchant for revenge Theo displayed during the afternoon had frustrated her, but Sadie had no intention of letting the others in on their confidential conversation.

"Lora, you've got to rethink your decision. Michael needs you. It would be in your best interest to join your son. Your self-esteem is so eroded you can't think straight." Sadie leaned toward Lora. "Choosing to go to your husband is the worst decision you could make. He's not going to change."

"Why does he need to change?" Rodney said. "Why can't she change? She needs to do what he says instead of moping around all the time. You're making him out to be the bad guy."

Theo scooted his chair over until his arm pushed against Rodney. He leaned within two inches of Rodney's face. "You are going to close that mouth and keep it closed until I tell you to open it. Is there any part of what I said that requires clarification?"

"Shit," Rodney mumbled in two syllables as he leaned away from Theo. "Just cuz you're a judge doesn't mean you can boss me around."

Theo put his hand on the back of Rodney's chair and whispered in his ear. "Yes, it does."

Jane opened the screen door and let Belly in. The dog checked his empty dish before ambling over to Theo and placing his jowls on the man's black slacks.

"Would you please remove your dog from my leg?"

"He's not my dog."

"Do you realize how idiotic that sounds?"

Sadie put her hands on her waist and jutted her left hip. "The truth is never idiotic. But those who can't interpret it may be."

Dismissing her comment with a look of disgust, Theo stood and opened a cabinet door. He pulled a box of dog treats from the shelf and placed several in Belly's dish.

"Don't do that. He's too fat already," Sadie said. "And besides, he's got gas from Jane's cooking."

"You might as well add vulgarity to your ever-growing list of shortcomings," Theo said. "I'd be willing to loan you a second sheet of paper. Or maybe you need a third."

"Bite me," Sadie said. "You're not perfect either."

"Were any of you successful in zeroing in on someone close to death?" Sadie listened to Theo and Tim discuss the pending death of two nursing home residents. Aanders added commentary when Tim left things out. She encouraged Aanders to be mindful of all the crossers, not just Tim.

"I have a question," Rodney interrupted, waving a fist full of mail at Sadie. "Why is your mail addressed to Fifilomine instead of Sadie?"

"Why were you going through my mail?"

"I was looking for money."

Sadie grabbed the mail and shoved it in a drawer. "My real name is Fifilomine. Actually both Jane and I have the same first name. Fifilomine. My mother chose that name to get even with the man who got her pregnant. He refused to marry her. It's that classic story of the man forgetting to mention he already had a wife."

Gesturing, she put her index finger on her chest. "My real name is Fifilomine Sadie and Jane's is Fifilomine Jane. It just so happens the man's wife was also named Fifilomine. Does that answer your question?"

"Now I know where you get your personality quirks," Theo said. "From your mother."

Puzzled, Tim and Aanders looked at one another. "What was your dad's name?" Aanders said.

"That doesn't matter. Actually our mother refused to tell us who our father was. All that mattered was that she got revenge."

"Was your mom the death coach who trained you?" The group strained to hear Tim's question.

"My coach was the man who took my mother in when her parents disowned her. Years ago it was a bad thing to have a child out of wedlock." Sadie looked at the boys. "That means you didn't have a husband."

"The man befriended my mother and offered her a job at his resort. Back then Witt's End was called Swanson's Resort. When that man died, she got the resort and renamed it Witt's End."

As memories washed over her, Sadie crossed her arms over her chest and leaned into the back of her chair. "I found out I was a death coach when I was twenty-four-years old. It was quite a shock. I had the same urge to deny it as Aanders has, but Mr. Swanson was patient. He taught me everything he knew. When I saw a rainbow at midnight, I became responsible for my own crossers."

"Do you think I could wait till I'm that old to do it?"

"No. That's not possible. You've got years of training

ahead of you. You could become an official coach at any time, but the training goes on for a life time. I still learn new things every day."

As she sensed Aanders' disappointment, she noticed a look of concern cross Tim's face. Tim slumped lower in his chair. Sadie put her arms under Tim's arms and pulled him up. "What is it, Tim?"

"You tell her," Tim said, looking at his friend.

The group turned toward Aanders.

Aanders joined Tim and sat on the edge of his chair. "Tim's upset because you won't believe his dad was murdered. He even knows who did it. He wants you to tell the cops."

"What?" Theo and Sadie exclaimed simultaneously.

"We've already talked about this, Tim." Looking at the others Sadie said, "It's natural to think murder could be an option. It's another way of justifying what he doesn't want to accept."

"No, I'm positive. I saw the rifle." Tim coughed, struggling to catch his breath.

"I bet things happened so fast, your brain didn't have time to register," Sadie said.

"No. I saw him. I saw the gun. And then after everything got quiet, I heard a motor start up. It sounded like it was on the other side of the woods."

Theo withdrew his arm from the back of Rodney's chair and leaned on the table. "Do you know who the man was?"

"Yes. It's the same man who was here the other day with the deputy. It's my dad's business partner."

20

"Miss Witt. Excuse me, Miss Witt," a resort guest shouted as she ran to catch up with Sadie and Belly.

"Excuse me. Excuse me." Rodney mocked. He was still angry that Sadie had chastised him in front of the other crossers. Rancid breath billowing, he slipped behind Sadie and leaned close to her neck. "You'll get yours, you witch."

Belly's ears flattened and he lunged toward Rodney. The crosser dodged the attack.

"The next time that dog growls at me will be his last," Rodney snarled.

Sadie pulled Belly to her side as she greeted the guest. The dog dropped to his haunches and raised his leg to scratch at the orange neckerchief. He leaned against Sadie's leg and tapped his foot in rhythm with the tempo of her fingers as she helped him locate the itch.

"Could you give us directions to the hospital? My daughter called this morning to tell me my aunt is hospitalized in Pinecone Landing. We'd like to stop and visit her." The woman held a pen over a small tablet, waiting for Sadie to begin.

Sadie pushed her orange-rimmed sun glasses up into her gelled spikes. With several grand gestures, she issued directions. "You can't miss it. It's one of the biggest buildings in that area." Sadie accompanied her guest as she walked back to her car. "I hope your aunt will be all right."

"I'm sure she will." The woman paused, keeping her gaze on Belly. "Why is your dog growling at me?"

"He's not growling at you." Sadie's eyes grew wide as she watched Rodney jump into the back seat of the woman's car. The woman's husband climbed in behind the steering wheel and put the key in the ignition.

Sadie hugged her arms over her orange polka-dot top, watching the car disappear down the drive.

Rodney let out a satisfied breath and snuggled against the soft blue upholstery. This fancy car had more to offer than that old van Sadie made him ride in every day. He wiggled his fingers at Sadie. Then he saluted.

Sliding sideways and leaning against the window, Rodney propped his feet up on the back of the driver's headrest.

"Home, James," he said issuing directions to the driver. "I'll take a beer. Make sure it's cold. On second thought, make it a whole case."

Rodney looked at the man's wife. "What's that? You have a daughter who thinks I'm a stud? That doesn't surprise me." He tapped the woman on the shoulder. "How about you? You want to do me the big favor, too?"

He watched the greenery fly by as the car headed down the highway. Rodney's elbow brushed against the electric controls on the armrest and he placed his fingers on the panel. He toyed with the silver buttons.

"What are you doing? It's too hot to roll the windows down," the woman said.

"I'm not doing anything."

"You must be. The window in the back seat keeps going up and down." She craned her neck toward the back seat. "Now they're both going up and down."

The man pulled the car over and shoved the lever into park. "Maybe it's a short in the wiring." He got out and opened the back door on the driver's side. His wife got out and opened the back door on the passenger's side. They both began pushing buttons along the armrests trying to get the windows to close.

"Are you sure you didn't lean your elbow on the front panel?"

"Of course I'm sure," he said. "I told you it must be a short in the wiring. Let's take the car back to the rental place. I'm not going to put up with this for a whole week. It's too hot."

They climbed back into the car. Rodney leaned into the front seat and cranked the radio's volume on high. He pointed toward the woman.

"What did you do that for?" she shouted. "You know how much I hate loud music."

Rodney pointed at the driver as the man turned the radio off.

"I didn't do it. There's something wrong with this car."

As the man finished his sentence, Rodney reached for the lever on the steering wheel and spun the wiper dial, kicking the wipers into fast motion. He spread his arms and propped them on the front seats, swiveling his head back and forth between the couple who was now embroiled in a fiery argument.

"I told you not to rent a cheap car. You and your stupid budgets."

"If it wasn't for my so called budgets, we couldn't afford this vacation," the man snapped.

"You can't take your money with you, if that's what

you think." She shot a nasty glare in his direction.

"Oh yes I can and there's not a single thing you can do about it. I'm going to install a hitch on my casket and take it with me." The man wrestled with the knob and continued down the sun-speckled highway with the wipers engaged full blast.

Rodney's impatience with the time it took to change cars at the rental place put him in a spiteful mood. He waited until the driver parked the new rental car in the hospital parking lot before setting the windows in motion again. After he honked the horn and flipped the window washers into action, he noticed a man in a black suit and a round, white collar climb out of an adjacent vehicle. The man tucked a Bible under his arm.

"Maybe this will be my lucky day." Rodney whistled through his front teeth. "Maybe I can end this stupid game."

The Bible-toting man appeared to be in a hurry. Rodney scrambled out of the back seat and hurried past the rental-car couple who tried to dodge the blue washer-fluid mist falling through the air.

Rodney followed the pastor through the front doors and stood behind him in the lobby. When the elevator doors opened, Rodney moved to the back of the elevator. Two other men joined them and one pushed the button for the fourth floor.

Rodney flicked the brim of one of the men's baseball cap with his index finger. It popped off his head and fell to the floor. The man looked sideways at the pastor before bending to pick it up and place it back on his head.

The pastor continued to stare straight ahead as the elevator made its ascent.

Rodney flicked the brim again sending the hat sailing off the man's head. It landed on the pastor's shoe.

The pastor grasped the Bible tighter and glanced sideways without moving his head.

The man again retrieved his cap and placed it on his head. He glared at the Pastor.

Rodney reached over and pushed the fire alarm, setting off a piercing alarm. An overhead page sounded, indicating a code red in the east lobby elevator. The page was repeated two more times. "That's this elevator," the Pastor said with a gasp. Three pairs of eyes widened in alarm.

One of the passengers stared at the red button pushed flat against the panel. He tugged on it to dislodge it. Rodney held his finger firmly on the button.

The overhead paging system again indicated code red. As the elevator rose to the fourth floor, the occupants heard static from a walkie-talkie. A voice shouted, "It just got to the fourth floor."

The doors swooshed open. Several nurses and a security guard ran toward them with fire extinguishers aimed at the opening.

"We didn't push the button. I swear," one of the passengers said. "I tried to make it stop, but it kept ringing."

As they exited the elevator, Rodney reached for the pastor's hand and placed it on the passenger's crotch.

"What the hell?" the man shouted. "What's wrong with you?"

Rodney fell into stride next to the pastor, who had paled. He followed him into a room and stood at the end of the bed while the pastor fought to catch his breath.

"I'm sorry I'm late. It's been quite a morning." The

pastor dabbed at the sweat beading on his face.

The woman smiled. "That's all right. Nothing could dampen my spirits today. The doctor just gave me my biopsy results and it appears the tumor was benign."

The pastor clasped the woman's hands. "Praise the Lord. I knew everything would be all right."

"Sheeeittt," Rodney moaned. He kicked the air with his foot. "That sucks."

Walking down the corridor, Rodney fell into pace behind a doctor headed for the intensive care unit. The physician held his identification badge over a wall-mounted scanner and the doors retracted.

Rodney stood behind the doctor as the physician pulled up a patient's data on the computer. He leaned against the nursing station and listened to a number of conversations going on around the monitors. What he needed most was to hear about a patient in distress.

When the doctor didn't discuss his patient's condition, Rodney wandered away from the nursing station. He lingered in each doorway, hoping to pick up signs of death.

"Oh, not you," he whined, noticing Lora sitting with a patient tethered to tubes and monitors. "Just what I need. Something else to ruin my day."

"Go somewhere else, Rodney. I was here first."

He crossed his arms over his chest. "I'm not going anywhere. I've got just as much right to be here as you do." Rodney blocked her path when she tried to step around him. "You're not going anywhere either."

Lora slapped at his hand and he grabbed her arm. "I told you not to do that." He raised his other hand and she cringed.

Rodney's taunting laughter was interrupted by two women and a man who entered the patient's room. They sat in the chairs at the foot of the bed. One of the women said, "What should we do about Mom's dog?"

The man placed a tray on his lap and eyed the food he had selected from the cafeteria. He passed out sandwiches, chips, and sodas to the others before contemplating the question. He took a swig from the soda can. "How old is Ranger?"

"I'd say about twelve or thirteen. Mom already had him when Eric was born and he's eleven now."

A nurse brushed past one of the women and checked the monitor's digital readouts. After checking the catheter bag, she shook her head. "I don't see much output. It looks like they're shutting down again."

Tears welled in one of the women's eyes. "Do you think Mother's in much pain?"

"I doubt it. The doctor increased her pain medication this morning." The nurse patted the daughter's hand. "I think she's comfortable."

The trio silently dwelled on the years they had spent cradled in their mother's love. The man wadded up what was left of his sandwich and wrapper and tossed it into a wastebasket. "I suppose we need to have Ranger put down. It's the most humane thing we can do. He's got arthritis so bad he can barely walk."

The youngest daughter said, "I don't think anyone else would put up with him. From what I understand from Mom's neighbor, he's been peeing on the carpet." She began to sob. "Will you take him to the vet? I just can't bring myself to do it."

"I suppose I'll have to," he said.

Rodney clapped his hands and jumped up in the air, causing Lora to shout out in fear. "Put the old mutt down. Put it out of its misery." Balling both fists into the air, Rodney shouted, "Yahoo. Why didn't I think of that?"

Lora slipped past Rodney and ran down the hall. She turned the corner and looked back.

Rodney caught up to her. "Didn't you hear what they said? Put the dog out of its misery." He feigned a pistol shot.

Lora wrenched away and continued down the corridor.

He matched her pace, walking beside her. "Don't you see? That solves everything."

"I don't know what you're talking about."

"Think about it. Put the old dog out of its misery."

"What do dogs have to do with anything? It doesn't make sense." She pushed at his stained hand when he reached to grab her.

"Yes, it does. What old dog do you know that should be put out of its misery?"

"No," Lora said. "You can't do that. Belly hasn't done anything to you."

The panic in Lora's eyes excited Rodney. He backed her against the wall. "You are really dumb, aren't you? It's not that stupid dog. It's Sadie. I'm going to put that old crone out of her misery."

"What," Lora gasped.

"I've got a rifle hidden in the woods behind Sadie's old fuel tank. Now we don't need to look for someone on the brink. When I finish with Sadie, I'm taking you to the parallel world."

21

Nan closed the folder and tapped her pen against her desk. "Oh, it's you," she said, a weary sigh escaping her lips. Paul walked toward her through the mortuary lobby.

"I'm glad to see you, too." Paul embraced Nan from behind and nuzzled his lips against her neck.

She leaned into the embrace. "I'm not enthusiastic about anything, I'm afraid. I have another body to prep. Then I've got a family coming later this afternoon for their first viewing."

"You can't continue to do everything yourself. You need to get someone to help you."

"I have someone. Mr. Bakke does a good job. I can't afford anyone else."

Paul turned her chair and knelt in front of Nan. "I'm taking you out to dinner tonight."

"Not tonight, Paul. I'd be lousy company."

"That's not true." He ran his thumbs over her hands as they rested in her lap. "You're always good company. And besides, I have a surprise for you."

Rising, Nan said, "I hit another dead end trying to locate information about that man my father was searching for."

"What man?"

"How come you don't remember the man? Mr. Bakke remembers. We were talking about it a few days ago. It's that man who took dad's invention and filed a patent. Dad thinks he took all the credit. I'm guessing the man made a fortune and dad found out about it."

Paul rolled his eyes. "I don't know why you torture yourself like that. That's in the past. If your father couldn't find him, what makes you think you can?"

"I won't find him if I don't try." Startled by her shrill tone, Nan reached for Paul's arm. "I'm sorry. I'm taking it out on you and it's not your fault."

Paul pulled Nan into his arms.

She reveled in his strength. If she lingered there forever, her troubles might evaporate. What was wrong with her? Paul had offered to help, yet she couldn't generate the enthusiasm necessary to commit. Had marriage to Clay ruined her?

"Everything that could go wrong today went wrong. I didn't need another hurdle." She breathed deep as if one hearty intake would replenish her resolve. "I'm concerned about Aanders. He's too chipper and he refuses to talk about Tim's death."

Paul tipped Nan's chin upward. "He's dealing with it the best he can. It's going to take time, so let him set his own pace."

"I'm thinking about booking an appointment with a counselor. Maybe he'd open up to a professional."

"You don't want to waste money on that," Paul said. "You've got more important things to think about."

"Waste money?" Nan pulled back from his embrace. "Aanders' wellbeing is my priority. I don't consider that a waste of money."

She drew in another fortifying breath. "But you're right. Money is an issue. It keeps me awake. After Sadie told me about Carl's lawsuit, I haven't been able to sleep."

"That's another thing you don't need to waste your time on," Paul said.

"How can you associate with a monster like Carl?"

"He's been my friend since high school. I don't necessarily agree with him, but I'm not going to end the friendship because we have a difference of opinion."

Nan wriggled free from Paul's embrace and moved toward the lobby. She sorted through a stack of stray brochures scattered over the credenza. After placing the brochures in the appropriate slots on the display rack, she gathered several boxes of tissues and placed them on the end tables.

"If Carl's such a good friend, why can't you talk some sense into him?"

"I've tried. Believe me, I've tried," Paul said. "But you know Carl. He thrives on controversy."

"I can't believe he'd do that to two old women. They've lived there all their lives."

"That's what I said, but he didn't care. He also said he's got plans for this building when he wins the lawsuit."

"You mean the mortuary?" Shocked, Nan dropped onto a long, tan sofa that separated the two visiting clusters. "Can't you tell him I'm trying to buy the land the mortuary sits on?"

"I did. But he won't listen. He's got a marketing plan ready to go."

"Carl's disrupting four lives and he could care less. What a creep."

"Quit worrying about the Witt sisters. They'll take care of their own problems. If the judge rules in Carl's favor, you've got a decision to make. I hope to be part of that decision." Paul perched on the back of the sofa and pulled Nan between his legs. He rested his chin on her head. "It'll get better. I promise."

"It doesn't seem like it." Nan tipped her head as Paul massaged the back of her neck. "It's one thing after another. Do you remember when I sent that letter to the patent bureau to see if a patent had been filed using the drawing I sent them?"

Paul nodded.

"Their reply came today. It's on my desk." She waved her hand toward the office. "They can't help me unless I can cite a patent number."

"I'm not surprised," Paul said. "Think of the volume of patents they process. They probably don't have time to sift through those files."

Paul never displayed an interest in her attempt to locate the information. His lack of empathy concerned Nan. "There's got to be a way to get that information. That was Dad's handwriting on the patent application and his drawings, so I know he designed the apparatus. I sent them sheet three of four. I never found the other three sheets, so I don't know what the device was. From what Mother said, she thought the man stole the idea and filed the patent in his name about six years ago."

"But you don't have the guy's name," Paul said. He drummed his thumb against her shoulder. "There's not much you can do without a name or a patent number. And you said your mom didn't seem to think it was important."

"Nothing about Dad was important to Mom. I already told you that. It was a love-hate relationship. All I want to do is talk to the man and find out what happened. Maybe it was just an idea that never materialized."

"You might as well give up. I doubt you'll ever find him."

"You're probably right. I've got enough to worry about."

The phone rang. When Nan returned from her office, she said, "The family is about five minutes away. I've got to pull a few things together before they get here."

Paul leaned on the French doors leading into the office. "I'm picking you up at seven and I won't take no for an answer. We'll work on eliminating one of your hurdles."

"Hook, line, and sinker." Paul sat in the cracked-vinyl visitor's chair in front of Carl's desk. "I think I'm about to reel in the big one. If Nan contacts you about continuing her land lease, don't talk to her. Tell her your attorney will contact her." Pointing at Carl, Paul added, "I want you to tell her all negotiations have to go through him. I don't want my plan to fall apart."

"You sorry sack of shit," Carl said. "You're preying on that poor woman's misery to get her to marry you. What kind of bottom feeder are you?"

A furrow of irritation creased Paul's forehead. "Same species as you. Except you're dealing with two old women you intend to put out on the street. But I don't need to remind you, do I?" If Carl wanted to take a position for the sake of arguing, he'd better choose his words wisely.

"Please. Remind me," Carl said. "It excites me. My middle initial doesn't stand for Raymond, it stands for Revenge." Carl's lips curved into a crooked smile as he put his hands behind his head and leaned back.

"I'm going to present an offer Nan can't refuse," Paul said. "I also bought another piece of land south of town on the highway. It would make a good spot for a new mortuary. She doesn't know about it, though." Paul stretched his long legs and crossed one foot over the other. "I'm keeping that surprise on hold in case I need ammunition. If she turns me down, I'll sell it to someone else."

"Is she still on a kick to find that man who screwed her dad over a patent?"

"She mentioned it again today."

"Do you think she'll find him?"

"I doubt it. I told her to give it up, but you know Nan. It's all about family loyalty."

The dispatcher entered the room and lifted the lid on a plastic container she carried. Angie waved the box under Carl's nose. "Try one. My daughter baked them this morning."

Carl inhaled one of the gooey cookies in two bites before grabbing a second one and stuffing the whole thing in his mouth.

Paul took a cookie and broke off small sections. Staring at the chocolate smears on Carl's lips, Paul placed a piece in his mouth before flicking at the crumbs on his grey slacks. He didn't want chocolate stains to soil his new three-hundred-dollar pants.

"By the way, Carl," Angie said, "I forgot to tell you Mr. Fossum's sister called yesterday. She won't be back for a few more days. She wondered if you'd keep an eye on the Fossums' property." Angie handed Carl three more cookies. "She's meeting a realtor out there when she gets back."

As Carl licked the chocolate off his fingers, Lon Friborg entered through the side door. Lon rummaged through the stack of papers in his hand, pulled out an envelope, and tossed it at Carl. The envelope slid across the desk and hit Carl in the stomach. "Here's the letter you wanted. It looks like the union's going to back your election."

"Holy shit," Carl said with a whoop. "It's about time they back the better candidate. With their vote and your campaigning, it'll seal my victory tighter than a virgin's ass."

"Congrats, buddy." Paul grabbed Carl's hand and pumped it. "Things are going your way."

"I wonder why?" Lon said under his breath.

Carl pulled the cookies out of Lon's reach. "If you've got something to say, say it to my face." He shoved a whole cookie in his mouth, glaring at Lon.

"I wonder why things are going your way. It wouldn't have anything to do with that fishing excursion with Judge Kimmer, would it?"

"That's none of your damn concern, Deputy," Carl said. "You better keep your nose out of my business. If your brain was as big as your ears, I wouldn't have to remind you."

Carl gestured with a stab of his finger. "You're trying to sabotage my election by conducting an investigation behind my back. You're going to get somebody in a whole shit load of trouble, and it ain't gonna be me."

22

Sadie draped her arm over the back of the driver's chair as she tried to interpret Lora's frantic ramblings. After calming the woman, Sadie stomped out of the van and marched through the sliding glass doors into the nursing home.

"Hi, Miss Sadie," a nursing home resident shouted as she hurried past him and continued down the hall. Her bare heels slapped against her sandals.

"I'll catch up with you later, Elmer." Sadie rounded a corner. Cursing her sandals for slowing her down, she paused in a doorway and kicked them off. She called out to Aanders.

A gnarled hand pointed in the direction of the dining room. "I just saw him pushing that empty wheelchair down the hall." The resident attempted to clear the gravel from his voice. "Don't that kid have nothing better to do than wander the halls all day?"

Sadie waved briskly as she passed a woman inching her way down the hall supporting her weight on a walker. Clutching her sandals, Sadie scurried past two more residents in wheelchairs. A conversation at the end of the corridor caught her attention. A funeral director from a town located seventeen miles north of Pinecone Landing loaded a body bag into his vehicle. Sadie watched him thank the nurse who had assisted him and hand her a sheet of paper. The nurse attached it to a clipboard and returned to the nursing station.

"You better be pushing an empty chair this time, young man," Sadie said under her breath. The dining room was filled with residents waiting for their evening meal. Weaving through the crowd, she spotted Aanders sitting at a table in the far corner. She balled her fists when Aanders shifted to the side and she saw Tim in the wheelchair.

Aanders pushed the wheel-lock lever into position before placing his hands under Tim's arms and hoisting him up. He uttered a cry as he felt a hand grasp his shoulder.

"I just had a conversation with Lora. I'm here to see if what she told me is true." She leaned close to Aanders so he could appreciate her anger. "The fact that Tim is still here tells me it is."

Aanders traced the leaf pattern in the table top with his finger.

Tim's head slouched toward his chest before he peeked up at her then back down to avoid the shards of rage emanating from the angry woman.

"Aanders, I'm talking to you." Realizing she'd attracted attention, she grabbed the handles on Tim's wheelchair and rolled him through the crowd. Looking back at Aanders, she jabbed her finger toward him and then down at her side. He fell into place next to her.

"Ma'am. Oh Ma'am," one of the dietary aides shouted. "You'll have to put your shoes on. You can't be in here with bare feet."

Dropping her sandals on the floor, Sadie slipped them on and gave the aide a look that could boil water. "Are you satisfied? I don't know what difference it makes anyway."

Sadie and Aanders left the aide standing in the dining room. "Blah, blah, blah," Sadie mocked as they rounded the corner and continued down the hall. The aide hurried to catch them, all the while reciting the merits of infection control.

Elmer and a few of his cronies watched Sadie push the empty wheelchair up to the van door.

"Help him into the van while I return the wheelchair," Sadie said.

Theo climbed down and took one of Tim's arms while Aanders grasped the other. They assisted Tim up the steps. Aanders avoided Lora as he walked to the rear of the van. Theo took his usual seat across from the driver.

"Sorry I don't have time to visit," Sadie shouted to Elmer. "I'll catch up with you next time." She pushed the door release and the door swooshed closed.

Elmer smiled and returned the greeting with a wave of his hand. The residents watched the van disappear around the corner. Elmer said, "Sure is hot today."

The woman with a straw hat said, "Sure is." Not one of them gave voice to what they had witnessed.

The tension in the van swelled as Sadie pulled away from the no-parking sign. She adjusted the rear view mirror so she could see Aanders. "Did you keep Tim from going through the light?"

Hearing no reply, Sadie raised her voice. "I'm talking to you, young man. If I don't get an answer, I'll pull this van over and hound you until you tell me the truth." Her voice faltered as she repeated the question. "Did you prevent Tim from going through the light?"

"Yes."

Sadie let out a disgusted breath. "I can muster four hours a day of being nice and I've already used them up."

When Aanders' eyes finally met hers, Sadie said, "I'm furious with you. You need to realize what a terrible thing you've done."

As soon as the vehicle came to a stop and the door folded open, Aanders bolted from the van and ran toward the mortuary. Theo assisted Tim up the steps and into the cabin.

"Why was Aanders running across the lawn?" Jane said, as Sadie pushed through the screen door. "It looked like he was crying."

"He was." Sadie dropped her purse on the table. "That young man is in a whole lot of trouble."

"Why?" Jane wiped the grease splatters that had peppered the stove.

Sadie strode over to Jane, bent over the cast iron pot, and took a deep breath. She frowned. She gave Mr. Bakke a questioning look. He shrugged and retreated behind his newspaper.

"It's what he didn't do that's making me madder than a wet hen," Sadie said.

Mr. Bakke chuckled. "Have you ever confronted a wet hen? I have. They're vicious."

"It's a good thing Aanders took off running because that's how I feel. I could spank his skinny butt."

"Sounds serious." Mr. Bakke pulled out a kitchen chair and sat down. Jane turned the burner down and waited for Sadie to explain.

After they cleared the supper dishes, Sadie called the crossers to the table. Lora fidgeted with the hem on her blouse and Theo drummed his fingers against his briefcase, waiting for the others.

Aanders hesitated by the screen door. Jane patted his shoulder and offered a consoling smile. "You'd better sit down. I think Sadie's looking for you."

"I know." Aanders sat next to Tim. "She told Mom she wanted me to run an errand. She shouldn't lie just cuz she's mad at me." He flicked a side glance at Tim. His foot buffeted the wooden base, setting the table in motion.

Belly plopped down next to Tim's chair and rested his head on his paws. His eyes turned upward to gaze at Tim.

"Do you see that?" Sadie pointed to the dog. "Even Belly is concerned about Tim's condition. What were you thinking, Aanders? Tim's death is at stake." She glared at him. "I need to know exactly what happened today."

Aanders buried his face in his hands, eyes welling with tears.

Tim reached out and put his hand on Aanders arm. "He doesn't want me to go…"

"I know he doesn't want you to go," Sadie interrupted. "But it isn't his decision. He's got a job to do. He needs to make sure you reach your destination." Sadie placed her water glass on the table and stood next to the sulking lad.

"He had the perfect opportunity to help Tim through the light. Instead, he turned Tim's wheelchair around and ran the opposite way," Lora said.

"Why? Why would you do that?" Realizing her voice had pitched two octaves above normal, Sadie fought to regain her composure. Fear of being disciplined would cause Aanders to slam the door on progress.

Tim rallied in Aanders' defense. "There was a light building behind this old man. Aanders pushed me closer.

When the noise got louder, I got scared. I asked Aanders to push me out of the man's room."

Aanders sat forward on his chair. "When I tried to turn the wheelchair around, the tunnel pulled at Tim. Tim shouted he didn't want to go. He said he had to tell Sadie something important. I pushed and we made it out of the room."

Sadie lifted Tim's limp hand. "Nothing is more important than getting you through that light. You may have made the biggest mistake you'll ever make."

"I hurried into the room when I saw Aanders running with the wheelchair, but it was too late," Lora said. "The light moved up into the corner. I ran up to it, but by the time I got there, it was gone." Lora glared at Aanders. "Because you fooled around, I lost my chance to go through the light, too."

"But we weren't fooling around." Tim tried to shout his defense, but his voice caught in his throat. "I needed to get Sadie to listen."

"You're not still thinking it was murder, are you?" Theo said.

"It was murder."

"I thought we put that to rest," Sadie said. "I thought you agreed it was your overactive imagination."

"No. There's a lot I haven't told you because you didn't want to hear it. I can prove Dad was murdered."

"If I listen, will you promise to make every effort to go through the light?"

Tim's shoulders drooped as he looked at Aanders. "I promise."

Sadie put her arm around Tim and pulled him close. He

sagged against her body. His strength was deteriorating and she wondered if he possessed the stamina to go on. "Aanders, do you know what Tim has to tell me?"

Aanders nodded.

"Because I want Tim to reserve his strength, I'm going to let Aanders tell me." She sat back and nodded for Aanders to begin.

23

Paul tucked the boat keys in his pocket as the dock attendant secured the rope to the post. "Make sure you put gas in it," he reminded the teenager.

"Will do, Mr. Brinks." The boy responded with a two-finger salute. "I'll keep a good eye on her." He grinned and watched Paul wave a twenty dollar bill before stuffing it back in his pocket.

After gassing the boat, the dock attendant wiped the surface clean. Bending low to inspect the area near the gas cap, he dabbed at a smear hoping to prevent an episode like last time when he had missed a spot. Tips of the twenty-dollar magnitude were a rare commodity.

The thirty-foot Sea Ray sport cruiser, named *Brink's Lady,* featured a Bimini top, full galley, sleeping berth, and a swim platform. The boat was Paul's most recent purchase. Two weeks earlier he had surprised Nan with the celebratory voyage around the lake where they toasted his new acquisition with a vintage bottle of Malbec from his personal wine cellar.

The capacity crowd at Yerry's on the Bay taxed the dock boys to the limit. Locals and vacationers boated to the restaurant, the finest in the upper Midwest, and moored in a sheltered cove just below the facility. The restaurant sat on the eastern shore of Pinecone Lake. A recent article in a national travel magazine featured Yerry's as offering the most romantic sunsets in northern Minnesota. Dining reservations were difficult to obtain.

A hostess welcomed Paul and Nan to Yerry's and ushered them past a large group of people waiting in line. The maître d' asked if Paul was satisfied with the location. At Paul's nod, he pulled Nan's chair out and waited until she was seated.

"How were you able to pull this off on such short notice?" Nan gazed at the spectacular view. "Window tables are impossible to reserve."

"The owner is a personal friend of mine. I manage his investments. My recommendations more than doubled his net worth," Paul said, "so he was happy to accommodate us."

The maître d' waited as Paul swirled the wine in his glass and brought it up to his nose. After inhaling the bouquet, Paul tipped the glass to his lips and drew in a sip. "That will do," he said. The couple watched the waiter fill each glass half full.

"I'm sorry it got to be so late. I was called out on a retrieval about the time you said you'd pick me up. Thanks for understanding." Paul had been unusually attentive and she liked this new approach. Being the consummate businessman, his tunneled focus reflected his demand for perfection as well as his refusal to be distracted. Tonight was different. Paul made her his priority.

A blush from the setting sun settled over Nan's face. Paul smiled at her. "Getting here later than I planned turned out to be even better. Look at that sunset."

Nan rested her chin on her fist. "It's almost surreal, isn't it? With those hues reflecting off the water, I feel like I'm surrounded by flowers." Even though the dinner hour was drawing to a close, the restaurant was full of patrons seeking the perfect sunset.

Nan wiggled her fingers in greeting to a recent client approaching their table. "How are you doing, Mrs. Boutain?" The woman clasped Nan's hand to express her gratitude for everything the funeral director had done in her time of need.

Paul patted the woman's hand as she clung to Nan. "I'm so sorry for your loss, Mrs. Boutain. If there's anything I can do, please let me know."

"Such a nice young couple," Mrs. Boutain whispered to her dinner partner as they were escorted to their table.

Strains of jazz filtered into the dining room from the lounge.

Nan sipped her wine. She grinned coyly. "Stop staring at me like that. You're making my mind wander."

"Good." Paul laughed. "But that'll have to wait till later. I need to talk to you." He raised his glass and waited until Nan's glass touched his. "Here's to an important evening. Here's to our future."

The maître d' led the waiter to their table and stood back as the server set their plates in front of them. After a gesture signaling Paul's satisfaction, the two men gathered the tray and exited the room.

"I love your hair pulled back like that. You look angelic." Paul rubbed his fingers over the top of her hand.

"It's the glow from the candles. Or maybe the wine's clouding your vision."

"You're beautiful whatever the reason," Paul said. "But I suspect it's because I'm in love with you."

Surprised by Paul's declaration, Nan set her glass on the white linen and placed her fingers in the arc of Paul's hand. "That's the first time you've actually told me you loved me. I've often wondered if that's how you felt, but was afraid to get my hopes up. Before when we talked marriage, you seemed so nonchalant." She cocked her head. "You're a hard man to read."

"It's hard for me to say, but that's how I feel. I'm in love with you Nan. I want to marry you."

The tender moment was interrupted by the waiter lifting their salad plates and replacing them with their entrées. "Enjoy your meal while it's hot," Paul said. "We'll discuss this after dinner."

The sound of Paul's voice warmed Nan as she listened to him chat about the day's events. He spoke with such fervor she stopped eating. Paul had ordered Chateau Briand with Béarnaise Sauce. Known state-wide for their presentation of beef tenderloin smoked over apple wood prior to being roasted, Yerry's on the Bay had won several national awards for their gourmet rendition.

The sun tickled the horizon adding to the room's glow. Candlelight shimmered in Paul's eyes and his Romanesque features disarmed her. When Paul entered a room, women lingered a bit too long attempting to portray an image he'd find appealing.

When Nan first met Paul, she denied the attraction. He could never be interested in her. Glamour had not been her forte because her profession didn't allow time for primping and even if it did, she wondered if she could live up to his expectations.

Paul oozed charisma. Nan had become self-conscious about her appearance when she noticed the caliber of woman Paul escorted around town. She had always been disillusioned with her curly blond hair. Even though it was natural, she wished for dark hair and piercing eyes like the other women Paul dated. Instead, she did nothing to change the pale features that were part of her heritage.

Nan was shocked when Paul had phoned her a year ago asking for a date. Her nerves had gotten the better of her during their first encounter and she wrote the date off as an utter failure.

Drastic changes had taken place in her life over the past several years. Her parents had died tragically in a boating accident and then she had taken on a financial burden by signing the mortuary land-lease with the Witt sisters. That lease could be her ruin. If the sisters lost the resort, she'd lose everything. Adding to her tangled situation, she now found herself contemplating marriage to a man she barely knew. Even though she spent ample time with Paul, she felt he held her at arm's length.

The maître d' waited for a signal from Paul before instructing the waiter to remove their plates. "Are you ready for dessert, sir?"

"I couldn't possibly eat another bite," Nan said. "I'm absolutely stuffed."

"Let's see what they've got. You don't have to eat if you don't want to."

The maitre d' smiled. "Yes, sir," he said as Paul pointed at the menu.

A business associate of Paul's stopped by the table and offered condolences on the recent loss of his business partner. "I suppose it's going to be a mess sorting through the legalities." Shaking his head the man added, "I still can't believe an entire family died in that accident."

"I can't either," Paul said. "Thanks for your concern."

Nan placed her hand on Paul's wrist as the man walked away. "Don't forget. If there's anything I can do to help sort things out, let me know."

"Thanks," Paul said. "I've got it under control."

The maitre d' placed Nan's dessert in front of her before setting Paul's glass on the table. The long stemmed glasses were rimmed with sugar and filled with strawberries. The maitre d' tipped Paul's glass to let champagne trickle down the inside of the stemware. He did the same with Nan's glass. He placed two long-handled forks next to the glasses before smiling at Nan. "I hope you enjoy your strawberries."

"You remembered," Nan gushed. "One good thing about our first date was the fresh strawberry I had in my wine. Everything else was a disaster."

"You knocked your plate off the table, your heel got caught in the sidewalk grate, and you slipped and fell outside the theatre," Paul said. "The only time you smiled that night was when you saw that fresh strawberry and you devoured it in one bite."

"That's because my dinner ended up on the floor." Nan stabbed at a strawberry and held it up to Paul's lips. He eased it off the fork and mimicked the gesture, lifting a sugared strawberry to her lips. The savory juices flowed over her tongue. She gathered another berry. "That maitre d' makes me nervous," Nan whispered. "He keeps staring at us."

"He's staring at you. The man knows a beautiful woman when he sees one."

"I think he wants us to hurry and finish so he can go

192

home."

"I doubt it."

She tipped her glass to find the next strawberry. Nan squinted, staring deeper into the glass. "Oh my God." Jerking her head up to look at Paul, she uttered, "Oh my God." She placed the fork gingerly into the center of the berry and lifted it out of the glass. "I can't believe it."

Paul reached for the strawberry and pulled it from the fork. He removed the diamond ring and said, "Give me your hand."

As tears began to pool in Nan's eyes, Paul slipped the ring on her finger. "Will you do me the honor of becoming my wife?"

Wiping her eyes, Nan gaped in disbelief. "I can't believe you. How did you manage this?" Nan looked toward the side of the room where several restaurant employees were lined up watching the event unfold. Nan mouthed a thank you in their direction before grasping Paul's hand.

"I've waited a long time to find happiness, Paul. I can't believe this." She dabbed under her eyelid, trying not to smear her mascara. "I can't believe this."

Laughing, Paul said, "You already said that."

"Of course I'll marry you. But…"

"I don't like the sound of that," Paul said, grasping her hand.

"I need to make sure you understand what you're getting into." She placed a hand on her chest. "You need to understand before you commit to a life with me."

"You need to give me some credit, Nan. I've thought this through. You're concerned about Aanders. You're worried how he'll adjust to having someone new in his life.

I also know you're concerned about your finances and you don't want to be a burden."

"That's exactly what I'm worried about."

"I'll make a deal with you. Let's not talk about this until tomorrow. Let's go to the boat and celebrate the way engaged couples should celebrate." Paul pulled Nan from her chair. "I promise tomorrow we'll sit down and map out a plan that will work for both of us."

"I wish you could spend the night. I don't want you to go," Paul whispered, his lips caressing Nan's neck.

"I have to go," Nan said. "I can't leave Aanders alone. You know how I feel about that."

Nan moved several items around in her purse, searching for her house keys. The evening on the boat had been magnificent and the scent of Paul's skin still lingered. He had truly knocked her off her feet when he told her he wanted to buy the land for the mortuary as a wedding gift. She had been giddy with joy. Her legacy would stay intact. Paul confessed he hadn't wanted to tell her about the land until later, but in the throes of passion, he divulged his secret.

Nan's purse tipped over, spilling the contents onto Paul's car seat. As she tried to push everything back into her purse with one sweeping motion, several items and slips of paper fell to the floor. She ran her fingers along the floor under the seat. Grasping the papers, she pulled them up, folded them and shoved them into her purse.

After returning home and placing the keys next to her purse on her kitchen table, Nan noticed note paper protruding through the purse clasp. She removed the items and carried them to Aanders' room. She pushed on the door and slipped into his room without a sound.

A hairy lump of dog sprawled in a U shape around Aanders' pillow. Five thumps of Belly's tail signaled he was aware Nan had entered their sanctuary.

Lost in sleep, Aanders lay on the far side of his bed with his video control resting on his chest. Nan switched the television off and placed the remote control on his dresser before bending to kiss his forehead. She watched his chest rise and fall in slumber, thankful sleep offered him a brief respite from the sorrow. She pulled the blanket up over his body.

Before Nan flipped the kitchen light off and surrendered to fatigue, she turned the papers over and paged through the notes. She wadded the first one into a ball and tossed it into the waste basket. She placed the second slip on the counter. She'd deal with it in the morning. She studied the return address on the final piece and realized she had picked up an envelope belonging to Paul.

Nan placed the envelope next to her purse. She'd give it to Paul when they got together in the morning to discuss their plans. She turned out the kitchen light, hesitated for a moment, flipped it back on, and lifted the envelope from the table. She ran her finger over the return address. "Gessal Life Insurance. Where have I heard that before?"

24

Failing to get the attention he felt he deserved, Belly grunted and dropped down onto the rug next to the screen door. He scratched at his blue rhinestone collar and stared soulfully toward the crossers. No one noticed. A pitiful whine erupted before he rolled over and closed his eyes.

"We'll leave you to your business," Jane said, glancing at her sister and Aanders sitting at the table. Jane placed her nose on the screen and peered back into the cabin. "Don't be too hard on the boy. You had to learn how to be a death coach, too."

Jane grabbed Mr. Bakke's arm and led him toward the steps. She suddenly turned back and shouted, "If I remember right, you made your share of mistakes as a death coach. In fact you made quite a few. I'd be willing to share them with Aanders."

"Thank you for those words of wisdom."

"Think nothing of it," Jane yelled from the bottom step.

"Has anyone seen Rodney today?" Sadie queried.

Everyone seated at the table shook their heads.

"Don't tell me he found someone on the brink. We couldn't possibly be that fortunate," Theo said. "At least I'd have a few tranquil moments before I go on to the next phase."

As Tim leaned on Sadie for support, Sadie directed the crossers' attention to Aanders. "Let's hear why Tim thinks his father was murdered." She shot a stern glare toward Aanders. "If you think this will buy you more time with

Tim, you're wrong."

Getting no response, she tapped the table top with a blue lacquered nail. "Aanders, I'm serious. You need to understand the consequences if Tim doesn't go though the light." Sadie tugged at her blue paisley halter top trying to resituate it against the strain of Tim's weight.

Aanders' foot twitched against the table leg setting the surface in motion. "I already know what will happen. You told me a million times. He'll disappear and never get to see his mom and dad."

"I trusted you, young man. You let me down. How will you ever earn your rainbow if you can't honor the rules?" Sadie's jaw tightened. "Someone obviously made a mistake when they selected you."

"I'll do it. I promise. If someone dies I'll make sure Tim goes through their light." Aanders' chest began to heave as he fought the inevitable loss. Giving in, he let the tears come. "I couldn't stand it if he didn't get to see his mom again."

The screen door slammed and Belly yelped as Rodney tripped over him. "Get the hell out of my way, you stupid dog."

A rumble erupted from Belly. The dog rose and walked stiff legged towards the surly man. Belly's jowls puffed a snarled warning while the rumble grew deeper.

"Belly. Go back to the rug and lay down." Sadie pointed toward the door when Belly looked at her in annoyance. "I said lay down."

A louder growl escaped the dog. He circled and then plopped back into his previous position. A snort finished his protest, but his eyes remained fixed on Rodney.

"It ain't raining," Rodney said. "You're talking about rainbows and there ain't a cloud in the sky."

Flicking at her blue gelled hair with his fingers, Rodney said, "You're losing it, old woman."

Sadie batted at his hand. "You're late. Sit down and join the session." She gestured toward an empty chair with her foot.

"I don't need to. I've got my plan ready to go." Rodney shot Lora a side-glance. He opened the door to the inner room. "I'll be leaving this dump real soon. You can count on it."

Lora winced as Rodney slammed the door. She crossed her arms over her chest and squeezed tight before taking a peek toward the inner room. Sadie's voice redirected Lora's attention to her fellow crossers.

"We need to hear why Tim thinks his dad was murdered," Sadie said. "I believe you told me he had proof."

"It isn't exactly proof. But he saw something that might make you believe it." Aanders sat forward and leaned his chest against the table.

"Before they picked me up to go to the movie, Tim heard his dad argue with his business partner. Tim's Dad accused Paul of doing something bad." Aanders paused, looked at Sadie. "Then Paul threatened his dad."

"Lots of people argue. But that doesn't mean they commit murder," Sadie said.

"I know that. He told Tim's Dad if he turned him in, it would be the biggest mistake of his life. He said he wouldn't live to see another day."

Theo leaned toward Aanders. "Son, you have to learn that people make threats they never act on. Threats are a way of scaring people. It lets them know they mean business."

Aanders looked at Tim for guidance. "When they were arguing, the man got so mad he pushed everything off the desk onto the floor."

Tim looked up at Sadie. "Mom cried when she helped Dad pick up the papers. She told Dad to call the police. She said things were getting out of control and she was afraid Paul would do something drastic."

"Paul's been dating my mom," Aanders said. "I need to tell her about this, but I don't know how. I'd have to tell her I talk to dead people. That will freak her out." He scowled at Sadie. "And you said I can't tell anyone."

With eyebrows raised in curiosity, Theo said, "Do you know what was on those papers that made Paul so angry?"

"Not really," Tim said. "Dad is Mr. Brink's bookkeeper. He does the books on our computer and won't let me play games on it because it's strictly for business."

"Do you know if the papers are still there?" Sadie pulled her arm from behind Tim. "Or did Paul take them with him?"

"I think they're still there. I didn't see him take anything when he left." Tim looked from Theo to Sadie. "After Mom helped him pick up the mess, Dad locked the papers in a drawer. But I know where he hides the key."

"That still isn't enough to prove he was murdered," Theo said.

"But Tim saw Paul shoot at them." Aanders shrunk back when all heads turned toward him. "He saw Paul with a rifle."

"What?" Sadie stared in disbelief. "You saw Paul with

a gun?"

"A rifle," Tim answered. "Mom saw him, too."

"You mean Paul brought a rifle to your house?" Stunned, Theo sat forward on his chair

"No. He was standing in the woods."

"Where?" Sadie said.

"Right near where we had the accident. After the movie we dropped Aanders off and headed home. I had my earphones in my ears. Mom told Dad I had my music on and couldn't hear them. They always tell secrets when they think I'm listening to my iTunes. She didn't know I hadn't turned it on yet."

Tim paused; Aanders took the lead. "She asked Tim's dad if he could prove Paul was stealing the old people's money. His dad said he had proof his partner bezzled."

"Embezzled?" Theo offered.

"That's the word," Tim whispered.

"But where does the rifle fit into this?" Sadie said.

"When Mom and Dad were talking about him stealing the old people's money, I saw Mom point out the window. When I looked, I saw Mr. Brinks pointing a rifle at us. He was on the edge of the woods. I knew it was him because he had on the same camouflage he wears when he shoots with Dad."

The group drew a collective breath trying to absorb the information.

"Are you sure, Tim?" Sadie asked. "You're not making this up?"

"See?" Tim's voice caught in his throat. He looked at Aanders. "I told you she wouldn't believe me."

"I believe you," Theo said, rising from his chair. He

crouched near Tim. "What happened after you saw Mr. Brinks with his rifle?"

"I heard a pop and then Mom screamed. She must have seen the flash from the rifle, too. Right after that, the car skidded toward the ditch. I could see Dad fighting with the steering wheel, but the car shot across the highway and into the ditch on the other side. It seemed like grass was flying everywhere. Then all of a sudden Dad's door flew open and that's all I remember."

Sadie's hand covered her lips. "Oh my God. Paul shot at Richard. That's what caused the car to go off the road." She looked at Theo. "Deputy Friborg was right. It wasn't an accident."

"Were autopsies done on the bodies?" Theo said.

"Just Richard's. But Nan didn't mention any bullet holes when she prepped their bodies. If they would have found bullet holes, it would have been considered murder. Everything I read in the newspaper indicated it was an accident. They think Richard swerved to miss a deer."

"That's what I heard them say," Tim whispered. "I could hear people talking. I tried to talk to them, but they wouldn't listen. I tried to tell them about Mr. Brinks."

"Maybe you were already dead," Aanders said.

Tim rolled his head to look at Aanders. "I wanted to tell them that after the car hit that tree, I heard a motor start up and drive away. Then I couldn't hear it anymore."

"You mean like another car's engine?" Theo asked.

"No. It was a four wheeler. It sounded just like the one Mr. Brinks has because it backfires a lot."

25

"You can't be serious," Jane said, as she listened to Sadie's plan. "What if someone catches you? Wouldn't it be safer if you called the sheriff and told them about the murder?"

Sadie stared at her sister while she let her impatience settle to a simmer. "That sounds like a good idea. I'll call Carl and tell him that Tim, who is deader than a doornail, told me all about a murder. Then I'll tell him the murderer, and his best friend, are one and the same."

"I don't get it," Mr. Bakke said.

"What do you mean you don't get it?" Sadie said. "Carl already thinks I'm loony. Telling him I've been talking to a dead boy isn't going to make things better."

Mr. Bakke folded the newspaper. "I mean about the doornail. Who ever came up with the saying doornails are dead? Or better yet, who ever thought they were alive?"

"I'm talking about murder." Sadie turned her disbelieving gaze from Mr. Bakke to her sister. "You two make a good pair."

Theo grabbed Sadie's arm as she dug for her keys in her purse. "I'm going with you." He spun her around. "You might get into something you can't handle."

She batted at his hand. "Why don't you say what you really mean? You don't think I'm capable of doing it myself."

"Precisely." Theo took her by the elbow.

Jane cocked her head. "It's not that I don't think you're

capable. I think it's too risky. Do you really think you'll find some evidence?"

"Don't you think Paul would have gotten rid of it?" Mr. Bakke said.

"Nan said Richard's sister isn't coming back for a few more days. I'm hoping that means no one's been in Richard's office. If there were signs of a break in, it would give Lon even more ammunition to investigate. I'm betting Paul's waiting for Richard's sister to let him in. Tim told me where his dad hid his desk key. If we can find a way to get in the house, the rest should be easy."

Jane wiped her hands on her apron. "Do you think I should go with you?"

"Theo's going with me."

"What can he do that I can't?"

"Drive the getaway car? Stay out of sight?"

"That's not funny," Jane said. "I can help you look for whatever it is you're looking for."

"Tell her there'll be less risk if one person is seen going into Richard's house," Theo said. "You could say you were getting some of Aanders video games. People would believe that."

"Theo's right, Jane. He says it makes more sense that you stay here. If I'm not back in an hour, you can come looking for me."

"Where's Theo sitting?" Jane said.

"He's standing by the door."

Jane and Mr. Bakke looked at the door. Jane wagged her finger. "You keep an eye on her. Don't let her do anything stupid."

Mr. Bakke tipped his head back and puckered his lips.

As Sadie glared at him, he turned an imaginary key to seal his lips. "I didn't say a word. Quit giving me the evil eye."

"I know exactly what you were thinking because death coaches can read minds."

"No they can't," Mr. Bakke said. "If that were the case, you'd have kicked me out years ago."

Theo hung on to the back of the van seat with both hands when Sadie cut the corner too close. "Don't drive so fast. You're going to attract attention." The rear tire hit the curb and bounced hard as the van bottomed out against the pavement.

Sadie adjusted the rear view mirror. "As long as Carl doesn't see me, we'll be okay. That fool pulls me over every time he sees me driving this van. If I fart, he makes a federal case out of it."

"Vulgarity." Theo exhaled deeply. "Don't you remember we talked about purging those words from your vocabulary?"

"Are you saying judges don't fart?"

"When and if we do, we don't talk about it."

"Didn't you ever have a chuckle over a good healthy fart?"

"Certainly not," Theo said.

Hearing scrambling in the back of the van, Sadie looked in the rearview mirror. "What are you doing here?"

Belly made his way to the front of the vehicle, trying to keep his balance although the ruts in the road made it difficult.

"You just went through a red light," Theo shouted, looking back at a man who gestured with his middle finger.

"I know," Sadie said.

"You could have killed somebody."

Belly rolled onto his side and stared at Theo.

"Your dog should be kept on a leash. Then he wouldn't pester your guests or go where he's not wanted." Theo braced his body as Sadie turned sharply causing the van to veer to the left. "Please keep your eyes on the road. That's a perfect example of why your dog should stay at home. He's distracting you."

"He's not my dog."

Holding his hands up at the futility of the conversation, Theo said, "Have you ever met any other death coaches?"

"Not really," Sadie said. "Just the one who trained me. Why?"

"I wonder if the experience of living with another death coach would have been as unorthodox."

"Probably," Sadie said. "You might have gotten a death coach who didn't give a rat's ass about you. Or worse yet, you wouldn't have the pleasure of my company."

"I'm truly damned then, aren't I? It's like one of those dreaded court cases–the kind where you're damned if it's assigned to you or you're damned if it isn't. There's always that need to control the outcome versus curiosity. Be glad you're not a judge."

Sadie turned the van into a narrow tree-lined drive and edged into the woods until the van was hidden by the lush greenery. She eased the door open and climbed down.

"I'd make a good judge. I've always wanted to wear one of those long robes. Just think of the things I could wear under them. Or not."

"Spare me the lurid details." Theo grabbed the back of

her shirt to stop her progress before she walked toward a clearing adjacent to the Fossums' yard. "How do you know nobody's in there?"

"You don't see any cars in the driveway, do you?" She pushed Theo's hand out of the way. "The Fossums have neighbors on the other side of the bushes, but they have a separate driveway." She looked back over her shoulder. "A good judge would have known that."

"I don't know the first thing about the Fossum's property, but I do know breaking and entering is against the law." Theo watched Sadie cup her hands over her eyes and peer through the front door.

"Nobody home," Sadie said under her breath. "I don't see any movement." She pressed the latch on the brass handle with her thumb, but the catch didn't release.

Theo followed her around the porch to the back door. The results were the same.

"Let's try a few windows," she said.

Theo ran his fingers along the wooden frame, attempting to find an indentation where his fingers could leverage the panel upward. The first four windows refused to budge. On the fifth attempt, the panel gave way and he forced it open. "I don't think I can fit through there. Are you willing to give it a try?"

Sadie placed her foot into Theo's cupped hand and pulled herself up. She placed a leg through the opening. "There's a shelf or some kind of board under the window." She wriggled in through the opening.

One thud and then another echoed from the dark opening. Sadie whispered, "I knocked a couple cans off the shelf. This must be their pantry." She felt along the wall for a light switch.

A light flooded the room. Theo looked through the window. "Are you all right?"

"I'm right here," Sadie said, coming up behind Theo. He jerked upright and screamed.

Catching his breath, he rasped in anger, "Don't do that. You startled me."

"Sorry. I thought you might want to come in through the front door. And take that stupid suit coat off. You look ridiculous."

"I look ridiculous?" Theo said. "I'm not the one wearing a mini skirt and a halter top. It's not me who's exposing a sagging abdomen with a tattoo of a worm."

"That's an asp," Sadie said. "Like the one that caused Cleopatra's death. I love that story, don't you?"

"I hadn't given it much thought. That tattoo actually looks more like a shriveled up worm."

Staring at Theo with her mouth askew, Sadie said, "My asp isn't any more shriveled up than your balls."

"My balls, Madam, are about as important to me as the Ides of March were to Caesar."

Opening her mouth to reply, Sadie paused, took a deep breath, and said, "I don't get it."

"I didn't expect you to."

Sadie closed the front door behind them and pointed toward an opening. "That must be his office. I see file cabinets."

Theo sat at the desk while Sadie rifled through a stack of papers on Richard's desk. "Where did Tim say the key was hidden?"

"Under a horse statue."

"There's got to be twenty horse statues in here." Theo scanned the shelves and pedestals featuring Richard's collection. "You start there and I'll take this side of the room." Theo began by lifting the smaller pieces of art. Leaning one of the larger bronze statues against his chest, a key dangling from a felt pad tumbled to the floor. "Eureka!"

Placing the key in the middle desk drawer, Theo pulled it open and ran his hands through the shallow drawer. He repeated the process with two more drawers. He inserted the key into a deeper bottom drawer and unlocked it.

"This might be it." He pulled a hard-bound checkbook from the drawer and placed it on the desk. He lifted a stack of folders and separated them into two piles. Pushing one pile toward Sadie, he said, "You start with this and I'll see what's in the checkbook."

Sadie opened the first folder and paged through the contents. The folder held several letters with envelopes stapled to the back of each piece of correspondence. "These are all addressed to Gessal Life Insurance at a Minneapolis address." Paging deeper, Sadie said, "Here's one from Mrs. Fading Sun."

"Who?"

"Mrs. Fading Sun. She lives in Pinecone Landing. Her husband died about six months ago." As she finished reading the letter, Sadie said, "This is a letter of complaint. Apparently she thought her husband had signed a $100,000 life insurance policy. But when he died, she got a check for $10,000." Sadie turned the letter over and tapped it with her fingers. "It looks like this letter was a second request. Here she says she previously asked for a copy of the original application, but never received one."

Theo held out a check. "Look at this. Here's a check written to Fading Sun for three thousand dollars. He's got a note clipped to it indicating it's the return of premium payments. The check's signed by Richard Fossum."

Sadie held up several more letters. "These are complaints, too."

"Give me their names," Theo said. He laid several checks on the desk's surface.

As Sadie read the names, Theo turned the checks over one by one. "There's a check here matching each of the letters in your hand. There are also envelopes with stamps on them. I believe Richard was getting ready to mail refunds to these people."

Opening another folder, Sadie whistled. "Looks like somebody's been making duplicate applications. Here's the original signed copy, and here's the one that actually got turned in." She pointed to the line indicating the dollar amount. "The original application says one-hundred-thousand dollars. The copy says ten thousand dollars. These polices were altered."

Sadie looked up in disbelief. "On this original policy it says to send the payments to a post office box in Minneapolis."

"And look at the insurance agent's signature," Theo said. "Paul Brinks. Gessal Life Insurance."

"Richard obviously got his hands on the paperwork sent to the Minneapolis office. That's what Tim heard them arguing about."

"Here's the proof we need," Theo said. He held copies of two bank reconciliation forms. "Paul had the policy holders pay their premiums for the larger policy to a post office box in Minneapolis. That money was deposited into a personal account Paul had down there." Theo looked up at Sadie. "Some businesses have their collections processed by holding companies and pay a fee for the processing."

Theo tapped on the second reconciliation form. "It looks like some of those funds were transferred from his personal account in Minneapolis to the business account Richard worked with here in Pinecone Landing." He pointed at the two forms so Sadie could see the progression from one account to the other. "Paul transferred enough from that holding account so Richard could record the receipt of premiums on the lesser policies and pay the bills. Who knows how long this went on before Richard figured it out. I would guess Gessal Life isn't involved in this scam. Gessal Life Insurance paid the larger death benefit to Paul and Paul paid the lesser benefit to the recipients."

"Do you think Richard was ever in on it?"

"I doubt it. I'm guessing he figured it out and worked through the process to prove it. He got his hands on Paul's personal bank account by tracking the account number the funds were transferred from. He must have requested copies by using Paul's official letterhead." Theo pointed at a stacking tray containing letterhead.

"Do you think he told Paul he was going to refund the money?"

"He must have. Either that or Paul figured it out. Tim heard Paul tell Richard he'd never live to see another day if he turned him in. A threat that serious means Paul was worried," Theo said. "Is that characteristic of him?"

"What are you getting at?" Sadie said.

"Did you ever think Paul was capable of murder?"

"Shrewd. Sneaky. But not a murderer. We've got to show this to the police. With this evidence, we can get them to follow up on the rifle Tim saw. If the autopsy didn't show any evidence of Richard being shot, then maybe we can convince them to look closer at the car. Something caused that car to swerve."

"It's not we, Sadie. It's you who has to convince them. In case you don't know it, you can't present evidence you've gathered by breaking and entering. That's against the law." Theo tucked the reconciliation sheets back in the folder. "You're going to have to convince them to look for the same information we found. But we've got to come up with something believable before you approach them."

A muffled bark came from outside the front door. "Oh, no. Belly followed us." Sadie hurried to the front door. Opening it a crack, she whispered, "Shush. Be quiet."

"Let him in before he barks, again," Theo said. "Someone might get suspicious."

Cracking the door to coax the dog in, Sadie's breath caught in her throat. "Paul's car just turned in to the driveway." She released the knob and eased the plunger into place before dashing to the desk.

Belly barked and dropped down on his haunches. Four wild tail hairs swept the porch floor in an arc.

"Hide in the other room," Theo whispered. He gathered the papers and shoved them in the drawer. "Hurry, Sadie."

Paul strode up to the house, studying the dog. "What are you doing here, Belly?" He held out his hand letting the dog sniff his fingers before patting the dog's head. Paul walked to the corner of the porch and looked around the side of the house before scanning the driveway. He turned his ear toward the road. "You sure get around. The last time I saw you, you were at the nursing home."

Belly whined his appreciation and pawed at Paul's leg.

Paul sauntered casually around the dog, looked from side to side, and then turned the knob.

Theo tensed. His hand stopped mid-air when he heard the latch click.

Realizing the door wasn't locked, Paul removed his hand and looked from side to side again. He pressed the latch again. It gave way as easily as it had the first time. He eased the oak door open and listened before poking his head through the opening.

As Paul entered the front room, Sadie squeezed in between the pantry door and the shelving. She held her breath, listening to Paul walk across the floor toward the office.

Paul pulled at the desk chair and rolled it back toward the credenza. Dropping into the chair, he lifted a key off a stack of papers and kneaded it in his fingers. He paged through two piles of folders. After placing them on the corner of Richard's desk, he added more folders to the pile before rummaging through the desk drawer.

Theo stood near the desk watching Paul's fevered attempt at locating the incriminating evidence. The crosser gasped when Belly nosed through the front door and waddled over to where he was standing.

Belly danced his glad-to-see-you dance around Theo's feet before pawing at the man's knees.

"You stupid dog," Paul said. He tugged on Belly's collar and pushed him toward the front door. "Get the hell out of here."

Belly veered toward the kitchen sniffing wildly. He circled the room trying to locate his buddy. Trotting into the pantry, his tail darted in double time as he nudged behind the door and butted his head against the Sadie's ankle.

Sadie pushed Belly back toward the door and tapped her finger to her lip to signal silence. She froze at the sound of Paul's loafers marching across the kitchen floor.

"You stupid dog. I told you to go outside." Paul grabbed Belly's hind leg and pulled him from the pantry. He spun him around on the slippery floor and grabbed his collar. "Quit growling, you worthless mutt." He unlatched the kitchen door and ushered Belly out with a shove from his left foot.

Paul locked the exterior door before striding back toward the pantry. He grabbed the doorknob. He stared into the darkness, muttered to himself, closed the door, and left the kitchen.

Sadie released her breath as the latch clicked and Paul retreated to the living room.

Paul made two trips to his vehicle to load his trunk with folders, bank statements, checkbooks, and ledgers.

Theo and Sadie watched their evidence disappear as Paul's taillights flashed red before he stepped on the gas and turned out of the driveway.

26

Theo waited until the nursing home administrator gathered her briefcase and made her way down the corridor before he entered her office. After making sure it was safe, he sat in the administrator's chair and moved the adjustment levers back and forth to find a comfortable position for his lanky frame. He drew a long, calming breath. He had finally found a location away from prying eyes where he could compose his final piece of correspondence.

Theo ran his hand across the finely crafted desk, searching for a pen. He didn't know how long she'd be away. It was crucial he make the most of his time before the woman returned.

During his years on the bench, Theo's business associates warned him about putting too much emphasis on his career and not enough on his personal life. They recommended he broaden his leisure horizons. Theo had disagreed. Why should he waste time on pleasure if the bane of his existence might accompany him? He'd done everything possible to avoid being with his wife.

Theo had given his life to the justice system. He was proud of what he achieved. He was also proud of several financial partnerships he had formed. If only he could feel the same about his personal life. His marriage had been a disaster and he had never forgiven himself for falling for the guiles of that horrid woman and her two children. How could he have been so naïve? The feeling of remorse more than deflated him, it devastated him. He fought to regain clarity to help him compose the most important document of his life.

He pulled a desk drawer open and searched for a sheet of paper. He found several sheets of nursing home letterhead, but pushed them aside in pursuit of a clean, unmarked sheet. Settling for a lined legal pad, Theo placed it on the desk. His fingers brushed over several writing instruments until he found the perfect pen and tested it on the corner of a financial printout. After wiping the space clean with a swipe of his little finger, he situated the tablet at an angle and began to write.

As my time on earth has come to an end, I must admit to a grievous error I made.

First you must understand my shortcomings. Obsession with my vocation and an unfortunate marriage distorted my belief in the justice system and turned me into the type of man I loathe.

I realize I will never be able to make up for what' I've done, but I hope with what I'm going to tell you, I can...

A burst of laughter rang from the hall, startling Theo from his concentration. He tore the sheet from the tablet and folded it in half before sliding it inside his suit coat.

The door opened as he rose from the chair. When the administrator entered her office and noticed the tablet in the center of her desk, Theo hurried out of the office.

Leaning against the wall to regain his presence of mind, Theo heard someone shout his name. He turned toward the plea. The urgency of his name being repeated made him rush toward the voice.

"Theo. Help me," Aanders cried. "I can't get Tim to wake up."

Aanders crouched over Tim, who had collapsed on the cold tile floor. "I tried to get him back into the wheelchair, but he was too weak."

Theo lifted Tim off the floor and started down the hall toward the front door. "Call Sadie and tell her what happened. Tell her to bring the van."

27

Nan knocked softly on the cabin door, waiting for one of the sisters to acknowledge her arrival.

"You don't need to knock. You're always welcome here," Jane said.

A weak smile crossed Nan's lips. She greeted each sister with a hug. She patted Mr. Bakke's shoulder as she joined the elderly trio at the kitchen table.

"What do you think of my new hair color?" Sadie asked. "The magazines say it's all the rage."

"Wow," Nan said, evaluating the new color as Sadie turned a complete circle. "Is it supposed to be mustard color?"

"Not really. Big Leon said I should wash it a couple times until the color fades." Gazing in the mirror above the sideboard, Sadie said, "Actually, I kind of like it. It goes nice with these shorts." She ran a hand over the leather fabric and looked up to see if Nan agreed.

"Big Leon told me to sprinkle this in my hair. It's supposed to give it that extra punch." Sadie held up a bag of silver glitter. "I think it might be a bit too much. What do you think?"

Before Nan could answer, Jane said, "You already look like a damn fool. If you added glitter, people would mistake you for a Fourth-of-July sparkler and light your head on fire."

"Coming from someone whose life revolves around the vibrant color of beige, I'll take that as a compliment."

"I don't see anything wrong with looking respectable," Jane said. "What's wrong with white and beige?" Seeking reinforcement, Jane said, "Mr. Bakke agrees with me." Getting no response, she batted his hand and growled through clenched teeth, "Don't you."

"Yes, dear."

"I see you're wearing the same depressing colors Jane's wearing. What happened to your plaid shorts?" Sadie said.

"Jane surprised me with a new outfit." Mr. Bakke looked down and sighed.

"If you want my advice, stick to what you usually wear. You look much better in plaid shorts and Hawaiian shirts than in those washed out colors. You and Jane look like twin cadavers."

"No, he doesn't," Jane said, dismissing the comment with a wave of her hand. "Quit telling him stuff like that. I don't want him looking stupid like you."

"Before Nan knocked on the door, you said you were in the mood for rhubarb crisp," Jane said. "Why don't you dish some up?"

"Why don't you? Just because you've got a crack in your ass doesn't mean your legs are broken," Sadie said. She crossed to the cupboard and selected four forks and placed them on the counter.

Belly pawed at her leg as she jabbed one of the utensils into the dessert pan. She offered a forkful of rhubarb crisp to the impatient dog. Belly lapped at the fork before snorting and backing away. He expelled a slobbery sneeze that sent crisp flying in all directions.

"You know you don't like rhubarb," Sadie said, swiping at a glob that had landed in her hair. "I don't know why you insist on tasting everything we eat."

Sadie pushed a plate toward her guest. Nan said, "None for me, thank you. It's one of my favorites, but I don't have much of an appetite."

"You've been awfully quiet," Jane said. "Is something wrong?"

"I'm not sure." Nan pulled a folded envelope from her pocket and placed it on the table. "I've got something to discuss with you. Actually two things."

Sadie placed forks in front of Jane and Mr. Bakke before setting their desserts on the table.

"I've told you before I've been dating Paul Brinks and that the frequency has intensified," Nan began.

Mr. Bakke shot a glance at Sadie before looking back down at his plate and grabbing his fork.

"You also know that with Carl's lawsuit pending, I might lose the land lease for the mortuary."

The elderly trio nodded their understanding.

"I'm afraid I find myself making a decision based on the love of my profession, rather than on what I should base it on." Seeing their concerned expressions, Nan said, "Unfortunately, because of Carl Swanson, I'm leaning toward a decision I might regret later."

"I don't understand what you're trying to tell us," Jane said. "What does Carl have to do with this?"

"Because of Carl, we're looking at an uncertain future." Nan's face tensed. "That was until last night when Paul asked me to marry him. We'd talked about marriage in the past, but I wasn't ready. This time his offer was so lucrative, I didn't think I'd be able to turn it down. But then I found this. Now I don't know what to think." She pointed at the envelope.

"Oh, my dear...," Jane began, but Sadie held her hand up to interrupt her sister.

"We have something to talk to you about, too," Sadie said.

"Maybe you didn't understand. Paul officially proposed last night." Noticing the serious expressions on their faces, Nan's concern deepened.

"We understood," Sadie said. She pointed at the envelope. "What's that got to do with Paul's proposal?"

"Do you remember when some of my clients were shocked to learn their life insurance polices weren't worth what they thought they were?" Nan pulled her chair closer to the table. "They were positive they had purchased policies with larger death benefits."

"I vaguely remember," Sadie said, hoping Nan would validate what she and Theo had discovered.

"It's happened twice recently. Both of the policies were with a company named Gessal Life Insurance. This Gessal Life envelope was in Paul's car. I picked it up by mistake."

Mr. Bakke shifted nervously in his chair.

Sadie nodded in understanding. Nan asked, "You're familiar with that company?"

"I am. And I'm afraid we've got bad news for you."

28

"Oh, now what," Sadie moaned, pulling the shuttle van up to the curb. She crossed her arms over her chest and assumed a defiant stance as she waited for Carl to get out of his cruiser.

Knuckles rapped against the sliding door. She stared out the windshield refusing to acknowledge him. After a second rap she shouted, "What's the matter, Carl? Are you so hard up you decided to frisk me?"

A voice said, "Pardon me, Sadie?"

Sadie grabbed the lever and the door swung open. "Sorry Lon. I'm so used to Carl pulling me over, I thought it was him."

Tipping his hat brim with his pen, Lon said, "That's quite the hairdo you've got there."

Sadie patted her hair. "Thanks. I like it, too. It goes nice with these shorts, don't you think?" She tipped her head and pointed to her glasses. "See the mustard speckles in these frames. Goes good with that, too."

The deputy raised his eyebrows. "Sure does."

Sadie's sandals slapped against her heels as she climbed out of the van. "I'm guessing you didn't pull me over for a friendly visit. But I'd be up for one if you've got the time."

"That won't be necessary." Lon grinned. He looked down at Sadie's high-heel clogs and flipped open the cover on the citation book. "It seems you didn't bother to stop at the last three red lights. You're lucky you didn't cause an accident."

"Oh I never stop at those lights. They're there for the tourists."

"Hmmm," Lon responded. "I thought everybody was supposed to stop when the lights turned red."

"Nope. Just the tourists. Those of us who live here know where we're going. That's why we don't have to stop."

"I didn't know that," Lon said, biting at his lip and turning to avoid eye contact with the mustard-embellished woman.

Sadie climbed back up the van steps. "Well now you do."

"Wait a minute, Sadie. I don't think you understand. I have to issue a ticket because you ran three red lights. In all honesty, I should issue three tickets."

Frowning as she backed down the steps, Sadie said, "You're just like that good-for-nothing Carl Swanson. You're harassing me like he does. And here I thought you were a nice young man."

"I guarantee I'm nothing like Carl. I'm not harassing you. I'm doing my job."

"Picking on a helpless, old lady isn't doing your job."

"Trying to make sure no one is injured when someone runs a red light is part of my job. You could have caused a serious accident." Lon shook his pen. "For your information, insulting me by comparing me to Carl won't help your case. That's hitting below the belt."

"I saw you going door to door campaigning for that loser yesterday. Why isn't he doing his own campaigning?" Holding a finger up and looking over the top of her glasses she said, "It's because he's busy playing the skin flute again, isn't it? I'll bet he's played every song ever written. My daughter told me he was always trying to get her to play it, too."

Smiling broadly as she observed Lon's shocked expression, Sadie said, "Why would you campaign for him if you don't like him?" The look on Lon's face answered her question. "He's got something on you, doesn't he? He's forcing you to do it?"

"Never you mind," Lon said. He wrote on the citation tablet.

"I bet I know what it is." Sadie's eyes darted with excitement. "My friend Elmer at the nursing home told me a rumor last summer about you roughing up an Indian and almost losing your job. Elmer knows everything. He gets the gossip from the nursing home staff."

"Carl framed me. He twisted the facts and made me take the blame for what he did. I couldn't afford to lose my job so I had to go along with it."

Sadie placed her hand on the citation pad and grabbed the pen. "I'll trade you information if you promise you won't write that ticket."

"I can't do that," Lon said.

"What if I've got something on Carl that might keep him from harassing you? All you need to do is tell him you know about it."

The change in his expression pleased Sadie. Cricking her finger to get him to follow her into the van, she said, "I've got something unbelievable to tell you."

After listening to her detailed suspicions and hearing what she had found at the Fossums' residence, Lon stared in disbelief.

"You got all this because one of Nan's clients complained about their life insurance policy?"

"Well, kind of," Sadie said. "I put two and two together…"

"But what made you think Paul was involved?"

"It's a long story, but it mostly boils down to Aanders telling me how Tim overheard Paul threaten his father."

"That's quite a stretch. They'll laugh me out of the station if I tell them I want to have Richard's car examined for gun shots."

Sadie watched a puzzled expression cross Lon's face. "The fact I could be right should be enough for you to investigate. With the evidence I saw on Richard's desk, it should prove Paul was scamming his clients. I'll bet you ten bucks Richard was going to turn him in to the authorities and Paul got scared."

"You were an idiot for breaking into Richard's house. I can't believe you did that. What if Paul had found you in the pantry? If he killed Richard, he could have killed you too."

"But he didn't. That's all that matters. Now we've got to figure out a way to get those papers from Paul."

"We?" Lon said. "You're done sticking your nose where it doesn't belong. I'll take it from here."

"But maybe I can help by making an appointment with Paul to talk about insurance. I can get Jane to stop in and distract him while I check out his desk."

"You've been watching too much television. It's not done that way. We need a search warrant, but before I can request one I need more evidence."

"Well you better hurry, because Paul will probably

destroy the evidence."

Lon paused as he sorted through what Sadie had told him. "A few things that happened recently are staring to make sense. Richard missed a golf date because he said he forgot. Richard lived to golf. Something drastic had to have happened for him to forget a thing like that. Now you're telling me Aanders said Paul threatened Tim's dad. Maybe there's something to that."

"There is. Richard figure out what Paul was doing and Paul had to stop him. Now you've got to figure out a way to examine the car."

"If Carl gets wind I'm investigating his best friend, he'll run me out of the department," Lon said. "I'll never work in law enforcement again."

"You can't let Paul get away with this. You owe it to the Fossums to at least check out their car. Something made them go off the road. It's too much of a coincidence they died just hours after Paul and Richard argued."

"I've got a friend who owns a repair shop. I know I can trust him to keep his mouth shut," Lon said. "If we find any evidence, I'll talk to the sheriff about a search warrant for Paul's office. We need to find the papers Paul took. I'll be in touch, Sadie. Don't do anything else foolish."

29

A small rental car pulled to a stop in front of Sadie's cabin. A wire-haired terrier yipped wildly as Erma Pouliot waved a greeting to Sadie and let the dog scamper toward the porch swing. The dog resumed his high-pitched greeting, bouncing excitedly in front of Sadie.

Sadie grabbed one of the swing's support chains and pulled herself up. As she walked to meet the Pouliots, the swing continued to sway and the dog continued to bark.

Gregg Pouliot flipped his sun glasses up and peered at the swing. "Your swing must catch a breeze off the lake. I wish we'd had that breeze. It's been hotter than a honeymoon this past week."

"Quit complaining. This was the best vacation we've had in twenty years." Turning toward Sadie, Erma said, "We had to stop before we left to thank you for the enjoyable stay. You've got a great place here. I've never been so relaxed in all my life."

"I'm glad you enjoyed your stay. We think of Witt's End as our little piece of paradise."

Gregg pulled a white handkerchief from his pocket and dabbed at his forehead. "That miracle we witnessed yesterday still has me reeling. I don't now how that kid made it to shore. By all rights his folks should be planning his funeral."

"It just goes to show miracles can happen," Sadie said, winking at Lora, who had remained on the swing.

"Yes, but there's no way that kid should have made it

to shore. He disappeared below the water line and then all of a sudden he was lying on the beach. Now you explain that to me."

"I wasn't there, but I heard about it," Sadie said.

Slipping her arm into the crook of her husband's elbow, Erma said, "The main thing is the boy survived."

Sadie joined them as they walked back to their car. Erma called to the dog, which had jumped up and settled comfortably on the swaying swing. The dog ignored Erma until his mistress said, "Come here right now, Mr. Twister. If you don't, you're going to have to ride in the back seat.

"We stopped at the lodge to make sure you remembered to book our reservation for next summer. The manager said it was taken care of." She squeezed Sadie's hand. "We can't thank you enough for your hospitality."

"Holy cats," Sadie blurted as she looked into their car through the rear window. "Did you leave anything on the gift shop shelves?"

"You know my wife," Gregg said. "She's always thinking of the grandkids. I bought a few things for them myself. I called my grandson and told him about that huge fish I caught. He insisted I bring him one of those yellow lures you sell in the bait shop so he could catch one, too."

Beaming, Erma said, "We've got eight grandchildren, you know. We have to treat them equally or we'd have a war on our hands."

"By the looks of it, you didn't forget anyone. Is your trunk full, too?" Sadie said.

Gregg patted his chest and Mr. Twister jumped into his arms. "The trunk's empty. We put everything in the back seat. That way the guy at the airport can load our stuff on his baggage cart and we don't have to worry about forgetting anything."

A voice from a few cabins away hailed the Pouliots. "Don't forget you promised to spend a couple of hours with us before you have to catch your plane. We've got some photos to show you."

Gregg looked at his watch. "Two hours. That's just about right. Do you mind if we leave the car here for a while?"

After the couple walked away, Sadie joined Lora on the swing and leaned into the gaunt woman's shoulder. "You did a wonderful thing saving that child's life yesterday."

"Anyone would have done it," Lora said. "I heard that man say he witnessed a miracle. But all I did was swim out and pull that child to shore. His friends were too young to know what to do." She shrugged. "Everybody panicked and just stood there. So I dove in."

"Did you ever think about what really makes miracles happen?" Sadie asked. "Since I've been a death coach, I've come to believe crossers have a big hand in making them happen. I'm not saying all miracles are crosser related, but I know for a fact some are."

Lora smiled in appreciation. "You have a way of making me look at things differently. If I could spend more time with you, I'd learn a lot."

"I know you don't like it when I preach at you, but I have a question."

"I've already lost Michael. I don't think any amount of preaching could make me feel any more miserable," Lora said.

"You didn't think twice about saving that child's life."
Seeing Lora shrug again, Sadie said, "What puzzles me is
why you insisted on forcing Michael to rejoin his father.
That's a complete contradiction. You recognized when
someone else's child was in danger, but you were willing to
lead Michael right back into harm's way."

A teardrop rolled off Lora's cheek and settled on the
back of her hand. "You're judging me when you don't
understand."

"There's nothing to understand, Lora. Your husband
was abusive and that pattern will continue. Why was
Michael able to sort through that cloud of uncertainty, but
you can't?" Sadie wiped at Lora's teardrop with her finger.
"I don't mean to be unkind, but Michael appears to be the
smart one in the family."

Rodney bounded up onto the porch. "You got that
right. Lora's an idiot. No wonder her husband left without
her."

"Zip it," Sadie bit back. "I've had more than I can
handle for one day. Go find someone else to bother."

"No can do," Rodney said. He wrangled his way onto
the swing between Lora and Sadie and put an arm around
each of them.

"Then I'll go," Sadie said, pulling herself from the
swing.

"Me too," Lora said.

Rodney reached across the swing and grabbed the
wooden arm, thwarting Lora's attempt. "You're not going
anywhere." He ran his finger across the back of her neck
and grinned. "When you gonna realize I might be a good
catch? You know I've been thinking about you."

Slapping at his hand, she tried once again to get out of the swing. "Leave me alone. I don't want to have anything to do with you."

"Now there you go hurting my feelings again. A loser like you shouldn't be so fussy."

Lora crossed her arms over her chest and stared at the cabin next door.

"You can ignore me all you want. But I'm still taking you with me. I need somebody to take care of the mansion I'm going to build in the parallel world."

Lora squeezed her arms tighter. "Mansion? Just how do you think you're going to do that?"

"It's a secret." He shifted his weight, leaned closer to Lora and buried his lips in her hair. "If you're nice, I might tell you."

"Do you spend all your time cooking up ways to make others miserable?" Lora leaned further into the wooden arm.

"I'm trying to get ahead in life."

"Life?" Lora said exaggerating the word. "Will you be alive in the parallel world? Will anyone?"

"Sadie thinks so. You heard her say there'll be some sort of life there. That's why we're given a second chance to better ourselves."

"So you think you're going to be rich if you go there? How do you intend to pull that off? You've never worked a day in your life. You were still living with your parents."

"Whoa, aren't you getting feisty. Full of piss and vinegar like my old lady." Rodney grinned. "I like that in my women." He set his heel firm against the porch floor forcing the swing to stop. "When I get my hands on what Theo's been trying to hide, I'm going to be rich."

230

"What does Theo have to do with it?"

"None of your damn business. But if you agree to go with me, I'll see to it you have everything you've ever wanted. Hell, I'll even let your brat live with us."

Lora turned toward Rodney and stared into his eyes. "How do I know I can trust you?"

"You'll have to wait and see."

He pulled a wad of fishing line from his pocket and held it under her chin. "I'm getting ready to go, so you'll have to make up your mind."

Lora took the fishing line and moved it around in her hands before looking at Rodney.

"Remember that dog I was going to put out of its misery? I've figured out a way to do it without using the rifle. It won't draw as much attention and will give me time to step into the light first. If I go first, I determine the path. I don't want to risk someone else choosing the alternative. Someone like you or Tim."

"I have no intention of following you into the light. Neither does Tim."

"We'll see," Rodney said, dangling the wad of fishing line in front of Lora.

"What are you going to do, choke Sadie?" Lora said.

"No. And keep your voice down. She might hear you." He looked toward the screen door. "That would attract too much attention, too. She'd put up a fuss and everyone would come running."

He rose from the swing and sat on the top porch step. Untangling the wad of fishing line, he stretched it out across the wooden decking. After folding the line in half to increase its strength, he tied one end around the bottom of the newel post and tugged on it to test the knot. "See? If I pull this tight, it's going to hit Sadie about ankle level. It'll trip her when she goes down the stairs." Pointing toward the ground, he said, "If I calculated right, she'll take a header into the concrete."

"There's no guarantee it'll kill her. Plus she'll see you when you pull the fishing line. She's not blind, you know."

"Not if I'm under the porch," Rodney said. "I've been under there experimenting with my timing and I think I've got it figured out. The line's transparent, so she shouldn't see it." Holding up a pocket knife, he said, "Whether she dies or not, the line's going to disappear. If she doesn't die, I've got the rifle under the porch. And won't everyone be surprised to find out that the shot that killed Sadie came from that deputy's rifle?"

Rodney wrapped the transparent line once more around the post before tucking it under the step. He rejoined Lora on the swing. "Soon. It's going to happen soon."

30

"Do you really think Carl will go along with it?" Jane said.

"It's worth a try," Mr. Bakke said. "With the new evidence Sadie's got, he can't afford not to. If the man wants to win the election, he'll do it."

Sadie double-parked in front of the city's municipal building and opened the van door. She leaned back in the driver's seat and held her palm against the horn.

Looking up from a pile of overdue reports, Carl shouted, "What the hell is that racket?" When no one responded, he again raised his voice. "Angie? What the hell is going on out there?"

The dispatcher shielded the sun from her eyes and looked through the glass pane. "It looks like that weird lady from the resort. She's holding her hand on the horn."

Grabbing his cap from a hook near the door, Carl snugged it down over his head and raced from the building.

Sadie saw Carl coming toward the van and lifted her hand off the horn. As he walked in front of the car she had hemmed in by double-parking, she pressed down, holding the horn in place with her thumb.

"Are you completely out of your mind?" Carl shouted, covering his left ear with his hand. Carl pulled the door open, climbed up into the van, and yanked her hand from the steering wheel.

"You're a flipping weirdo." His voice rose two notches

higher and cracked as he lost control. "You should be locked up in the nut house." His nostrils curled with the spiteful words rolling off his tongue. "My mother told me you were trouble. She'll be right there celebrating when I get the deed to the resort."

Tipping her head in thought, Sadie said, "I really don't think that's going to happen. But speaking of your mother, how is Oink Etta the Wonder Pig? I haven't seen her for quite some time."

"Leave my mother out of this," Carl shouted. "This conversation is about you disturbing the peace."

Sadie displayed a toothy grin. "Well Carl, if you're in the mood to talk..." She rammed the door lever into the locked position and turned the key in the ignition.

"What the hell are you doing?" Sadie's foot slammed against the gas pedal. Carl grabbed the door post to brace himself.

"Taking you for a nice, long ride."

"The hell you are," he said, dropping down into the stairwell and attempting to insert his fingers into the seal surrounding the door.

Sadie turned the steering wheel sharply, causing Carl to drop onto the top step. "Calm down, Carl. I'm not kidnapping you. I just want to talk to you. I don't want anyone to hear what I have to say."

"Let me out right now," Carl said, "or I'll break this door with my foot."

"I wouldn't do that if I were you. After you hear what I've got to say, I think you'll be singing a different ditty."

Sadie parked the van under a pine tree at Nordeen

Point and opened the door. "Feel free to escape if you want. But if you do, I'll go to the newspaper about Richard's murder."

"Murder?" Carl said. "Murder? Richard wasn't murdered. He died when his car went off the road."

"The evidence proves different," Sadie said. "The evidence points to cold blooded murder."

"You think someone planned to kill him? Are you crazy?"

Jutting her chin out and glaring at Carl, Sadie said, "You ask me that same question every time you see me. I'm going to settle it once and for all. The answer is no." Enunciating slowly, Sadie said, "I am not crazy. Are you capable of understanding that?"

"You're as squirrelly as a two-peckered loon. Everyone knows that."

"Well then you better pay attention. Apparently only a crazy person is smart enough to figure out Richard was murdered." Irritated that Carl turned his back on her and descended the steps, she raised her voice. "Richard was killed because he was about to go to the police."

Sadie detailed her suspicions and told him about the evidence she found at the Fossums'. Carl sank into the seat next to the door. He slowly shook his head from side to side in disbelief as Sadie continued to explain.

"You're telling me I'm supposed to believe you because you saw evidence on Richard's desk, but you don't have anything to show me?"

"You must not be listening," Sadie said. "I told you I don't have anything to show you because that murdering partner of yours took it."

"Partner? Paul was Richard's partner, not mine."

"Oh you're his partner, all right. I had someone do some checking with the State and they found old partnership papers stating you're one of Paul's silent partners. So don't tell me you're not his partner."

"We formed that corporation years ago. I haven't had anything to do with it for over a decade." Carl moved to the edge of his seat. He removed his cap and wiped the sweat from his forehead. "You can't possibly think I had anything to do with this story you're making up."

Slamming her fist against her leg, Sadie said, "I'm not making it up. I saw what I saw."

"Can anyone else verify your story?"

Throwing her head back with a moan, she said, "Noooo. I already told you that. Nobody can verify what I saw."

"Sounds to me like you don't have a case. If you're trying to involve me in this, you're wasting your time." Carl grabbed the overhead support bar next to the door and stood up.

"You're going to be involved in this one way or another. I'm not finished yet. I'm here to barter with you."

"Really?" Carl droned in disbelief. "You don't have anything I want. Why would I barter with a dried up old hag like you?"

"If you want to become sheriff, you'll barter with me."

A throaty laugh spurted from Carl's lips. He lifted his cap and scratched his bald spot. "I'm already going to get the resort. So there's nothing else to talk about."

"You're not getting the resort. You're going to drop your lawsuit and settle for winning the election."

With mouth gaping, Carl craned his neck forward. "That confirms it. You are crazy." Fidgeting with the brim of his cap, he said, "You really don't get it, do you? That resort belongs to me. If someone's been feeding you a line of bull about winning this lawsuit, you'd better face facts and prepare to move on. Next week you're losing title to the resort."

Sadie held her fingers out to admire the anchor decals she had applied to her nails. "I don't think so. Like I said before, if you won't barter with me, I'll take my information to the newspaper. You'll not only lose the resort, you'll also lose the election."

"Then you better do it. That way when you leave the resort, everyone will agree it was for the best. Half the town already knows you're crazy. If you go to the newspaper with that asinine story, it will confirm it for the other half."

"Going to the paper will make everyone adore me even more than they already do."

Carl puckered his lips and rolled his eyes. "Sure it will."

"When I tell everyone Lon helped me solve the case, maybe he'll be elected sheriff. Heaven knows he deserves it."

With a quick side glance, Carl said, "What does Lon have to do with this?"

"If you hadn't been so nasty over the years, maybe he wouldn't be so eager to prove it was murder."

Sadie beamed, tipped her head, and toyed with an anchor earring. "I haven't had this much fun in years. I've got you right where I want you. Actually, I've never wanted you. But seeing you this uncomfortable is better than sex."

"That's it," Carl shouted. He pressed the call button on the speaker attached to his shoulder. "Angie? I'm on the east end of Nordeen Point. Send a cruiser to pick me up."

Static blared through the speaker as Angie said, "You're where?"

As Carl pressed the button to repeat his location, Sadie said, "The rim on Richard's tire has a bullet hole in it."

Carl released the button. "What?"

"Well not actually a bullet hole, but evidence a bullet struck the rim. Lon's friend towed the car from the junk yard to his garage and found an indentation on the rim. They went back to the scene of the accident and did a thorough search."

Thrilled that she had piqued Carl's curiosity, Sadie continued, "They searched the area this time as if it had been a crime scene. They gathered the rubber tire shreds you didn't even bother to look for."

Dropping down on the top step, Carl leaned his head against a support pole and closed his eyes.

"They tested the rubber shreds and found traces of lead fragments. And you know what else they found?" Sadie watched Carl's right eyelid pop open. "They used a metal detector and found some shell casings. Lon said they were able to match the casings and fragments to the type of rifle used to fire the shot."

Releasing a deep sigh, Carl stared straight ahead. "It's a Winchester .300 Win Mag, isn't it?"

Clapping her hands together, Sadie said, "Give that man a prize. Isn't it peculiar Paul owns the same type of rifle? Lon also told me it was the same type you use when you compete in contests. He even said Paul's rifle was in your possession more often than it was locked up in Paul's gun cabinet."

Grabbing the support bar and pulling on it, Carl said, "Now wait just a second. If you think I had something to do with Richard's murder, you're wrong. Dead wrong."

"Murder? You're admitting it was murder?" Sadie jabbed a finger toward him. "That's what I needed to hear." Pointing toward the seat next to the passenger door, Sadie said, "Sit. Now we're going to barter."

Carl stared at his feet. "What do you want?"

Smoothing the fabric on her shorts and tugging at her shirt hem, Sadie wagged her head in contemplation. "Here's exactly what I want. If you drop the lawsuit against us, I won't go to the newspaper. I'll even let you be the hero for solving the case. That, of course, comes with the stipulation you stop harassing Lon. He didn't rough up that guy last summer, you did."

"I'm going to take credit for solving this case by myself," Carl said, before Sadie could draw a breath and start her next sentence. "No one would ever believe you were capable of solving it."

"Lon's ready to back me up. He'll tell everyone I was the one who came forward with the proof and you failed to find the evidence. And don't forget you're Paul's partner. If Paul committed fraud, and if news gets out that you're in cahoots with him, you'll not only lose the election, you'll lose your job. You'll be named as an accessory."

Grinning, Sadie said, "Don't you just love those legal words? Lon educated me on what to tell the authorities in case anything happens to him."

"You bitch," Carl muttered under his breath.

239

"Now was that nice?" Sadie bent down to gaze into his face.

"It fits."

"It may fit, but you forgot to put 'clever' in front of it. Once Lon listened to me, it didn't take long for him to locate the evidence. The hard part was finding information on Paul's business holdings and tracking down his cash flow."

Sadie smiled at Carl's discomfort. "Don't look so surprised. Did you really think he'd stop digging once he had proof the tire was shot? Once he discovered that, he couldn't wait to look deeper into Paul's business holdings. What excited him most was finding your name buried deep within Paul's corporate records."

"That doesn't prove I was involved."

Gesturing with an open palm, Sadie said, "It also doesn't prove you weren't involved. Or that you weren't aware of what was going on. I would guess being a silent partner is enough to sway people's vote."

"How do I know I can trust you?"

"You don't. That's the beauty of it," Sadie said. "I've got you either way. If you take the resort away from us, I'll go to the press and your career will be over. If you agree to drop your lawsuit now, but try to get the resort at a later date," Sadie explained as she reached into her purse, "I've got a signed copy from Lon verifying your silent partnership with Paul and my involvement in solving the case."

Sadie waved the folded paper under his nose. "I'm not stupid. I've got copies in my safety deposit box. You might end up owning the resort, but you won't be able to enjoy it from prison."

240

She tucked the sheets back in her purse. "Don't forget there'll always be a record of your involvement in Paul's corporation. It might interest you that a client of Paul's who was cheated out of money is Mrs. Fading Sun. Does that name ring a bell? You wouldn't want the diversity crusaders to find out you're Paul's partner."

"Oh, and one more thing," Sadie said. "There's no guarantee I've told you everything. Maybe I've got a little tidbit tucked away for safekeeping."

Sadie turned the key in the ignition. "I expect you to be at my cabin by ten o'clock tomorrow morning with a signed statement indicating you've agreed to drop the lawsuit. If you're not on time, I'll go to the newspaper and tell them what I know."

Carl closed his eyes in resignation.

"My favorite restaurant is Yerry's on the Bay. I believe a gift certificate for three dinners will be an adequate apology for all that nasty name-calling you did earlier."

31

Sounds of laughter and rejoicing drifted from the cabin as Jane, Sadie, and Mr. Bakke hugged and offered congratulations to one another on their pending victory.

"What if Carl backs out? What if he decides to go to the newspaper by himself?" Jane said.

"From what Sadie told us, I'd bet Carl's dropping the lawsuit as we speak." Mr. Bakke pulled Jane to his side and kissed her cheek.

Sadie bobbed her head from side to side as she danced an impromptu jig by the kitchen sink. She held a hand out to Theo to join her as she celebrated.

Theo reached for her hand, grasped it, and held it to his lips. After placing a gentle kiss on her knuckles, he said, "To quote our eloquent friend, Rodney, you're one hell of a broad." He twirled her around the room, dipped her in a graceful sweep, and escorted her to the table. He bowed low as she took her seat.

"Will wonders never cease?" Sadie said. "Theo just complimented me."

"He did?" Jane said.

"He did." Sadie relished in the glow of Theo's compliment, a hard-won morsel of praise.

"Who else is here?" Mr. Bakke asked.

Sadie looked around the room. "Just Theo. I think Lora's out on the porch with Rodney. Tim and Aanders are in the inner room resting because Tim's stamina is almost gone. Guilt is getting the better of Aanders. He's afraid he ruined Tim's chance of going back through the light."

Sadie walked over to the window, parted the white curtains, and looked out at Lora. A tiny chipmunk sat on Lora's lap. His paw rested against her stomach, his head bobbing with each stroke of Lora's finger. Belly's legs trembled with excitement and he pranced at Lora's feet trying to convince her he needed some quality time with the animal, too. Lost in concentration, Lora ignored Belly's pleas.

Belly finally retreated to the top porch step and plopped down in defeat. His ears twitched erratically and he cocked his head from right to left, focusing on the faint movement beneath the porch.

Mr. Bakke bolted from his chair. "Oh, no. I forgot to take the meat out of the freezer. I better get over there or we'll have frozen fish for dinner."

As Mr. Bakke waited for Jane to join him, Sadie heard a plaintive cry from Rodney. "Sadie. Come here quick. Something's wrong."

Sadie hurried toward the screen door.

"Sadie. I'm over here by the trail," Rodney shouted.

Sadie crossed the porch. Lora yelled, "No! Don't…"

Rodney wrapped the end of the fishing line around his hand as footsteps clinked across the porch decking. He yanked on the line. An ankle slammed against it, jerking his hand wildly. He scrambled to find the knife to severe the fishing line. A thunk echoed as a body hit the concrete slab at the bottom of the steps.

Jane screamed. She grabbed the railing and hurried down the steps. Kneeling, she called out, "Dial 911. Get an ambulance."

Jane's plea registered with Theo, but he concentrated on Lora's frantic movements.

"It's Rodney. He's hiding under the porch," Lora screamed, pointing toward the sidewalk. "He told me he was going to kill Sadie."

Lora followed Theo down the stairs. He bent to see under the porch.

Theo dove head first under the structure as Rodney's boots disappeared into the darkness. Clawing at the ground, Theo inched along the damp dirt until he grabbed Rodney's ankle. Rodney's heel swung wide and caught Theo in the jaw. Theo yelled in pain and surprise.

Theo ducked avoiding Rodney's second kick. He pulled on Rodney's leg with all the strength he could summon. Grunts emanated from both men in their struggle. Jamming his foot against a porch brace for leverage, Theo pried the culprit out of the darkness.

Wide-eyed with rage, Theo shouted to Lora, "Get something to tie his hands."

Lora scrambled past the body on the sidewalk, now surrounded by others who stopped to help. Her shaking hands matched her frustration. She bobbed in place. "What do you want me to get?"

"Here, use this," Theo shouted. Lora ran to assist him. Theo had wrestled Rodney to the ground and held him face down while he knelt on his back. "Pull my belt off. We'll tie his hands behind his back."

Kneeling in front of Theo, Lora unfastened the buckle and yanked the belt through the loops. She dodged Rodney's flailing feet, wrestled his hands into position, and looped the belt tightly around his wrists.

"You bitch. You bitch," Rodney shouted, spitting dirt from his mouth. "I thought you were going with me." He jerked from side to side, trying to rid himself of Theo's weight.

Theo removed his suit jacket and secured it around Rodney's ankles. "You're not going anywhere. If it's the last thing I do, I'll see you never leave this place."

Lora's head jerked up. She shouted, "The car. Those people left their car. We can put him in the trunk."

"No," Rodney screamed, writhing back and forth.

"That's a rental car and they'll be leaving it at the airport this afternoon. Their suitcases are in the back seat. They won't need to open the trunk when they get there." Lora gasped for breath, the words tumbling from her lips. "I heard them tell Sadie there's no hurry to get the car back because it's scheduled to have work done on it. It wouldn't be rented out for another two weeks." Seeing Theo's confusion, Lora explained, "By then Rodney's time will be up."

"No. Don't do it," Rodney yelled as he watched Lora check the trunk latch. "You're supposed to go with me to the other world. I'll give you anything you want." Lora continued to grope frantically at the latch. Rodney shouted, "I'll kill you. I'll kill you, you bitch."

Lora's hands trembled as she continued to search the trunk's seal. "I can't find the latch." She felt again and then looked toward Theo. "The keys. I saw those people give Sadie the keys before they went to visit their friends."

After retrieving the keys from the kitchen table, Lora hurried to the driver's door, unlocked it and felt along the driver's seat for a lever. Locating the lever, she lifted it and the trunk popped open.

"Grab his feet. Help me lift him into the trunk." Theo stooped to slide his arms under the angry crosser. Rodney bent his knees and thrust his feet toward Lora. "Watch out," Theo shouted. Lora stumbled and fell backward.

Rodney's feet slammed against the ground when Lora dropped them. She stood, set her jaw, and stomped against his knee cap. Ignoring his cries of pain, she looped one arm around his ankles and lifted them off the grass.

Rodney writhed back and forth by bending and then straightening his knees. His captors, bobbing in sync with each thrust of his body, shuffled toward the trunk. Bursts of air issued from Lora's lips.

Shouting to be heard above Rodney's cries, Theo said, "When I say three, lift." Theo spread his legs to gain better balance. He forced his arms under Rodney's arms and clasped his hands together in front of Rodney's chest. Theo began swinging Rodney's body; Lora mimicked his rhythm. She gasped for air against the burning strain.

Grimacing under the weight, Theo rasped, "One. Two. Three."

As his body was hoisted into the trunk, Rodney clamped his upper arms tightly against Theo's arms and pulled Theo in with him.

Theo's feet left the ground. He sprawled on top of Rodney. Theo struggled to regain his balance and free his arms.

Lora stuck her fingers in Rodney's nostrils and yanked. Then she yanked again.

Screaming as his chin rose to meet Lora's hand,

Rodney released Theo's arms. Theo put both hands on the trunk and slammed it. He turned toward Lora. "Are you all right?"

A breathless Lora nodded. She joined Theo and tucked her trembling hands next to her elbows. The two turned their backs on the trunk and leaned against it.

Profanity spewing, Rodney issued every threat he could contrive. "Let me out, you worthless piece of shit." He banged his knees against the trunk. "I'll fade away if you don't let me out."

"Really?" Theo said. "What a shame that would be."

"Didn't you hear me? I'll fade away."

Theo waited for the banging to stop before he responded, "You should have thought of that before you tried to kill Sadie."

"At least that bitch is dead." Rodney let out a haggard laugh, a laugh meant to disguise panic. "Who needs her any way?"

"You made a big mistake," Theo said. "By killing Sadie, you ruined any chance of going to the parallel world. Be sure to let me know what it's like in oblivion."

More profanity escaped from the trunk. Lora grimaced and looked away.

Theo joined the crowd kneeling over the body and made his way to Sadie's side. He drew in a somber breath. His eyes grew moist as he placed a knee on the ground and stared at the body.

"Nooo. Please, nooo. Don't go. Don't leave me," Jane moaned, cradling the bleeding head. Tears flowed down her cheeks, dropping in small splats against her arm. She gently held the still hand, rubbing her cheek back and forth against the bruised skin. Her head dropped back as a piercing wail escaped.

Aanders appeared at the door and realized what had happened. A guttural cry rumbled forth as he ran to the people gathered around the sidewalk.

Trembling, he knelt next to Jane. He reached out and touched the body. "Please don't die." Brushing tears from his eyes with the back of his hand he repeated, "Please. Please don't die."

Aanders' pressed gently on Sadie's shoulder fighting to regain his composure. "It's time. It's time for Tim to go. I need to get him."

Jane wailed as Aanders' words registered. She pulled Mr. Bakke closer to her chest. The man's head fell against her shoulder. She placed kisses on his forehead.

Aanders' breaths came in spurts, suddenly understanding the finality of his statement.

"Hurry. We don't have much time," Sadie said, fighting the acid inching its way up her throat. The roar of her pulse pushing adrenalin through her system was deafening.

"Why did this have to happen to him? Why couldn't it have been me?" Jane said grasping her sister's hand.

Sadie looked toward Lora who leaned against the rental car's trunk with her arms crossed tightly over her chest. Lora's lower lip trembled. She nodded toward Sadie. The frail woman stood sentry over the trunk, ignoring the threats emanating from within.

Tim appeared in the doorway with Aanders bracing him on one side. Theo ran to assist the pair.

"Just a little farther," Aanders whispered, encouraging Tim to take a few more steps. Aanders helped lower Tim to the ground and sat behind him to prop him up. He swiped at his tears with his hand.

The sound of sirens in the distance caught Jane's ear and she looked at Sadie.

Sadie shook her head in reply to Jane's unspoken question.

"Noooo," Jane said, as she caressed Mr. Bakke's hand. "Noooo." She bowed her head and placed a final kiss on Mr. Bakke's cheek.

Aanders, Sadie, and the crossers looked on as a glow began to form and a gentle breeze swirled around Mr. Bakke.

Tim managed a forlorn smile. He looked up at Aanders who lifted him into a standing position. He mouthed "Thank you," but the words were barely audible.

Aanders sobbed, trying to fight the consuming emotion.

"You know I don't want to leave you. But I have to. Mom and Dad need me."

"I know," Aanders said, bracing Tim's sagging body. "I'm sorry I kept you from going through the light the other day. That was wrong."

The wind's intensity grew as the tunnel began to rotate with increased momentum.

Mr. Bakke rose and placed a kiss on Jane's head before he turned to gaze at the vivid aura building in the background. Wisps of his thin, white hair danced excitedly in the wind. He reached out to Tim and beckoned with a motion of his fingers. "Let's go son. I think I know two people who are anxious to see you."

Tim released Aanders' hand and grasped Mr. Bakke's

arm. The elderly gentleman pulled him to his side.

Brilliant rays danced like lightning. The power of the light drew them deeper into the vortex. "Please remind Jane how much I love her and take good care of her. Tell her we'll meet again," Mr. Bakke shouted, waving farewell to Sadie.

"Thank you, Sadie," Tim said. "Thanks for taking me in." Tim stood straighter as his strength increased. He placed his right arm behind Mr. Bakke and together they began the journey they had chosen. Tim looked back over his shoulder. He scanned the group gathered around Mr. Bakke's body. "You'll always be my best friend, Aanders. Don't ever forget that."

Sadie wrapped her arms around her sister and placed her chin on Jane's shoulder. "He's gone now, Jane. He took Tim with him. They've completed their declaration."

Jane hugged Sadie fiercely in return and let her anguish flow.

A young paramedic gently encouraged the twins to move to the side while he knelt next to Mr. Bakke's lifeless body. After checking for a pulse, he shook his head. He pulled the stethoscope from his ears.

Jane, Sadie, and Aanders accompanied the paramedics back to the ambulance and watched them release the spring-loaded mechanism and push the stretcher into the ambulance. "I'm sorry, Ma'am," a paramedic said, tenderly prying Jane's hands from the gurney. "I'm so sorry."

After the deputy finished interviewing Jane and Sadie about the accident, the sisters retreated to the porch swing. Jane rested her head on her sister's shoulder. Sadie kept the swing in motion with the tips of her toes. She and Jane reflected on the afternoon's tragedy.

Sadie raised a hand and waved at the Pouliots as the rental car laden with luggage, and a crosser who would soon slip into oblivion, rounded the corner and disappeared from view.

Belly lay near their feet and watched with soulful eyes. Each time Jane began to sob, he let out a high pitched whine. "It sounds like that silly goose is yodeling," Jane said between sniffles. As the flood gates opened once again, she said, "How could he do that? I just don't understand how someone could do that to Mr. Bakke."

"Mr. Bakke wasn't his intended victim. I already told you Rodney was trying to kill me," Sadie said. "He told Lora about his plan to put me out of my misery. Because Mr. Bakke realized he'd forgotten the fish in the freezer, he headed down the steps in front of me."

"Are you sure Rodney won't ever get out of that trunk?"

"All we can do is hope that what the Pouliots said about the rental car is accurate. By the time the trunk is opened, Rodney will have faded away." Sadie patted Jane's hand. "He can kick and holler all he wants. No one's going to hear him."

Tears dropped into Jane's lap. "I'm really proud of Mr. Bakke. He was such a kind man."

"I know you are," Sadie responded, pressing her nose against Jane's cheek.

"Mr. Bakke and I both decided we'd go to the parallel world if we had to make a decision. It was unselfish of him to accompany Tim back through the light so he could find his parents. But it doesn't surprise me. He always loved helping people. I hope I'm fortunate enough to meet up with him again." Jane smiled up at Sadie.

"If we're lucky, we'll all be together. Mr. Bakke wanted me to tell you how much he loved you and that he'd see you again."

"Do you think he'll be lonely without me?"

"Of course he will," Sadie said.

Jane leaned her head against Sadie's shoulder. "Do you think death coaches will have a different role in the after life once they leave earth?"

"I guess I'll have to wait to find out," Sadie said. "Maybe you'll have to worship me as a goddess and wait on me hand and foot."

"Then nothing will change, will it?" Jane's attempt at humor was lost in another torrent of tears.

A family of four walked past the cabin and waved at the sisters. They briefly stopped to offer condolences. After they left, Sadie said, "You know what else shocked me today?"

Jane dabbed at her eyes and shook her head.

"Lora didn't go through the light with Tim."

Gasping in amazement, Jane said, "Are you sure?"

"Of course I'm sure. She's sitting right there." Motioning toward Lora on the porch step, Sadie continued in a whisper, "Lora knew Tim had chosen to return to his parents rather than go to the parallel world. If that's really where Lora wanted to go, she'd have taken advantage of Mr. Bakke's death and gone with Tim. Apparently she's had second thoughts."

32

Aanders body jerked as a clap of thunder jolted him from a troubled sleep. Closing his eyes and burrowing deeper into his pillow, he tried to block the sound of rain hammering against the side of the mortuary. Lightning sizzled outside his window. As if competing with nature's fireworks, a deafening clap of thunder exploded through the darkness before fading into a distant echo.

Aanders' bed sheets were clammy from the heavy humidity. He heard his mother hurrying from room to room, shutting the windows against the driving rain. After sitting on the edge of his bed to get his bearings, he rose and pulled the window frame down until it met the sill.

Nan wrapped on his door. "I need to check your window."

"I just shut it," Aanders said. "The floor didn't get wet."

Nan lingered outside the closed door. "Are you okay? Are you getting any rest with all the racket?" Nan turned the knob and poked her head into Aanders' room. "Do you mind if I come in?"

Aanders retreated to the privacy of his covers and pulled them tight over his head.

After securing her robe ties around her waist, Nan sat on the side of her son's bed. Running her hand along his back, she said, "You've had a terrible day. I'm sorry I didn't get to spend more time with you after Mr. Bakke died. I'm here if you want to talk about it."

Aanders pulled his shoulder away as his mother smoothed her hand over the outline of his arm. "Sadie said you were a real help when Mr. Bakke died. I know you always thought of him as a grandfather." Nan smiled. "I did too. He was a wonderful man."

Aanders drew his knees closer to his chest. Nan said, "You can't avoid talking about Tim's death forever. I'd like to know how you feel."

Nan shuddered as lightning crackled near the window. "Wow. That was way too close." She cautiously looked through the window. "I'm always ready to listen. Just let me know if you need me."

A few sniffled gulps broke through despite Aanders' attempt to hold his breath against the sobs threatening to escape. His mother tugged at the edge of his sheet. He didn't want her to invade his privacy. It was his cocoon. It was the one place, the only place he could seek refuge from the sorrows of the day. Tim was gone. Gone forever.

Prying the fabric away from his grasp, Nan uncovered her son's head and placed her cheek against his. "I'm so sorry about Tim's death. He was my friend, too. And now we've lost Mr. Bakke. I'm going to miss them both."

Aanders' chest heaved with sobs. Nan freed him from the tangled sheet and slipped her arms under his body. Swaying gently with her son in her arms, she let her tears flow, too. Wishing desperately for a black hole to open up and swallow him so he wouldn't have to face another day without his best friend, Aanders sank into the safety of his mother's arms. "He's gone," he gasped, trying to draw air into a chest heavy with grief. "Tim's really gone."

Nodding understanding, Nan held him tighter.

Beth Solheim

"Why did it happen? Tim didn't hurt anyone." Aanders' chest rose and fell sharply, spasms rocking his body. Trying to make sense of the injustice, he said, "I heard Sadie tell you about Paul. Why do people do bad things like that? Why did he have to shoot at Tim's Dad?"

With Aanders' head cradled against her, Nan stroked his hair. "The evidence is going to come out over the next few days. Maybe then we'll understand what happened."

Nan dropped her head back and closed her eyes. "I feel like such a failure. I almost subjected us to life with a man I never really knew. And now they think he might have murdered Richard Fossum." She ran her finger under her eye to stem a tear. "I'm sorry Aanders. I made a mistake."

"That's okay Mom. You didn't know."

As the night wore on, the two propped themselves against the headboard and talked about things on their minds.

"Can we go visit Tim's grave again? I need to make sure he's doing okay."

"Of course. Any time you want," Nan said.

"Maybe I can take over Mr. Bakke's duties. I mean helping you with funerals like he used to do. Tim's Dad used to pay him to work in his office. Maybe I can earn money like that, too."

"Sounds like a good idea," Nan said. "Let's get through the next few days first. Then we'll make a plan."

Nan waited for Aanders to slip into sleep before removing her arm from behind his back. She propped a pillow under his head. Tiptoeing from his room, she looked back through the crack in the door. "You've come a long way, little man." Patting her lips and sending a silent kiss of

255

admiration, she closed the door and returned to her bed.

Fifteen minutes passed before Aanders woke to the gentle rustle of leaves outside his window. Turning toward the illumination, he saw a bright rainbow arcing in the distance. He untangled his legs from the covers and rushed to the window.

The rainbow radiated the most vibrant colors he'd ever seen. Waves of blue, red, and yellow rose and fell, dancing above each arc as the colors grew in intensity. "A rainbow at midnight," he whispered. "It's a rainbow at midnight."

A pebble pelted against his window. Startled, he jumped back from the sill. He cautiously peeked over the window ledge. Another one tinkled against the pane. Scanning the ground he tried to distinguish the shadows from the trees and noticed a shadow edge along a Norway pine. He strained to see through the pale light of the rainbow. The shadow moved again. It was Sadie. He slowly raised the window and pressed his nose against the screen.

Signaling with the wave of her arm, she whispered excitedly, "Did you see it?"

Aanders followed the point of her finger. "I see it." Grinning broadly, he released the screen's latch and swung it wide. He put a leg through the opening, lowered himself to the ground, and joined Sadie under the tree.

The pair followed the rainbow's arc toward the shore, commenting on the ripples rising off the bright colors. A few more droplets fell as the clouds returned to their pre-tempest buoyancy.

Sadie put her arm around Aanders and hugged him to her side. "You did it. I'm so proud of you. By setting your sorrow aside and making sure Tim made it through the light, you earned your rainbow at midnight."

Hues of color danced around them. "I'm glad he's with his mom and dad," Aanders said. "He really missed them." He cocked his head toward his left shoulder and gazed questioningly at Sadie. "Did you notice Lora didn't go with Tim and Mr. Bakke? Do you think she decided to go to the parallel world to find her son?"

"Let's hope so. Let's hope she's got the sense to do that."

Aanders held his hand out. "It stopped raining."

"They've quit crying," Sadie said. She pointed toward the sky. "Look at that glow from the rainbow and then look at that billowy cloud behind the rainbow. That's called a cloud of crossers." She watched Aanders look back and forth over the horizon. "It's full of crossers lost. When you see billowy clouds during a rain storm, it's the crossers lost crying for the future they never realized. Tonight they were crying tears of joy."

"It's always cause to celebrate when a new death coach earns their rainbow," Sadie said. "For all we know, you're the youngest death coach ever chosen. I'm sure the crossers lost are pleased with the sacrifice you made." Lifting his hand off the bench, she cradled it to her cheek. "A new journey begins tonight. Do you think you're ready ?"

"No. But Tim and I talked about it. I'm going to do what he asked me to do." Aanders' gaze fell upon the lake. "Sometimes Tim was so smart, it was scary. He told me it'd be easier for me if I always pretended he was walking beside me."

"He's right, you know," Sadie said.

Aanders sighed deeply. "That's what's so scary."

33

Sadie hurried up onto the porch, opened the door and waved the newspaper at Jane, who sat lost in concentration at the kitchen table. Nan had asked Jane to prepare an obituary for Mr. Bakke. Jane sighed with exasperation, wiped the eraser back and forth over her last sentence. Struggling to find the proper wording, Jane had queried Sadie several times before Sadie walked over to the lodge to buy a newspaper.

Mr. Bakke had spent the last fifty years of his life as handyman and caretaker at the Witt's End Resort. Vina, the twins' mother, had hired him when he was a young man. He never realized the desire to seek alternative employment. Taking a leave from the resort, he had served four years in the Army with the knowledge his position would remain open until his return.

Vina had treated the shy, unremarkable little man as a son. When Vina passed away, Mr. Bakke pitched in with unwavering vigor to make sure the twin's transition to resort owners went as smooth as possible.

"I've never seen such a buzz over the headlines. People stood five deep at the counter buying copies of today's paper," Sadie said. The screen door slammed behind her. A muffled bark caused her to retreat and swing the door open to let Belly in. The dog sauntered over to Mr. Bakke's chair and sniffed vigorously before looking toward the kitchen table.

Jane dabbed a tear with the edge of her napkin before rising and walking to Mr. Bakke's chair. Squatting down to pet the dog, she whispered, "You miss him too, don't you fella?" She pressed her cheek against the chair and cried softly. "What am I going to do, Sadie? I feel so empty. He was part of our lives for so many years I can't remember what it was like without him."

Sadie knelt next to her sister. "He's watching you, you know. He knows how you feel. He told me to take care of you. He told me that as he was going through the light."

"You?" Jane laughed. "He must have lost his mind when he hit his head." The conflicting emotions made Jane cry even harder.

"He told me to throw your clothes away and take you shopping," Sadie said. "He insisted I buy you a thong."

"Now I know you're pulling my leg."

"It was worth a try," Sadie said. After helping her sister into her chair, Sadie listened while Jane read through the obituary, pausing from time to time to sniffle and wipe her nose.

"Because he didn't have any family, Nan asked me to make decisions. I've got most of the stuff picked out for the funeral," Jane said. "I think he'll be happy with what I've selected."

"Of course he will. He worshipped you. His goal in life was to make you happy."

"He didn't take a shine to me until he realized you had no intention of going out with him," Jane said. "It took him a year to get over your rejection. Poor man. He hardly came out of his cabin for a month."

"But that was forty years ago," Sadie said. "If you

hadn't catered to him back then and made a fool of yourself drooling on his doorstep, he'd have eventually come around and asked you for a date on his own."

"I doubt it," Jane said. "You totally deflated his ego. But once he got to know me, he realized I was the better catch."

"Bull," Sadie responded. "He just settled for less. And besides, he was too horny for me. All he talked about was sex."

"Not to me," Jane said with a huff. "That's because he realized I was pure and worth taking time to get to know."

Sadie's red glitter glasses slid down her nose as she lowered her head and scrutinized Jane. "You need to see a psychiatrist. You've lost your grip on reality." Sadie spread the newspaper over the table.

The headlines read *Local Business Man Indicted on Murder Charges*. "Look at that," Sadie said, slapping the front page with the back of her hand. "That rat Carl took all the credit."

"That's what you agreed to, wasn't it?"

"It was. But you'd think Carl could have mentioned my name in there somewhere."

"I think you're going to have to settle for the fact Carl dropped the lawsuit. He exchanged the lawsuit for your silence."

"That just frosts me," Sadie said. "I did all the ground work, but he became the hero."

"I'm surprised he was willing to take a chance that people wouldn't find out about his business dealings with Paul."

"Unfortunately, I have to agree with him. If they

haven't discovered the information by now, they're not going to find it. I'd still like to see him hang by those itty bitty balls for all the grief he caused Mrs. Fading Sun when her husband was arrested. Those diversity crusaders would love that tidbit of information."

"You've always got that to fall back on," Jane said.

"You should have seen Carl's face when I told him that very thing. What goes around comes back to bite you. But in Carl's situation, his prejudice ended up slapping him across the face. If Mrs. Fading Sun hadn't mentioned the policy, I would never have put two and two together. At least it will keep Carl in line until the next crisis." Sadie bit at the inside of her cheek. "If he wins the election, it'll give him power. And power makes him crazy. That's when he'll cook up another scheme to get his hands on this resort."

Jane nodded in agreement. "I'm afraid you're right. Everyone knows he needs money. His wife goes through money like water. You can tell she thought their wedding vows said for better or for purse." Jane forced a smile. "At least we have the satisfaction that Paul will never see daylight again. Lon said Paul will probably get three life terms for murdering the Fossums. With everybody concentrating on the trial, it gives us time to get things in order. If Nan can come up with enough money to buy the mortuary and the acreage it sits on, that'll be one less thing for Carl to get his hands on."

"Is that hole in your head getting bigger?" Sadie asked, frowning at Jane's lack of comprehension. "Weren't you listening when Nan told us there's no way she's going to get a loan? The bank turned her down flat. That's why she was ready to accept Paul's proposal."

"That poor woman." Shaking her head Jane said, "She's so embarrassed she couldn't even look me in the eye when we were picking out Mr. Bakke's urn. I told her no one blamed her for what Paul did. It's going to be a tough road until the gossip dies down."

"I heard Carl tell her the same thing after he questioned her. I think he was trying to cover his own ass by seeing if Nan knew anything about his relationship with Paul."

Jane set her jaw and rapped her fist against the table top. "He was worried about his own hide so he faked his concern about Nan. That man makes me so mad I'd like to kick him all the way to Tubuktim."

"You mean Timbuktu," Sadie corrected.

"No, I don't," Jane said, glaring at her sister.

Drumming her fingers against the table, Sadie decided not to educate her sister in the finer points of geography and opted instead to help Jane with her project. Pushing a scissors across the table, Sadie said, "There's an article about Mr. Bakke's accident on page three. You might want to cut it out and add it to your scrapbook."

Tears flowed once again. Jane reached for the wadded-up napkin as she read the article. "That's so nice of them to mention he was a well-respected member of our resort staff. If they only knew how important he was." She slid the scissors across the top of the article. "What would we have done without him?"

Sadie held the scrap book open so Jane could insert the article between two vinyl sheets.

Jane stood and retrieved a faded box from a shelf in the book case. "I went through mother's trunk this morning and found her old memento box. I remembered seeing her scrapbooks in there after she died. I was hoping to find something about Mr. Bakke's discharge from the Army."

The women paged through the scrapbooks, selecting several photos and articles written during Mr. Bakke's life at the resort. They arranged them on the table in order by date. "I'll send one of the dock boys to town to get a sheet of tag board so we can create a collage," Jane said.

Laughing, Sadie pointed at one of the photos. "Remember the day Mr. Bakke was in the outhouse before we had indoor plumbing and that storm blew the top off the outhouse? All we could see was his head sticking up over what was left of the wall."

"I sure do," Jane said. "He was so mad at you for taking that picture he didn't talk to you for two days."

"And do you remember he wouldn't repair the wall until I gave him the photo?" Sadie said. "Little did he know I had a duplicate."

Jane removed the articles and photos one by one, stacking them in the order she wanted to apply them to the tag board. "There. That's ready to go." She slid the stack into a large envelope. She gathered the remaining loose sheets. As she lowered the scrapbooks into the memento box, a yellowed envelope fluttered to the floor.

Sadie bent to retrieve the envelope and placed it on top of the keepsakes. "What was in the envelope?"

"What envelope?"

Turning it over, Sadie noticed the familiar flair of her mother's handwriting. She smiled. "It's got our names on it."

Jane looked over Sadie's shoulder while Sadie pulled two sheets from the envelope and unfolded them. "It looks like mother wrote a birth announcement," Sadie said. "She must have planned to put it in the newspaper because it's written on newspaper stationery." Pointing she said, "Look at that. Those numbers must be the size of the announcement and how much it was going to cost."

"She must not have had them print it, because we didn't find a newspaper clipping in her scrapbooks," Jane said. "And you know mother saved everything. Maybe she didn't dare do it. There has to be some reason she never told anyone who our father was."

Sadie read the birth announcement to her sister.

Vina Witt proudly announces the birth of twin daughters, Fifilomine Jane and Fifilomine Sadie, born on the Eleventh of July, Nineteen Hundred Forty Five.

Sadie placed the announcement behind the second sheet before gazing at its contents. Gasping, she said, "It's our birth certificate."

"Let me see," Jane said, pulling it from Sadie's grasp. Her eyes zeroed in on the line indicating paternity. "Oh my God. Oh my God," she whispered.

Sadie wrenched the form from her sister's hand. Jane dropped into the chair. "Swanson?" Sadie shouted. "Ingmar Swanson?" Rereading the words, Sadie said, "I'm shocked. Ingmar Swanson is our father."

Jane's shoulders began to shake as she cupped her hand to her mouth.

Standing to embrace her sister from behind, Sadie said, "It's not that bad. Don't cry."

As her shoulders heaved with each breath released, Jane said, "I'm not crying. I'm laughing." Rising to face her sister, she said, "Don't you know what this means?"

"That the man who owned the bank where mother used

to work is the one who got her pregnant?"

Pausing to catch her breath, Jane again burst into laughter. "That's part of it. But don't you remember hearing some talk about a scandal at the bank, years and years ago? I always thought it meant Ingmar embezzled and that's the reason he uprooted his family and left town. But I'll bet it's because his wife found out he got our mother pregnant. Think back on the time we went to the museum and saw Ingmar's family photo on the wall. It was in the founding-father's section."

"So," Sadie shrugged. "What does that have to do with this?"

"Remember the names under the photo?"

Losing patience, Sadie said, "Are you serious? Why would I remember the names? It's been thirty years since I've been to the museum."

"Well I remember because I thought it was so strange a lady was named Fil. I always thought it was a misspelling and that it should have been Phil. Back then I thought her name must have been Phyllis. But I'll bet it was Fifilomine."

Nodding at the possibility, Sadie said, "What's so strange about that?"

"Nothing," Jane said. "I just got distracted as I was sorting it out in my head."

Scrunching up her mouth and glaring at Jane, Sadie growled, "Will you please get to the point."

"Well, Miss Smarty Pants," Jane said, as she craned her head toward her sister. "For once I'm one step ahead of you. I know something you don't."

"What?" Sadie rolled her eyes upward, sighing in frustration.

"Swanson," Jane responded. "Who do you think about when you hear the name Swanson?"

"That's a dumb question," Sadie said. "Who else would I think of besides Oink Etta's love child?" Tingles spiraled through Sadie's spine. "Don't you dare think that way. There's no way Carl can be related to Ingmar. Swanson is a common name and not every Swanson is related."

"For your information Sister Superior, Ingmar is Carl's grandfather's brother. He must have been the black sheep of the family because he had an affair with our mother. I remember hearing they banished him from their lives. Ingmar owned the bank and Carl's grandfather owned the resort. After Ingmar left, the family acted like he never existed."

"I can't believe it," Sadie said. "To think our mother had to bear the shame of being taken advantage of by a married man. At least mother got a snippet of revenge."

"I bet it was more than a snippet," Jane said with a grin. "When folks found out what mother named us, I'm guessing Ingmar had a lot of explaining to do."

"I'm glad she had Carl's grandfather on her side. He was kind enough to offer her a job and give her a place to live. Not many men would have done that for a woman who had just given birth to twins."

Sadie wished she would have paid more attention to the man who provided them with a home after her mother found herself in dire straits. Even though Mr. Swanson was always visible around the resort while the girls were growing up, she never thought to sit down and have a serious conversation with him. A small smile crossed her lips. Mr. Swanson must have had an ulterior motive for offering their mother shelter. She hoped it had involved affection. Even if the motive was limited to a brother's revenge, Sadie was thankful Mr. Swanson made the offer.

"All these years we've thought our connection to Carl was his desire to get his hands on his grandfather's resort," Jane said. "We're related to Carl and we didn't even know it."

Hanging on to the kitchen sink, Sadie jigged her happy dance as she said, "Can't you just imagine what he's going to say when we tell him?"

34

Sadie stood at the screen door and eased it closed to keep it from slamming shut. Jane was asleep on the davenport with a pile of sympathy cards at her side and one lying open on her lap.

Sadie crossed the room and sat on the cushion next to her sister. When Jane stirred, Sadie put her arm around her and pulled her close. Jane drew in a few sharp breaths like a child after a lengthy cry.

Resting her head against Sadie, Jane said, "That sure was a nice funeral, wasn't it?"

"The best," Sadie whispered. "He'd have been so proud to know all those people showed up to honor him."

"Yes, he would," Jane sighed.

"I especially enjoyed the gun salute the Veterans performed to commemorate his years in the army," Sadie said. She read two more sympathy cards before passing them to Jane. "Who was that guy who fell into the grave after he saluted you and gave you the flag?"

"I don't have a clue," Jane said. "But I think he'd been drinking. Did you notice how out of step he was when they marched up to the grave?"

"I think he had his vest on inside out, too," Sadie said. "All I could see were the pin portions of his medals poking through the fabric."

Jane lifted a twenty dollar bill out of one of the sympathy cards. "What kind of memoriam should we create in Mr. Bakke's honor?"

"Probably some kind of fishing contest. Maybe we could host an annual contest each winter. Ice fishing was his favorite."

"I really like that," Jane said. "Elmer and his group from the nursing home would like that, too. Wasn't that nice of those nurses to bring the old folks to the funeral?"

Sadie leaned her head back on the davenport. "Who was that man who screamed when the gun salute went off?"

"I didn't recognize him, either," Jane said. "That goes to show you the guys with the guns shouldn't stand behind the crowd. Nan should insist they stand in front. At least it would give people time to prepare instead of being scared to death."

Sadie reflected on the day's events. "He's gone."

"I know, dear," Jane responded. "I was at his funeral."

"I don't mean Mr. Bakke. I mean Theo."

"He is?" Jane said. "Are you sure?"

"I'm pretty sure," Sadie said. "He didn't get on the van when I went to pick them up. Neither did Lora. When we drove to the nursing home this morning, I heard them talking about someone who had taken a turn for the worse. I waited an extra half hour, but they never came out."

"You're going to have to speed up your trips with the crossers. I don't think it's appropriate to make our other guests wait just because you're toting around a bunch of dead people," Jane said.

Sadie huffed with exasperation. "I agree. How many times have I told you we need to buy another shuttle? Why is it okay when you suggest it, but it's a dumb idea when I bring it up?"

"Because you're options are ridiculous. We need another respectable shuttle, not a used hearse."

"Why? What's wrong with that? We can convert it to seat eight people. We'll make it plush like a limo with velvet and a bar. I bet our guests would love to be picked up at the airport in a unique shuttle. I know just where we can get a good deal on a used one."

"Over my dead body," Jane gasped.

Nan hung up the receiver and turned to face the Witt sisters. She shook her head and sank into the desk chair. "I've spent the past few days filling out loan papers with a different bank. One of the loan officers called this morning and said the papers were ready to be signed. I was going to do it this afternoon. Then, I got a call from the bank saying they'd decided to decline my loan for the mortuary land."

Nan stood and walked over to the window. "When I called him to find out why, the receptionist said he was with another client. He finally returned my call and told me I can't get the loan because I don't own the land the mortuary sits on. That means I can't use the mortuary as collateral. Their underwriter said they had to rescind the offer because he didn't realize the land the mortuary sits on and the land I'm trying to buy are one and the same."

"I thought you explained that to the loan officer," Sadie said.

"I did, but he didn't relay that information to the underwriter." Leaning her head back, Nan groaned, "What a mess my life has become. I must be the most naive woman in the world."

"You and our mother," Jane said. "She was taken in by

270

a man, too, you know."

"At least he wasn't a murderer." Nan buried her face in her hands. "People were staring at me during the funeral. I can about imagine what they're thinking. I'm surprised I'm still getting calls to schedule funerals."

"It'll pass," Sadie said. "They'll forget as soon as the next big scandal hits the streets."

"We're so sorry, dear." Jane patted Nan's back. "It's been one hateful summer, hasn't it? It's hard to believe so much sorrow can pass through such a small community."

"I suppose we better get back to the cabin," Sadie said. "We wanted to see how you were doing and tell you about our idea for Mr. Bakke's memoriam. We're glad you like it."

After ushering the sisters to the door, Nan grabbed the stack of mail Aanders had retrieved from the mailbox and paged through it. She sorted the envelopes into categories, placing the business items in one pile, her personal mail in the middle pile, and the junk mail in another. Trying to decide the category for the final envelope, she turned it over looking for the return address. The upper left hand corner was blank. There was no stamp on it, either. She turned the envelope over to see if anything was imprinted on the envelope flap. The flap was bare.

Resting her knee on one of the sofa cushions in the lobby, she slid her finger along the flap to unseal the glue. Dropping all the way onto the sofa, she pulled the contents from the envelope. She unfolded the sheet of paper. Her lips moved silently as she began to read.

My Dearest Nan,
As my time on earth has come to an end, I must admit

to a grievous error.

First, you must understand my shortcomings. Over the years, an obsession with my vocation and an unfortunate marriage distorted my values and turned me into the type of man I loathe. I had every intention of approaching your father and confessing, but am now unable to do so. I realize I will never be able to make up for what I've done, but I hope with what I'm going to tell you, I can make amends.

When I was a young man, I formed a partnership with your father. His zest for life and his keen ability to formulate ideas led me to believe that with my funds backing the venture, we'd be successful beyond dreams. In the midst of our haste to grab the golden ring and move forward with our plan, your mother found out she was pregnant. Your father's attentions turned to finishing his mortuary science degree and building a life for his family.

From time to time your father wrote to inquire as to the progress of our patent application. Shamefully, I must admit I wasn't altogether truthful in my reply. I told him they rejected our idea. That was partially true. They rejected it, but asked that it be reconfigured with a few adjustments. I altered your father's original drawings and resubmitted the patent without your father's name on the application. The patent was granted and a number was issued. I then sold the rights to a medical device company and reaped the reward of your father's hard work. For that I am truly sorry.

When I graduated from law school and subsequently became a judge, I no longer harbored an urge for confession. It wasn't that I didn't feel remorse; it was the fear of losing my prominent standing in the judicial system that kept me from admitting fraud.

Upon hearing of your father's death, I attended his funeral. It was then that I realized how despicable I had been. Your father had lived a meager existence carrying on his dream and preparing his daughter to continue the legacy. Those were the exact words you used in praise of your father during the ceremony. I now see that your love for you son and the wish to continue in your father's footsteps consume you as they did your father.

My dear Nan, I truly apologize for my lack of judgment, my greed, my cowardice. I am ashamed.

Because my will stipulates bequeathal of my assets to my wife, patent ownership flows to my heirs and assigns as well. You will never realize a stipend from your father's efforts. I can, however, offer something in its place.

Please check the lower left hand corner of the top drawer of your file cabinet in your office. You will find a small black velvet bag. The contents within were given to me by an appreciative client. Cash them in. Their value is more than enough to enable you to purchase the mortuary land. Even though I deprived your father of the income he so rightfully deserved, and subsequently caused stress in your life, I ask that you accept this as a token of forgiveness.

You have been blessed with a child who will go farther than you can ever imagine. Your strength will guide you. Never doubt you are walking the correct path.

By the time you receive this, I will have gone on to my final destination.

Respectfully,
Theopholis Jamison Peter.

Nan held the letter to her chest before rereading it. Her finger traced the signature. A tear welled and landed on her hand. How could someone have done this to her father?

Standing, Nan turned the envelope over and wondered where it had come from. She walked over to the file cabinet and tugged on the top drawer. She pulled the file folders forward as far as they would go and felt along the back of the drawer. There it was. Her fingers curled around the soft bag.

35

"I still can't believe it," Jane said. "Did you verify the diamonds are legitimate?"

"Absolutely." Nan said. "I took them to a diamond broker in St. Paul. He offered to buy them on the spot, but I got a second opinion. I sold them to the highest bidder."

Sadie sat against the back of one of the sofas. Nan, Jane, and Aanders sat on the opposing sofa in the lobby.

Aanders' exuberance had him bouncing from a sitting position to standing at the edge of the sofa to squatting on his knees by the coffee table. When he couldn't contain himself any longer, he repeated the circuit before plopping down next to his mother.

"Mom said I can get a new bike and we're going to take a trip and I get to..."

Nan interrupted, "Settle down, young man. You're going to pop a blood vessel with all that excitement."

Squirming, he started up again. "A man left a bag of diamonds to Mom. The man cheated grampa out of lots of money and felt guilty so he gave Mom the diamonds."

Holding a hand up to silence Aanders, Nan said, "I'll tell you all about that in a few minutes. First I've got something to tell Sadie and Jane. I'm obviously in a position to purchase the mortuary land if you'd still like to sell it."

Jane looked at Sadie as her sister nodded in agreement. "Of course we'll sell it."

Sadie smiled and returned Nan's embrace as Nan

hugged her in appreciation. "I'm so happy for you, dear. We both are."

"Thank you, Sadie. You don't know how relieved I am. Our future is finally secure. I'll never be able to thank you for all you've done." Her fingers kneaded the envelope resting on her lap. "You've been part of our family ever since I can remember. I know my father would agree. I couldn't ask for better friends."

"Me either," Aanders said. "You're like a grandmother to me. You, too, Jane."

"Tell us all about it," Jane said. "I can't wait to hear everything."

"It's right here in this envelope." Nan waved it in the air. Grinning, she added, "Can you imagine this letter and a tiny black bag can hold the key to someone's future?"

She pulled the letter out and unfolded it. "May I read it to you?" Seeing their nods, she added, "Aanders hasn't heard everything yet, either. I've not told him the details."

Jane sat on the edge of the sofa and put her arm around Aanders. She pecked his cheek and smoothed his hair as Nan began to read.

After reading a few paragraphs, Nan paused. "Are you doing okay, Aanders?"

Aanders nodded. He signaled for her to continue.

She finished reading and held the letter to her chest. "I know my father would be pleased. I still don't know how he got wind that Theopholis Peter had filed the patent it in his name. I guess I'll never know. But the fact that Mr. Peter admitted it would make my father happy."

Sadie smiled her 'isn't that wonderful smile' at Nan and crossed her arms over her chest, trying to hold her composure. The last three words Nan read had thrown her for a loop. A double loop. Theopholis Jamison Peter.

How could Theo have hidden the fact that he knew Nan's father? He hadn't wanted her to figure it out and had used generic references when he commented on his past. Sadie was astounded. Had she lost her edge? The last time she saw Theo, she still believed he intended to take the diamonds with him.

It was rare Sadie's crossers deceived her, but this time she'd gladly admit to being the fool. She had lectured Theo on the hopelessness of seeking revenge and trusted her words had played a part in his change of heart. Now she understood the real reason Theo had landed on her porch. Sadie regretted not giving him the credit he deserved.

Jane sat with her mouth wide open as Aanders gasped, "What?"

Their heads swiveled back and forth while they looked at each other and then at Sadie.

Nan repeated, "Theopholis Jamison Peter. That's quite a fancy name, isn't it?"

"Theo," Aanders said quietly, staring at Sadie.

Sadie nodded and then turned toward her sister. "Close your mouth, Jane. You're teeth are going to fall out again. You don't want to walk around for a week without dentures like you did last time."

Jane's head slowly rotated toward Sadie. Seeing the warning glare, she said, "No. No, I don't." Under her breath she looked at Sadie and said, "Theo?"

"I suppose that was what he went by," Nan said. "Theopholis is hard to say. It's a tongue twister."

Jane sat back and pulled Aanders with her. She took

his hand and held it in her lap. Reaching across Aanders, she said, "Can we see the letter?"

Sadie watched the two reread the letter. She winked twice at Aanders as he looked up for reassurance.

"I'd have given anything to have talked with my father about his patent design. I'm not surprised the patent was related to the medical profession. He was always trying to improve upon medical devices," Nan said. "I wonder if Theo was in the medical profession too. He must have been. If only Aanders and I could have met him."

Sadie smiled at Aanders. She stood to embrace the young man who in the past few minutes had come to realize the intricacies of dealing with the crossers. They not only held secrets, they carried the potential to deeply impact the future of the living.

This was a turn of events she couldn't have predicted. Theo had grown during his journey, overcoming the armor of bitterness he built over the years. Rodney met the fate he deserved. Tim and Michael followed their hearts–Tim rejoined his parents and Michael braved the unknown. Lora apparently chose to rejoin her son.

Relaxing against the softness of the sofa, Sadie gazed out the window toward Cabin 14. A man in a hospital gown stood on her porch. A breeze parted the back of his gown, raising it above his waist. The man tugged at it pulling it tight around his hips. He edged closer to the railing and scanned the marina. He backed up as Belly butted through the screen door to greet him and sniff his bare feet.

Watching the man peer through the screen door, Sadie rose and said, "I guess I better get back to the cabin. It looks like I've got a new guest."

Like the main character in her Sadie Witt mystery series, Beth Solheim was born with a healthy imagination and a hankering to solve a puzzle. She learned her reverence for reading from her mother, who was never without a book in her hand. Her lifelong interest in figuring out how things worked was a natural transition into weaving a tale.

By day, Beth works in Human Resources at a hospital. By night she morphs into a writer who frequents lake resorts and mortuaries and hosts a ghost or two in her humorous paranormal mysteries. In her writing life she's been a sheriff's deputy, a funeral director, a child, a death coach, an embezzler, a ghost and a chef who's been banned from cooking at the Witt's End resort. With those characters traipsing through her mind, there are still numerous stories yet untold.

Raised in Northern Minnesota, the setting for her stories, she resides in lake country with her husband and a menagerie of wildlife critters that frequent her patio. She and her husband are blessed with two grown children and two grandsons.

Beth welcomes you to dangle your feet off the end of the dock and reel in a hefty dose of humor as you enjoy the Sadie Witt mysteries.